Joan,
Enjoy!
Kathy

THE TWENTY-FIRST FLOOR

KATHLEEN ORMOND

First published in the United States of America, 2020
Copyright© Kathleen Ormond, 2020
All rights reserved

LIBRARY OF CONGRESS CATOLOGING
IN PUBLICATION DATA

Ormond, Kathleen (Kathy H.)
The Twenty-First Floor

Kathleen Ormond
ISBN 978-1673188530
Printed in the United States of America

The scanning, uploading and distribution of this book via the
Internet or via any other means without the permission of the
publisher is illegal and punishable by law. Please purchase
only authorized electronic editions, and do not participate in or
encourage electronic piracy of copyrighted materials. Your
support of the author's rights is appreciated.

This is a work of fiction. Names, characters, places and
incidents either are the product of the author's imagination or
are used fictitiously. Any resemblance to actual persons, living
or dead, events, or locales is entirely coincidental.

CHAPTER ONE

Arthur was the personification of confidence and trust with his staff until betrayed, then his retribution was swift. He had no tolerance for deception or ineptitude and the mere thought of a traitor within the ranks of his Board of Directors had him on edge. Someone was leaking information to a corporate rival who threatened to take away his bank, his entire career, and he was ready for battle. Thirty years before, Arthur had been named CEO of First Community Bank, a title he held dear to his heart. He gained approval to change the name to Barrington Bank within two years and had insisted they keep his name as long as he was head of the bank. He built it into a regional Midwest financial institution with twenty-seven offices throughout Illinois and two in Indiana. He still worked with many of the same people, trusted associates who had become friends he cared about. He felt a responsibility, not only to them to ensure their jobs, but also to the shareholders of the bank and his Board of Directors. He was in for the fight of his life.

Bartel Bank, had made an offer to merge with them and Arthur flatly turned it down from the start. The bank was his lifeblood and he intended to remain in charge. He was sixty-two years old, far too young to consider retirement and the thought of taking a backseat while someone else made the decisions was out of the question. Bartel was one of six major banks in the nation with headquarters in Atlanta and their history of mergers and acquisitions was aggressive. They had him in their sights and would lie in wait for any opportunity to force his hand. That possibility had reared its ugly head thanks to a group of Wall Street analysts who reduced Barrington's rating due to a transitory move in derivative margins last quarter. Arthur was furious. He had recouped the deficits and the fiscal yields were impressive.

His assistant tapped on the open door. "Good morning Mr. Barrington." He peered over his glasses and waved her into the room. Lillian had worked for him twenty years and knew when to be silent. "Lillian, cancel my appointments today. Call Jordan and ask if he can come for lunch at twelve-thirty, just the two of us.

I need the Bartel file and an update on this month's numbers as soon as you can get them." He turned back to his computer and Lillian closed the door behind her, a sign he was not to be disturbed. She returned ten minutes later with the reports he requested, set them on his desk quietly and left. She took no offense to his mood.

Lillian admired Mr. Barrington immensely. Twenty years before, she was divorced and nearly penniless when Mr. Barrington hired her as his secretary, a term no longer allowed at Barrington according to the human resource department. They insisted on the term of executive assistant. Lillian had worked tirelessly to learn the ins and outs of the corporation and struggled with complicated telephone systems and computer classes. She finally gave up and flatly told the computer gurus she intended to go back to using her electric typewriter.

Arthur watched her progress and admired the effort she put into her job, 'one of a kind' he often told his wife. He insured she was rewarded each year with a sizable increase in salary and a Christmas bonus and soon she felt much more secure with her life.

Lillian was old school, restrained in every aspect of her life; her mannerisms, diet, voice and appearance. Tall and thin with silvery gray hair pinned into a perfect chignon, there was a stern elegance about her. Her life had been regimented since childhood. She never had children and did not regret it for one moment, could not imagine sitting at home with a child all day. Her entire world had been Barrington for twenty years. She had watched them come and go, hot shot MBAs from Wharton who skipped from one financial institution to the next for the best deal, no loyalty or respect for Mr. Barrington. She could easily spot them now and if asked her opinion would give it freely, only to Arthur, and found she could undermine a career with subtle comments and innuendos. Over the years she developed a reputation of wielding power within the bank that made men cringe at the thought of trying to get past her to Arthur.

"Mr. Banks is here to join you for lunch in the East dining room." Arthur put on his jacket. "Send him back."

He met Jordan at the door and they walked to the dining room together. Arthur sat across from Jordan as Della served their lunch.

"Please close the drapes Della, the sun is blinding me." She went to the wall of windows. "Yes sir, Mr. Barrington." She closed the drapes and left the room. "Thank you for coming Jordan, I want to talk with you about Bartel. What's your take on them?" Jordan Banks was Mayor of Chicago, elected two years before with the backing of Arthur and a cloistered group of city leaders. Arthur respected him, a man of integrity and moral character rare in a politician. "I think you're in for a fight Art. The New York analysts' reduced rating last quarter will stir up renewed interest from competition like Bartel. They will come with an offer that may well be too hard to turn down. They want Barrington and they'll make it sweet for you and your officers to walk." Arthur threw down his napkin. "I don't want their money!" Jordan knew the fight Arthur was up against and worried the directors of the bank would give in to pressure. "Then let's get moving to gain the support you need. I'll talk with Barnett. He's your biggest worry. He's counting on me to endorse his senate campaign and needs my support. I may be able to persuade him to help us out. Dunhill could also be a problem I'll look into."

Arthur said nothing; he thought he had Dunhill on his side, now not so sure. "Thanks Jordan, I'll get with my officers this afternoon and tell them in no uncertain terms what is on the line. Where do they think they can go? The positions they hold here are not that easy to find."

"Thanks for lunch Art. I'll call you tonight and let you know what I find."

"Lillian, I need to see you." He scribbled some notes and checked the computer as she came in. "I want a meeting with Swan, Conlan, Douglas and Lawrence at three-thirty today in the Boardroom. Set up a dinner meeting with Dunhill and Preston and tell Dan to get me to the club at six. How are you doing?" Lillian looked up from her tablet, "I'm fine Mr. Barrington, thank you."

Clark Barnett and Roy Jensen showed up for a two o'clock meeting and Lillian showed them to Arthur's office. Barnett gave her a gushing hello as he always did, the cad, he was someone she didn't like. She realized she had not stopped for lunch and went to the kitchen where Della and Mary were cleaning up and ready to go home.

"Did you forget to eat again Miss Lillian?"

She loved to tease Lillian and was one of the few who could get by with it. "Yes, I guess I did." Della brought a bowl of tuna salad from the refrigerator, placed some on a dish with a hardboiled egg and carrot sticks. "Here, sit and enjoy your lunch, we're going home."

Dan was Mr. Barrington's driver, security guard and general all-around gopher. He was on-call for any and all emergencies, business and personal for Arthur and his wife. Dan loved his job; Mr. Barrington treated him well and trusted him completely. He had been trained in defensive driving techniques and the official car was equipped with bullet-proof glass and puncture-proof tires. He liked the idea of subversive activity and secretly hoped for an opportunity to use his training as he felt sure he could escape any situation. Mr. Barrington frequently insisted on driving his own car and Dan would be required to follow at a safe distance for security purposes. He liked to complain about some of his duties but was careful not to say anything at work, only to his wife and friends on his own time.

Arthur flew to New York the next morning to discuss the Bartel problem with his friend, John Meier. "This threat is real, John. I need some time to set my defense."

"Give me a day or two and I'll see what I can do. I have a friend at the newspaper who owes me a favor. Hold tight till I get back to you."

Dan stopped by Lillian's desk that afternoon. "Mr. Barrington seemed to be in a good mood when they landed. I drove him to Mr. Banks office and he told me to take a break and be back there by five."

"Thanks, Dan. I'll see you in the morning."

Lillian thought of the unfolding events. The meeting the day before with Mr. Barrington's staff must have shaken some of them. Bill Lawrence would stand by whatever Mr. Barrington decided, true to the end. Doug Swan would be undecided, waiting for the best offer. Diane Conlan would wait to judge the winner and be anointed part of whatever team emerged. Tom Morrison would side with Mr. Barrington. He had nothing to lose, he would be happy to retire to Montana with his wife and horses.

John Douglas was a loner, on one hand he seemed loyal to the corporation but on the other hand he seemed to hold a dream for something greater, more important with greater influence. She knew Mr. Barrington was going through the same process of elimination.

Bill Lawrence, executive vice president at Barrington was one of Lillian's favorites. Tall, thin and balding which looked somewhat distinguished on him, he had a glimmer in his eyes and a charm about him that was intoxicating. He walked with the halting measure of a man with a bad back from a horrible boating accident years before in which his wife was killed. Bill had re-married just last year to an attractive blond, a former model ten years younger than he. His friends teased him about keeping up with her but he laughed it off telling them they were jealous. He had worked at Barrington for fifteen years and had come to Arthur's rescue more than once in battles with the Board of Directors. He stopped by Lillian's desk after lunch. "Is Arthur going to make it in today?" She never mentioned where Arthur was, who he was with or when she expected him and Bill knew that. "You should call his cell phone and ask him."

"Touché Lillian, loyal to the end, I like that in you. Have you ever considered working for the KGB?"

"I'll think about that." Bill laughed and walked away. At least he has a sense of humor, she thought, the others were afraid to talk with her, afraid what they said would make its way back to Arthur.

Doug Swan had been with Barrington for three years as Senior Vice President of Retail. He liked to stay to himself and showed his insecurities at the most unexpected times. There was a law on the twenty-first floor that no one was to have food or beverages in their office, a result of a spill on some rather important documents years before. Doug ignored the rule and brought a thermal cup of coffee in his briefcase each day, his form of rebellion.

Diane Conlan was the newest member of the executive team on-board eighteen months before from a job in London with the World Bank. She believed her experience in Europe gave credence to her reputation and should provide a certain level of aplomb. She was married to a one-time Olympic athlete who owned a public relations company.

Lillian was not impressed. She viewed Diane as phony and self-absorbed with an ego-maniac personality of enormous proportions.

Tom Morrison, another senior vice president, was in charge of mergers and acquisitions; an ambiguous position of secrecy and intrigue he seemed to enjoy. His whereabouts was always a secret as he may be meeting with a potential acquisition candidate. A receptionist had been fired years before because she mentioned to a caller that Mr. Morrison was in Dallas for the day. The caller surmised why he was in Dallas and managed to stall a potential deal in as a result. Tom was strictly ivy-league, a graduate of Princeton and Wharton; he had the credentials to take him to the top. At fifty-one he was tall, trim and athletic, worked out at the club three mornings a week, played tennis with his wife on weekends and had climbed Mt. Everest the year before with his brother. He was energetic and always on the lookout for a new challenge in his personal life as well as in his work.

CHAPTER TWO

"Bartel faces SEC Investigation", front page of the morning paper. The story detailed reports of inappropriate fee charges and misuse of funds. "An unnamed source told reporters the securities commission was investigating alleged criminal activity." Arthur walked briskly through the lobby and into his office. Bill Lawrence tapped on the doorframe. "Looks like some good news for us today." He was holding a folded newspaper in his hand. "Bill, come in. This news couldn't come at a better time, now we have to work on some changes around here. We dodged a bullet on this one, at least for now." Bill was as relieved as Arthur. "Let me know if I can help."

The members of the Board arrived for the ten o'clock meeting. Dan was on alert for the day to greet and assist in anyway needed. Mr. Jensen was the first to arrive and Mr. Barnett the last as usual.

Mr. Dunhill, Chairman of the Board, conducted the meeting. They began with the rudimentary agenda, boring to everyone who cared a whit about the company. Arthur sat quietly and scrutinized the people at the table, there was definitely an agenda at hand, he could feel it. "Mr. Douglas please present the quarterly report to the Board." John Douglas stood. "I'm happy to report the latest numbers show significant improvement in our return on investment. The past month's figures show growth in retail and trust accounts. Please turn to page four in your report for a graph showing improvements in these areas. The economy will continue to be a major factor in determining eventual performance. However, assuming the economy stabilizes at or near its current level, our expectation is that we could return to profitability sometime during the next year." There was silence in the room as each person turned to the report. "Mr. Chairman, may I speak?" Clark Barnett stood. "I have read the quarterly report and am dismayed at our position. How can we possibly expect to gain the market share we need with our current course of action?

We've been hit hard with market decline, shareholder resentment and a retail slide that makes it impossible to compete. I feel we need to consider a merger with a company like Bartel to strengthen our position. It's time for a change at Barrington." He sat down to silence. The members of the Board scanned the report he passed to them, each deciphering his own conclusion. Arthur didn't open his folder but watched the others as they read the information. Damned fools, he thought, can't they see through Barnett? He's trying to kick me out and sell my bank. No one spoke for ten minutes. The silence was deafening. Mr. Dunhill finally stood. "If there is no further business…" Arthur couldn't stand the charade any longer. He stood. "Mark, I have a question. Who in this room wants to see Barrington Bank survive?" He waited in silence as bowed heads fought with their thoughts. David Siegel spoke. "I do, Arthur. Barrington has been through worse times than this." Roy Jensen agreed and next came Mark Dunhill. "I don't like what I'm hearing. You have my vote Arthur." Hiram Baker followed suit and next was Pete Preston. Arthur's attention turned to Barnett.

"And you Clark, are you ready to sell us out?"
Barnett looked around the table obviously upset
with the show of support for Arthur. "We who are
in positions of answering to our shareholders
should take this possibility into consideration."
Arthur glared at him. "Clark, you are out-voted."
Mr. Dunhill stood. "Is there any further
business?" The room fell silent. "If not, this
meeting is adjourned." Arthur left immediately
through the side door and went straight to his
office. He sat at his desk and turned to look out
the windows. Barnett had to go.

Arthur called John Meier to tell him about
the Board meeting. "Barnett took a shot but the
other members stood beside me. Of course, the
Bartel news helped a little." John laughed. "Yes,
I imagine it did. Odd, isn't it, how one well-
timed news item can change the tone of a
meeting. Keep me posted."

Arthur met monthly with each of his
executive staff members individually where they
reported on their areas of responsibility. Lillian
spaced the five meetings around his calendar to
make it less grueling for him.

Diane Conlan showed up promptly at nine a.m., dressed to impress in an elegant turquoise suit and carried a scarlet red leather portfolio. "Good morning Arthur, beautiful day isn't it?" He stood to shake her hand. "Yes, it is. Have a seat Diane." He showed her to a comfortable chair in the seating area of his office and sat opposite her. "Tell me what you've been up to." She smiled and opened the portfolio. "The good news is in the Trust Department. We brought in a charitable trust worth $50 million last week with a family in Michigan and picked up three accounts from United totaling $14.5 million. Our fee revenue increased ten percent." Arthur listened carefully and noted she began with 'the good news.' He waited for the other shoe to drop. "Great, keep it up. Find out what's going on at United, there's a reason people are moving their accounts and we can take more of them." She made a note and continued. "Insurance made modest gains last month, up five percent and Security Corp is flat due to market conditions." Arthur stopped her. "Market condition is no excuse Diane. Steve had some problems with an equity fund I know but our blue chip and small cap funds should have covered that.

You need to keep an eye on him and let him know his performance is critical this month." Diane jotted more notes. Her pulse was racing as she didn't like Arthur questioning her ability to control her direct reports. "How's Tim doing in Wisconsin?" She took a quick breath. Arthur was really pinning her down today. He knew Tim's numbers were down last month and he had shown little improvement. "I met with him last week and told him I need an increase of fifteen percent in contracts by the end of the month or he's gone. I don't think he'll make it and I want to move Joe Reagan in to replace him." Arthur watched her as she talked; she was backpedaling, trying to take control. She continued. "Reagan's background in leasing is impressive and I know he can do the job." Arthur stroked the arms of his chair. "I want to know before you let Tim go. Are there any other issues?" She closed the portfolio and placed her hands on it. "No, that's the status for now. I do have a question. I have a meeting in Louisiana next week where I need to get out and back the same day and can't do it commercially. Is it alright to take one of the corporate planes?" Arthur laughed. "I have no control of the planes.

You have to go through Lillian for that, she is in charge. Good luck." He stood and walked Diane to the door. She returned to her office, closed the door, tossed her portfolio on the sofa and stared out the window. Damned, she thought, Tim is out for sure, I'm not going through that again and Steve is on very thin ice, I will not take the fall for him. She sat at her desk and pushed the intercom. "Leslie, bring me last month's Security Corp file and write a letter to Mr. Barrington thanking him for our meeting today. Call David Reagan and tell him I want to see him tomorrow at eight-thirty and tell Lillian I will need one of the bank planes next Wednesday to fly to New Orleans." Leslie brought the file she asked for along with a red folder of letters needing her signature. Diane opened the red folder. "These should have gone out yesterday, what took you so long? Here, wait, I'll sign them now and I want you to walk to the post office and mail them yourself." She handed the folder to her assistant without another word and picked up the phone to make a call as she turned her back to Leslie as a sign to leave.

Leslie waited for the elevator when Dan walked by. "Leaving so soon?" She held up the stack of letters. "I've been dispatched to the post office because Ms. Conlan didn't sign these yesterday and they must go out today." Dan took the letters from her. "Go have a cup of coffee and take a breather. I'll take these to the post office." Leslie thanked him. "I could use a breather, thank you Dan." Leslie stopped by Lillian's desk on her way back from coffee. "Do you have a moment Lillian?" She looked up from her computer. "Certainly, sit down. What is it you need?" She liked Leslie and felt sorry for her being treated so poorly by Diane Conlan. "Mrs. Conlan would like to take one of the corporate planes to New Orleans next Wednesday." Lillian took off her glasses. "So, she sent you to ask me? Tell Mrs. Conlan I need a request in writing with the names of all passengers, the business reason for the trip, what time she needs to arrive and if it is overnight. I will check the schedule and if a plane is available, I will give the departure time, airport location and tail number." Leslie wrote as she spoke. "Thank you, Lillian, I'll let her know."

Lillian watched as she walked away. She liked Leslie from the first time they met. She had interviewed her for the job of executive assistant to Diane Conlan and had been pleasantly impressed with her sense of style and refinement. She was poised, well-dressed, sat up straight and had a delightful way of smiling as she spoke. Lillian had explained the position was as executive assistant to a woman who was coming in to head up the bank holding companies. She remembered how excited Leslie was on her first day at work when Lillian gave her a tour of the twenty-first floor. They toured the two executive dining rooms, the kitchen, the conference rooms, the ladies lounge and Lillian introduced her to the other assistants. She had watched Leslie's progress over the past few months as she gained confidence in her role and displayed professionalism in her duties. She was an excellent addition to the twenty-first floor.

Diane returned from her lunch meeting. "Come in Leslie, I want you to get these files off my desk." Leslie followed her. "Mrs. Conlan, I talked with Lillian about the plane." She explained the details she needed. Diane glared at Leslie.

"You know the meeting is at eleven, so she should plan however long it takes to drive from the airport to the meeting, the business reason is my presentation to the New Orleans Trust department. What else do you need?" Leslie reminded her. "The names of who is going and if you want breakfast catered." Diane dropped the stack of files on her desk in front of Leslie. "Of course we will want breakfast. The passengers will be me; Steve and Doug Swan is coming along too. Is that all?" Leslie picked up the stack of files. "Yes. Lillian will let us know if the plane is available." She turned and left the room.

Joe Reagan showed up the next morning at eight fifteen for his meeting. The receptionist rang Leslie to tell her he was there and she buzzed Mrs. Conlan. "Mr. Reagan is here to see you." Diane replied, "I'll be right there." Leslie saw the phone line light up and knew Diane had placed a call. She began her work for the day and glanced at the light on the phone occasionally. It was nine-thirty and Mr. Reagan had been waiting over an hour. Thirty minutes later Diane opened her door. "I am ready to see Joe." Leslie went to Mr. Reagan in the lobby. "Ms. Conlan is ready to see you now."

She felt like apologizing to him for the wait but decided against it. She showed him in to Diane's office, closed the door and returned to her desk thinking how rude it was to keep someone waiting so long. It became a regular occurrence that Leslie resented. Diane would summon her direct reports for monthly meetings. They would arrive by eight a.m. for an eight-thirty meeting from New York, Dallas, Phoenix or Wisconsin only to be kept waiting until ten or eleven o'clock in the reception area. They had been up since five a.m. for a seven o'clock flight to Chicago only to sit cooling their heels until Madam Chairman saw fit to allow them to enter her chamber. Leslie announced their arrival and watched as she played her game of cat and mouse. She stalled, acted too busy to see them, and enjoyed her control over them.

CHAPTER THREE

Lillian buzzed Arthur's intercom. "Mr. Banks is on line two." He picked up the phone. "Jordan, thanks for calling. Sorry I missed you last night. How was your discussion with Barnett?"

"He was guarded as usual. I asked him about his business, you know, to get him talking about himself, his favorite subject." Arthur laughed. "That must have taken a while."

"Humility is not his strong suit. I asked him what was new at Barrington. He was cautious because he knows you and I are friends but told me he thought it was time for a shake-up, new blood to improve the company."

"He thinks he has all the answers. I'd like to shake him up."

"Art, I have a suspicion he has an interest in Bartel. Why else is he being so insistent on this change he wants? He knows the Board supports you and he will have a tough job changing their minds."

"I'd like to agree with you Jordan, but money talks and that's the only important thing to him. You never know who will turn on you if the incentive is big enough."

"Of course, he told me how well his campaign is going and that the polls show him leading by a significant margin. I know he was hoping I would offer my endorsement. I suggested we could possibly help each other."

"Good job, Jordan, he'll think about that."

"I'm having dinner with Dunhill next week. I'll let you know what he has to say. I have a meeting in ten minutes, Art, I'll keep in touch." Arthur walked to Bill Lawrence's office, "Busy Bill?"

"Hi Art, of course I'm busy, up to my ears, I have to keep my job you know. I'm joking, come on in. What's up?" Arthur took a seat. "I want to talk with you about Barnett, what do you think he has up his sleeve?" Bill got up and closed his door. "The walls have ears Art." He sat down beside Art. "I've been working on that. I hear he spent two million of his own money so far on his campaign and needs to raise more funds fast. He is so hell-bent on winning the senate race.

There's also talk he's thinking of selling off one of his companies. You wouldn't know it to talk to him, he tells everyone how great he is doing, but there are some who think he may be in trouble. Do you think he has a connection to Bartel?"

"Wow, I'd like to prove that! We could unseat him from the Board with that news." Art stood. "Let's work on it, there has to be somebody we can get to talk."

Arthur returned to his office and checked his email messages. His friend John Meier planned to be in Chicago for the weekend. "Any chance you and Ann are available for dinner Saturday night?" Art picked up the phone and called him. "John, Art here. I just read your email and we are free Saturday, how about dinner at our house at six? You don't want to stand in line at a restaurant and Ann makes a mean beef tenderloin."

"You're on, I'll be there at six, thanks Art." Arthur dialed his house. "Ann, I just talked with John Meier and invited him for dinner at the house Saturday night at six, okay with you?"

"I haven't seen John for months, of course it is fine. Can you pick-up some wine?"

Arthur and Ann lived in an exclusive gated area on the far north side. Their large Colonial-style house comprised every luxurious appointment one could dream of; a large kitchen equipped with the finest cabinetry and appliances and a wall of windows overlooking the wooded back lawn. There were four bedroom suites, a media room, great room and a dining room with a magnificent glass table and eight chairs upholstered in sherbet colors of pink, kiwi, aqua and orange. Ann had rejected a formal living room as she knew they wouldn't use the space. A large solarium with leaded glass windows and stone floors overlooked the manicured gardens and a three-car garage housed Arthur's restored Alfa Romeo as well as their new cars.

Arthur and Ann met at Northwestern in their junior year and married as soon as they graduated. She was petite, only five feet three inches tall, with short brown hair and bright blue eyes. She was full of energy, played tennis, golf and dabbled in watercolor paintings when she had the time. They had no children much to their regret, but were extremely close and crazy about each other. Ann volunteered with local charitable foundations and the children's hospital.

She loved to cook Arthur's favorite foods and watched his diet as closely as possible without torturing him about his cholesterol level. They had an active social life and were highly respected in the community with influential friends. Arthur downplayed his stature and promoted an image of being modest and humble, true to his Midwestern roots. He tried to keep up with Ann's athletic activities but had given up tennis the year before after a nasty sprained knee that bothered him for months. They owned a vacation home in Canada where they relaxed, fished and went boating on summer holidays and a condo in Montana where they went to ski and have time alone.

John Meier arrived at the Barrington home at six-thirty. "Ann, hello. You look great as always." He gave her a kiss on the cheek and shook hands with Arthur. "Sorry I ran late, that GPS took me around the other side of the lake." Ann put her arm around John and led him to the great room. "Come here and relax, we're having a glass of wine." Arthur brought a drink to John and sat on the sofa beside him. Ann passed a tray of steamed shrimp and olives.

"I do hope you have your bags with you, we're counting on you staying with us for the weekend." Arthur spoke up, "I probably didn't mention it John, just assumed you would."

"My bags are in the car but I do have a reservation downtown." Ann stood, "Which hotel John?"

"Here is the confirmation, I would much rather be here with the two of you."

"I'll cancel it right now. You two can talk about all of your business secrets while I'm gone." John watched Ann leave the room. "Arthur, you found the perfect woman you know."

"You're right John, nobody else would put up with me. Isn't it about time you start seeing someone?" John's wife had died three years before and he had been alone ever since. "You took the best one Art, there aren't any others like Ann." Arthur poured him another glass of wine and filled him in on the latest developments with Bartel and his Board of Directors. "That press release made them retreat for now, gave us some time to recoup our position. What I need is some scoop on Bartel, a relationship with Barnett."

"I have a friend who has known Barnett's family for years, since he was in college. I'll see what I can find out."

"Dinner's ready you two." Ann led them to the kitchen table set for three, with a platter of rare beef tenderloin, a salad and roasted vegetables. "This is where we have family dinners as the dining room is too big."

"Family sounds good to me, thanks for including me in that description." They talked for hours about old times and shared vacations. "I remember those fishing trips to Canada. I haven't relaxed that much in years." Arthur agreed. "We're going again in June, why don't you join us, the fishing will be good and you know Ann's cooking can't be beat."

"You're on, just let me know the date. I'll dust off my fishing gear."

"John, remember how the three of us went bar hopping in Old Town when we were in college? You and Arthur introduced me to gin and tonics and I had the worst headache of my life."

"I know Arthur and I had a few hangovers from those nights too, but it was fun.
I remember how cold it was walking downtown. We nearly froze!"

They talked until eleven when John said he said he was ready to retire. "Thank you both, dinner was great as always. I'll see you in the morning."

Sunday morning breakfast was waiting when John came downstairs; pancakes, sausages, fresh fruit and bagels set out on the countertop. Arthur pulled out a chair for him. "It's about time you got up. How did you sleep?"
"Your home is wonderful. I slept like a log and I'm starving." Ann joined them and poured fresh orange juice. "You should come visit more often John. We miss you." Arthur and John went for a walk after breakfast and talked about business. Arthur told him about his suspicions of Clark Barnett. "It's a matter of time Art, if he is involved with Bartel it will come out eventually. Let me know what happens." John left for his flight at two o'clock.

Lillian was surprised to find Arthur in his office when she arrived at seven-thirty. She tapped on the doorframe and said good morning to him. "You're in early, is everything okay?"
"Surprised you huh? Yes, everything's fine, my breakfast meeting was canceled. Jensen was in a minor fender bender this morning so I came on to work.

Do you think you could sneak a cup of coffee in here?"

"Give me ten minutes." Lillian went to the kitchen and made a pot of coffee. She found some banana bread in the refrigerator that she sliced and put on a small tray with the coffee. "Don't tell anyone where you got this or there may be a mutiny." She set the tray on his desk. "Thank you, Lillian, I won't say a word. Have a seat and tell me what you've been up to, we haven't had much time to talk." He took a sip of coffee. "This is nice without everyone eavesdropping to hear what we're saying. You should come in early more often. I went to Wisconsin Saturday to visit my niece and her family, two daughters, three and five years old who never stop. I was so glad to get home Sunday afternoon, I was exhausted. I have been thinking about taking a trip to New York in the Spring to see some shows and do some shopping. I would only be gone three days." Arthur raised his eyebrows. "We must be paying you too much if you can afford to shop in New York. I'm joking, go whenever you want and have a great time. You need to get away from all of this once in a while."

"Thank you, Mr. Barrington. I'll put the dates on your calendar. Are you and Ann planning any trips?" He glanced at the picture of his wife on the desk. "We are planning a few days at the cabin in June for some fishing but I don't have exact dates yet. I'll talk it over with Ann and let you know. In fact, I have an invitation here from our friends in Louisville who have box seats at the Kentucky Derby. I forgot to mention it to Ann and I know she will want to go. You know, it's a chance to buy a new hat." Lillian laughed. "It sounds like fun. I think I hear the troops. I'd better get back to my desk. I'll have Dan sneak the tray back to the kitchen later. We can't let them see you with coffee in your office." The 'no beverage' rule on the twenty-first floor had been Arthur's idea. Lillian passed Dan on the way to her desk. "There's a tray in Mr. Barrington's office, would you please take it to the kitchen when he's finished? There's banana bread in the refrigerator, help yourself." Dan was always hungry.

Arthur checked his calendar for the day. His first meeting was with Doug Swan at nine for his monthly review. "Good morning Arthur, are you ready for me?"

"Good morning Doug, yes, come in and have a seat." Arthur got up and motioned to a club chair. Doug sat down and smoothed the crease in his slacks as he crossed his legs. Mr. Perfectionist, thought Arthur. "How are Kay and the family?" "Everyone is fine, thank you. Jack will graduate from high school this year and has been accepted at the University of Kentucky. Sally is about to turn sixteen and can't wait to get her drivers' license much to my chagrin. You know how you worry about them." Damn, he thought, Arthur doesn't have kids. "I'm sure she'll do fine." Arthur noticed the faux pas and decided to put him at ease. Doug rambled on. "Kay has been in Maryland for a month visiting her sister." Arthur decided to get down to business. "What do you have for me?" Doug seemed relieved to talk about work instead of his personal life. "The rise in credit card interest rates is generating millions. We have another year before Congress tries to reign us in with some reform program.

If and when that happens, we will have greatly increased profits. Customers were angry at first but they soon learned we weren't the only bank leading the charge. There is nowhere for them to turn if they want credit.

We made a deal with Jefferson Foods, exclusive rights to add ATMs in twenty-two stores in Indiana and Ohio that will bring in fee revenue of two million annually." He paused for Arthur's response. "Good job Doug, we get our name in the stores and make banking convenient for shoppers." Doug nodded and went on. "We're working on a deal with a major beer brewery to market our card for Spring break in Florida, Texas and New Orleans. No national publicity because of the lobbyists, but we can count on ten to twenty thousand new accounts with annual fees of half a million plus interest charges and late fees estimated at one million the first year. Arthur smiled. "Spring break ain't what it used to be."

"I have a big surprise you will want your staff to see." He handed a copy of a report to Arthur. "It's a major hit for us, a new design for a thumbprint reader that will eliminate the account number from our cards improving security. We've tested the prototype and it's foolproof. Consumers are going to go wild for this. If we can come out of the gate first with this, we should be able to count on two and a half million new accounts nationally in the first six months."

Arthur scanned through the presentation with details of the card reader and profit analysis. He leaned forward with his hands on his knees. "I want to see this thing. When will it be ready?" "I put Deborah Harris in charge of working with Dynamic Editions for production. They're telling her six months and I'm asking for two." Arthur stood, walked to his desk and pushed the intercom. "Lillian, call Deborah in marketing and ask her to come up here." He sat back down. "I want you to set-up a presentation for Friday with the entire staff, check with Lillian for my schedule. We have to get this done now. We can't wait. If we're not first with this we'll lose out big time." Deborah Harris came to the door. "Mr. Barrington, you wanted to see me?" Arthur stood. "Yes Deborah, please come in, sorry to interrupt you but we need to discuss something." She said hello to Doug and sat on the sofa. "Doug was telling me about the thumbprint reader you're working on. We have to get moving on this. What do you need to get it done now?" Deborah pursed her lips, uneasy at being pushed.

"Mr. Barrington, I have been working on this day and night for six weeks since our research department came up with the configuration."

"I didn't ask how long you have been working on it, Deborah, I'm asking what it will take to get it done now." Arthur wanted an answer to his question. "Okay, the prototype has been approved and we contracted with Dynamic Editions for production of the first twenty thousand machines for delivery in May. I will need to give them an incentive to move up delivery, I'd guess twenty-five to fifty thousand."

"Done. I want to see the prototype as soon as you can get it to me, before Friday. I'll call George and tell him to give you the funds you need. You work with Dynamic, tell them we want to increase the first production to fifty thousand and call me first thing tomorrow morning to let me know what they say. Thanks Deborah." Arthur stood and showed her to the door. He turned to Doug. "You get on the phone with your guys in the field and get everything ready for set-up in two weeks. I want a major national media blitz on this one."

"I have Manning Media working on that. I'll have them here for the meeting on Friday."

Arthur called his chief financial officer and told him to get the funds marketing would need immediately. "Get a check to Deborah today." Arthur knew this was a remarkable advantage in the credit arena, an advantage he intended to capitalize on for as long as possible. He sat at his desk and made some notes in Doug's folder, 'major expansion not handled properly', 'negligence with timeline', 'poor leadership skills', 'thumb print production follow-up'. He closed the folder and looked out the window. He couldn't believe Doug Swan had let something like this slide, he hadn't even mentioned it at last month's meeting. He thought about their conversation, Doug said his wife had been in Maryland for a month, maybe they were having trouble. He decided to keep a closer eye on Swan. He didn't want any more slip-ups.

CHAPTER FOUR

David Siegel had been a Director of the Barrington Board for five years. He was a highly successful businessman who traded in world monetary markets with the instincts of a Wall Street predator. He was as powerful, if not more so than any national banker, with a keen understanding of shadow finance and the skills to leverage investments to enhance his balance sheet. Arthur sought his opinion and valued his insight as well as his friendship.

David was somewhat of an enigma in Chicago; wealthy, charming, attractive and a confirmed bachelor at fifty-one. Many women vied for his attention over the years but he focused his energies and attention squarely on business as he built an empire. He was a meticulous dresser, tall and thin with an athletic build and hair beginning to gray at the temples. He was rarely seen in public except for occasional charity events.

His time was filled with private clubs and corporate Boardrooms. He had a penchant for the utmost security, refusing interviews and photographs whenever possible which only served to make the media more determined to catch him off guard. They tracked his every move hoping for a look behind the walls of privacy.

He and his brother had inherited sizeable fortunes from their parents and David wielded his power to invest in real estate with the prowess of a seasoned sage. He had grown up in New York and moved to Chicago ten years ago but still maintained financial liaisons there. He kept his family's attorney on retainer and still used New York banks to finance his investments. His move to Chicago was purely for business reasons, to establish a foothold of real estate investments in and around the city. The prices in New York had become impossible to compete on the scale he had in mind. In ten years, he had purchased downtown office towers he leased to major corporations, high-rise condominium buildings on the north shore, industrial warehouses and several thousand acres of land on the northwest side of Chicago.

He built his own corporate headquarters on forty acres of ground near the airport, a building easily recognized in the familiar matte gray and glossy silver that adorned the logo of his company. His newest venture had been in the works for four years. It would consist of a luxury destination hotel with specialty shops. There would also be restaurants and entertainment, a massive development that would draw people from surrounding states. The demographics predicted a plethora of consumers he couldn't ignore. David began by purchasing tracts of land through a fictitious corporation for rock bottom prices. Most were farmlands where owners were happy to unload the struggle of working long hours to eke out a living. One owner had monitored the sales and surmised whoever was buying up the land would want his property and knew it was an opportunity to make a huge profit. David's agent approached the owner with an offer he quickly dismissed insisting he was not interested in selling. David studied the plat maps and arranged to fly over the property the next day. He could see the land had not been farmed for years.

Two aging barns and a large farmhouse stood in a clearing half a mile from fenced pastures with Black Angus cattle and a handful of horses. Most of the land was forested with oak, hickory and pine trees he could sell. "Run a check on him, I want to know what he owes on the property and his weak spot." The agent reported back to David that the owner had two mortgages on the farm totaling $80,000. "He is seventy-four years old and struggling to make ends meet. He is holding out for more money." David looked over the offer once more. "The old fool should be happy for the chance to unload it. Increase it by $100,000. No, make it $50,000. I will up the offer if necessary. I want his land and I'll get it one way or another." David phoned Arthur Barrington. "Art, do you know the head of First Savings Bank?"

"Sure, he is Charlie Denton. I've known him for years." David explained the problem he was having with the land owner. "I have made a fair offer to him and I'm sure the bank would like to unload those loans before he eventually defaults." "I'll call Charlie. He owes me a favor. Maybe he can convince the owner to reconsider the offer. I'll let you know."

The following week David's agent phoned with the news that the owner accepted the latest offer to sell. "I don't know what pushed him over the edge but we finally got him." David smiled into the phone. "Good job. I just saved $50,000 and the timber on the land will sell for nearly that amount. Let's get this wrapped up before he changes his mind." David called Arthur. "Thanks for your help Art, I got the land. Now I can move forward with my plans." He invited Arthur to join him for lunch the next week at his offices. "I want to show you the plans for this project."

David proudly showed Art the topography model of Brighton that held center court in his office. The scope of the project was impressive and David's enthusiasm for the venture was contagious. He pointed to the southern border of the development. "Here is the last tract of land you helped me win, one hundred acres of pristine farmland." Arthur was impressed at the size of the project and the planning that had obviously taken years of work. "How soon can you get started?" David explained the zoning approvals took time and expected a wait of four to six months before construction could begin.

Five of the zoning requests sailed through but the final request was stalled due to a title check. David met with his staff and his group of architects and gave the go ahead to begin construction on the approved acres.

He had assembled a top flight staff of pros experienced in development planning and insisted on weekly progress updates. He devoted the majority of his time pouring over timelines, maps and design changes.

Ten months into the project he began feeling pressure to speed up the work. The price tag was staggering and delays cost him tens of thousands of dollars each week. He had managed to nail down the initial financing through his contacts in New York but needed a large line of credit to complete the project. He approached Arthur Barrington. "Art, the development of Brighton is proceeding nicely. I am going to need financing for the final touches, a credit line of $5.5 million." Arthur didn't hesitate. "I will make the arrangements David. The plans are phenomenal, I can't wait to see it completed and it's all Ann talks about." Insider lending was not uncommon for the bank. They regularly made loans to the Board of Directors and their families.

They provided funding for real estate developments, medical buildings and any number of ventures for the directors. Outside business owners would need to provide volumes of tax and financial information, business plans, blueprints, legal documents and wait months for the bank's approval or rejection. The odds of obtaining funding for a project the size and scope of Brighton would be slim.

The final hurdle David faced was the zoning board meeting at the end of the month and his main focus was to get the final request approved, one way or another. He sent one county commissioner a leather-bound box of Private Reserve Cuban cigars, facilitated a job in a top-flight law firm for the daughter of a state representative and invited the head of the zoning board to use his home in Mexico for a month. David knew how to get what he wanted. The request was approved unanimously by the zoning board.

David had been involved in a romantic relationship with Barbara Ornstein for nearly two years; a relationship of convenience for him, someone to accompany him to social functions, someone to see when he chose, she was attractive, discreet and could be charming when she wanted. She would marry him in an instant, he knew, but couldn't imagine spending his life with her mood swings and erratic temperament. He sometimes thought of calling it off but didn't relish the idea of going through one of her angry scenes. He provided her with a luxury condo on the north shore, a car and a monthly allowance that kept her happy most of the time. They spent occasional weekends in New York and once or twice a year flew to his home in Mexico.

David went to New York often, sometimes twice a month to meet with his investment reps or his attorneys. His most recent visit held a pleasant surprise in the form of Isabelle Sachs. She was a stunning beauty with silky brown hair, a creamy complexion and the bluest eyes he had ever seen.

He saw beautiful women every day but the charm of Isabelle rose above beauty; she was intelligent, soft-spoken and sophisticated with a warmth and gentleness about her that was enchanting. Their meeting had been brief, a quick introduction in the lobby of his financial advisor's office, but he couldn't stop thinking of her. He asked his advisor Martin, about her background. "She is an obstetrician in a small Manhattan practice. I knew her father who died just last year and I am helping with his estate. She got her medical degree at Harvard, is single and thirty-four years old. She is a charming young woman, unpretentious, smart as a whip and not bad to look at, don't you agree?" Martin knew David would be interested, what man wouldn't, but there was an age difference that could be a problem. "I do agree. She is absolutely lovely. Do you think you could arrange a dinner, you know, for two or three of your favorite clients?" Martin put his hand on David's shoulder. "I think I just may be able to work that out. I'll let you know." David flew back to Chicago and thought about seeing her again.

Martin phoned him the next week and told him the dinner was scheduled for Saturday, the fourteenth. "I'll pick you up at your hotel at seven o'clock."

David had planned the coming weekend with Barbara, a drive to a favorite getaway Saturday night and back home on Sunday. Suddenly he did not feel like being with her and decided to make an excuse. She flew into a rage when he called to tell her something had come up and their plans had to be postponed. She pouted about how she had looked forward to seeing him and tried to make him feel guilty, but finally regained her composure and asked him to call her on Sunday. David hung up the phone and decided he had to stop seeing her for good. It would not be simple to end their relationship but it was time to call it quits, she was far too clinging, whining and temperamental and he was tired of dealing with her.

The first thing on Arthur's schedule Monday morning was to check with Deborah in marketing on the status of the thumbprint project. As soon as he got to his office Doug Swan appeared in his doorway. "Good morning Arthur, do you have a minute?"

"Sure, come in Doug."

"I have some good news for you. The manufacturer of the thumbprint machines agreed to the deadline of two weeks and the increase to fifty thousand machines. We only had to give them twenty-five thousand to step up the delivery. I have been on the phone all weekend with the media group to formulate the press releases to go out with the implementation of the project. We're all set to go."

"That's great Doug. Good work. Have you talked with Debra this morning?"

"Not yet, I left a message for her but haven't heard back yet."

"Keep me posted, I want to get this nailed down today." Doug agreed and left for his office. Arthur called Debra's office only to get her voicemail message. "Lillian, clear the decks for today and the rest of the week, we're cooking a big one. I want to see Debra as soon as she arrives and ask John Douglas to come see me."

"Right away Mr. Barrington." John Douglas came to Arthur's office immediately. "Good morning Arthur. What do you need?"

"Hi John, I want your advice on a couple of things.

Has Swan said anything to you about a new card reader?"

"Yes, a few weeks ago he asked me about a patent attorney in Washington for the card reader. How's that coming?"

"You won't believe this John, I just heard about it yesterday. He should have told me about this before contracting for the machines." John shook his head. "You know Swan, he wants every detail nailed down before opening up with anything. He worries too much about failure but I can't believe he took this as far as he did without talking with you."

"I'm not happy with this. Swan isn't going to fly solo with my company. He needs to follow procedure. I shouldn't have to pry information out of him and I won't." His intercom rang, "Mr. Barrington, Debra is here to see you. Shall I send her in?"

"Yes Lillian, thanks." John stood to leave. "I'd like you to stay for this John. Debra, I've been waiting for you. What do you have?" She set a box on the corner of his desk, opened it and lifted out the card reader. "I have been at Dynamic this morning to check on production and pick up this reader.

50

They agreed to increase our numbers and move up delivery. Here, let me show you how this works." She gave a quick instruction on the thumbprint reader and Arthur was impressed. "Look at this John, pretty impressive don't you think?"

"What an idea, no account number on the card, but how does the consumer use the card over the Internet?" Doug Swan appeared at the door. "Arthur, may I come in?"

"Sure Doug, come on in. Debra brought the card reader." Debra went on to answer John's question. "There's a code on the back of the card that can be entered when necessary, online or somewhere with outdated equipment." Doug Swan sat down beside John. "What do you think John?"

"It's pretty exciting, wait until the directors see this." Arthur spoke up. "Doug will give us a full presentation Friday morning with the media group here to show us the advertising campaign. Is it all on schedule Doug?"

"Yes sir, Art, we're ready to go."

"Thank you, Debra, I'll keep this one. I want a status report every day until we launch this to the public.

Doug, I'd like to talk with you if you have a few minutes."

Debra and John took the cue to leave them alone. Arthur opened the folder he kept on his meetings with Doug. "I looked over my notes from our meeting last month and can't believe you didn't mention this to me. I don't like it Doug. You took too much liberty to go it alone on this one." Doug bit his lip. "You're right Art. I got so wrapped up in it when I saw the potential in the market. I wanted to get it set in stone before anyone else beat us to it." Art closed the folder and looked at Doug. "I will only tell you this once Doug, the decisions at this bank are mine. The Board holds me responsible and I must have confidence and trust in the people working for me. Do you understand?"

"Yes sir. It won't happen again."

"I want to review your presentation before Friday's meeting. Be here at ten Thursday morning."

"Thank you, Arthur. I'll have it ready." Doug returned to his office and closed the door. His palms were clammy and his head throbbed. He sat at his desk, closed his eyes and thought about what Arthur had said to him.

He had managed to go to the top of Arthur's list of red flags, a position where his every move would be scrutinized and his ability to perform the job questioned.

Arthur glanced at his watch. He had thirty minutes before Beathe Billingsly would be there for lunch. He took a deep breath. He wasn't sure he was up for her today. She would talk incessantly about her charity fundraiser at the end of the month and describe in length details about which Arthur could care less. The bank had pledged $25,000 for the charity and he had the check in his pocket to present to her.

Lillian announced Mrs. Billingsly's arrival and Arthur met her in the reception area. She was flustered, complaining about the weather as they walked to the dining room. "Oh Arthur, it is a monsoon out there! I was nearly blown away and I must look a fright." Arthur assured her she looked elegant as always but thought how over-dressed she was, with too much jewelry and make-up. Arthur guessed she must spend hours in front of the mirror. She launched into a saga of her recent trip to India, how oppressively hot it had been and the crowning blow of the airline losing her luggage.

"There I was in the Mumbai Palace with only my traveling clothes. It was devastating! The concierge was a *fabulous* fellow who sent in local couturiers with their collections and it cost a small fortune to select a wardrobe for the remainder of my stay." Arthur rang for Della to serve lunch. "I'm sure you're happy to be home. Tell me about the charity ball." She threw herself into details of the black-tie event, "Set Sail on the Magnificent Mile." The performing arts center will be transformed into a fabulous yacht, resplendent with a formal dining salon, a nightclub with dancers flown in from Broadway, a casino lounge, a tree-lined promenade and thousands of tiny lights simulating a star-filled sky. She droned on and on about the tons of flowers, the costumed Captain and crew and the caterers, "the best" in Chicago, of course, who promised voluptuous cuisine from around the world. Arthur congratulated her and told her how excited he and Ann were about attending. He handed the check to her. "Arthur, how generous of you! The committee will be extremely grateful. You won't be disappointed darling. It will be the event of the season and I can't even hint as to what the magnificent favors will be.

It's a monumental surprise!" Arthur finished his lunch and noticed Beathe had hardly taken a bite, she was so busy talking. Della cleared the dishes and replaced them with dessert of chocolate mousse with fresh raspberries. Beathe waved her away. "Thank you my dear but I must watch my figure carefully." Once behind the closed kitchen door Della straightened her back and sashayed across the kitchen with her nose in the air as Mary covered her mouth with her hand to muffle her laughter. "That woman could use some sweetening up."

Arthur stood as a sign to Beathe that lunch had ended. He helped her from the table and thanked her for joining him. "I'll tell Ann about the ball. She will be thrilled." Beathe kissed Arthur on the cheek. "Oh, yes, please do. Dear Ann will just adore what we're doing! Lunch was *fabulous* darling, thank you so much. Now I'm off. Tata!" Arthur returned to his office shaking his head.

Ann Barrington had stopped in during lunch and talked with Lillian. "I was out shopping and thought I'd pop in to see Arthur." Lillian told her he was having lunch with Mrs. Billingsly. "Shall I let him know you're here?"

Ann rolled her eyes and mockingly put her hand to her brow. "Oh, pleeeze no, Lillian. I'm sure he is engrossed in their conversation." She smiled, held out a shopping bag and whispered to Lillian. "I'm just going to leave this for him and run." She went to his office and set the bag on his chair. He would be thrilled with the first edition she found at the bookstore. She picked up the notepad from his desk, planted a lipstick kiss on it and set it down. She knew he would laugh when he saw it. She waved to Lillian on her way out. "Thanks Lillian, take care." Arthur returned to his office and found the book Ann left for him. He saw the lipstick kiss on his notepad and smiled. Ann had a way of lifting his spirits unlike any other person on earth.

CHAPTER FIVE

Lillian had set-up the Boardroom for Swan's presentation Friday morning and the tech department installed equipment needed for the media group ad campaign. Della set out coffee, fresh fruit, rolls and bottled water on the credenza. The executive staff assembled at eight-thirty, took their usual chairs and Doug Swan began his slideshow promptly at nine. Arthur watched Doug intently as he explained the program, the costs, the market share he anticipated and the annual revenue projections. He knew the project inside and out and answered every question with confidence. "Consumers want the latest and greatest technology and they will love this. We can add transaction fees to offset our start-up costs and they won't blink an eye. It's a prime opportunity while we have the lead in the market." There was a round of applause and they took a short break before the media group's campaign.

Arthur was pleased, the advertising blitz would hit newspaper, television and radio markets simultaneously with the rollout of the program to the public. There was another round of applause as the media group finished their program and handed out new cards around the room. "Groundbreaking", "Unprecedented", "Ingenious", the comments were enthusiastic and optimistic for the program. "Good job Doug." Art patted him on the back and returned to his office. Bill Lawrence was right behind him. "Got a minute Art?"

"Sure, come in. What did you think?"

"Pretty cool. If technology keeps going like this, you'll soon have robots running this place. Actually, this is just what we need now. The revenue from this will put us over the top, out of reach of Bartel. Does Barnett know about it?"

"Not yet. I want to see the look on his face when he sees the numbers."

"Lillian, I need to see you when you have a minute."

"Right away, Mr. Barrington." She gathered his mail and phone messages and went to his office.

"Jordan Banks wants you to call him and Tom Morrison wants to meet with you whenever you have time. I hesitate to bother you with this but I had a call from Paul this morning. He told me he had his hands full yesterday with Diane Conlan. The plane was delayed for takeoff due to fog. Mrs. Conlan became angry and demanded he keep checking with flight control for permission to take-off. He said she ranted and raved about being late for her arrival, until he threatened to cancel the flight if she didn't calm down." Arthur shook his head. "That's not good. Call Paul and tell him it won't happen again. I won't have my staff members acting that way. I'll speak with her. Thank you for telling me." Lillian smiled, pleased that Mrs. Conlan would be reprimanded for her behavior. "We had a great presentation this morning, here, take a look at this when you have time." He handed her a copy of Swan's presentation. "I think you will find it interesting." Arthur liked to keep Lillian up to date on things as big as this. "I want to keep my schedule as open as possible for the next couple of weeks until I'm sure we have this under control.

Now down to business. Please send a letter to the head of Dynamic Editions thanking them for stepping up production on the card readers. You'll find everything you need in the report. I want to see the file on Bartel again and the Leasing report for the last six months." Lillian took notes and asked if that was all. "That's it for now, thank you." Lillian returned to her desk to retrieve the files he wanted. "Tom Morrison will be in tomorrow at ten o'clock and here are your files." Arthur was reading something on his computer and didn't answer her. It was a news report from the Securities and Exchange Commission on the Bartel investigation. "The commission has found no basis for the charge of excessive fees; however, they are still investigating allegations of misappropriation of funds." Arthur read it again. Maybe Bartel was up to something illegal. He opened the file Lillian had placed on his desk. He searched the listing of officers again, looking for any correlation between them and Barnett. Nothing. He would have Tom Morrison look at it again, he had contacts all over the country.

Arthur dialed Jordan Banks. "Jordan, Arthur here returning your call."

"Arthur, thanks for getting back to me. I have some news for you. Can you stop by this afternoon?"

"I'll be there at three, okay with you?"

"Three o'clock is good, see you then." Arthur hung up the phone and wondered what Jordan had uncovered, something he obviously didn't want to discuss over the phone.

He thought about what Lillian told him about Diane Conlan and decided to talk to her. Diane had a reputation of being self-righteous and discourteous to her staff. He went to her office. "Diane, do you have a minute?" She looked up from her desk. "Of course, Arthur, please come in."

"I understand there was a problem with your flight to New Orleans yesterday." She put down her pen. "Oh yes, it was ridiculous. I was nearly an hour late for my presentation. I was irate." Arthur had obviously caught her off guard. "We sat on the plane waiting for over forty-five minutes." Arthur watched her demeanor. She was outraged by her inconvenience, totally oblivious to why he was there.

"Diane, my pilots are in total charge of the corporate aircraft, they make the decisions. They are responsible for the safety of the planes and the passengers. I will not have their judgment questioned or second-guessed. You were out of line and I do not want it to happen again." She turned scarlet. Arthur stood. "I suggest you write a letter of apology to the pilot."

"Yes sir."

"Good." Arthur left the room and returned to his office. She sat there and stared at the door, dumfounded. She could not believe what had just happened. She was the one inconvenienced, she was the one who had to apologize to the New Orleans trust department for being late, she was the one who went without lunch until two o'clock because of the delay. Arthur was out of line in her opinion. He had the audacity to defend a pilot rather than understanding the problems he had caused her. Okay, she thought, if this is how the game is played, I will go along. If his pilot goes running to Arthur with every little bit of gossip, I will find some way to have him fired. She buzzed her assistant. "Leslie, come here at once." Leslie had heard every word Mr. Barrington said to Diane.

She had sat quietly at her desk enjoying the reprimand. It's about time someone took her to task, she thought. She is rude and demanding and needs to be admonished. Diane dictated a letter of apology to the pilot. "Get the address from Lillian and I presume this will stay confidential?" "Of course, Mrs. Conlan." Leslie returned to her desk and joyfully typed the letter to the pilot. She made a copy for herself and buzzed Lillian for the address.

Lillian knew why Leslie asked for Paul's address. Arthur had insisted on a note of apology. Great. Mrs. Conlan needed to be brought down a step or two. Arthur wouldn't forget this, she knew. She had planted a seed of suspicion in his mind, purposefully.

Dan drove Mr. Barrington to city hall for his meeting with the mayor. "Wait here for me Dan, this won't take long." Arthur stepped out of the car and into the lobby of the mayor's offices. The receptionist recognized him. "Good afternoon Mr. Barrington. Mr. Banks is expecting you." Arthur thanked her and walked to Jordan's office. "Arthur, come in." Jordan stood to shake his hand and closed the door behind him.

"Thanks for coming Art, I have some interesting information on Barnett. I was talking with a friend of mine at the SEC. I asked him about the news story on Bartel, the misappropriation of funds that was in the paper. He told me they found a suspicious loan in the millions to a corporation they are trying to trace. The tax number is fictitious as well as the corporate identity but the money was transferred to a New York bank where our friend is known to deal. It may be a coincidence or it may be the connection we're looking for."

"It sounds too good to be true but it would explain a lot, our friend siding with Bartels attempted buy-out, trying to kick me out of my bank."

"They'll track the transfer and find out where the money wound up, probably through a series of phony accounts."

"Good work Jordan, you've made my day. If they can link him to this, I'll have him kicked off the Board and out of my hair for good. I owe you one."

"My pleasure Art, I hope it pans out the way you want. I'll let you know if I hear anything."

Arthur called Lillian from the car. "If there's nothing urgent blowing up, I'm heading home for the day. Call if you need me." Lillian hung up the phone, pleased that Arthur was on his way home to spend the evening with his wife. She sometimes wondered how he kept up with the pace of work and the constant demands on his time.

Diane Conlan was in her office when Leslie arrived for work at seven forty-five as usual. She could hear her talking on the phone, so went about preparing for the day. Mrs. Conlan's calendar showed lunch with Joe Reagan at the Ambassador Club at noon, a two o'clock meeting with Mary Lawson and a three-thirty appointment at Simon's for a dress fitting. Leslie smiled. Diane would be gone by three for the day and she could relax and think about her weekend plans.

The intercom rang. "Leslie, please come in." She picked-up the mail and walked into Diane's office. "Well, good morning Leslie, don't you look nice today. Have a seat." Leslie placed the mail on the desk and sat down, surprised that Diane seemed pleasant and shocked to receive a compliment.

Diane leafed through the mail and set it aside. "I have nothing scheduled until noon I see. Good, because I have a project for you. My husband and I are planning a dinner party at our house next month. I want you to prepare a guest list of my direct reports, their wives or husbands, and of course you too Leslie. Is there a 'Mr. Leslie' or a guest you would like to bring?" Leslie clinched her teeth at the attempt to pry into her life. "Thank you, Mrs. Conlan. I will be happy to attend and will be coming alone. What is the date?" Diane opened her calendar. "It is Saturday, the 20th. We'll have cocktails at six and dinner at seven-thirty. Mary Lawson will take care of all the arrangements, the invitations, caterer, etc. Please get the list of names to her by the end of the week and make sure all the names are spelled correctly." Leslie scribbled a note to herself, 'list to Mary Lawson, Friday.' The telephone rang and Diane picked it up. "Hello? Roger, what a nice surprise." She waved-off Leslie as a sign to leave her alone.

Leslie made a note on her calendar about the party and began making phone calls around the country to get the names of spouses and alert their offices of the date of the party.

This was indeed a command performance no one would miss. Unfortunately, that included her. There was no excuse good enough to get out of attending this one.

Mary Lawson was the events coordinator for the corporation and was good at her job. She planned the annual shareholder meetings, all corporate and charitable events, as well as all personal entertaining for the executives. Her list of resources was impressive and only she knew just how impressive as she kept top secret records of key contacts. This would be the first time for Mary to work with Diane Conlan and Leslie knew it would be a monumental task to impress her.

Leslie thought about what she would wear to the Conlan party. She went shopping on Saturday from store to store disappointed with the selections, when at last she saw a green jersey dress that caught her eye. It was conservative yet well-made with a good hand as they would say in New York. The fabric wouldn't wrinkle and the price was right. She found a pair of pumps in the same color and returned home pleased with her finds.

Leslie dressed for the Conlan party and checked the directions to their home once more. She didn't like driving at night when she wasn't sure where she was going. She drove past the whitewashed fences and iron gates that guarded the secluded homes and pulled into the circular drive of the Conlan home where parking valets were stationed to assist guests. Diane Conlan was in her glory as the hostess. She gave tours of her home, a two-story brick mansion, custom-built with the finest of everything. Very staid, in Leslie's mind, not a comfortable home but true to Mrs. Conlan's personality.

Mary Lawson was there, in charge of every detail. She had designed the invitations, hired the caterers and musicians, ordered the flowers, commissioned personalized favors for guests and supervised the placement of the tent. After cocktails, Diane announced to the guests that it was time to move outdoors to the back lawn. There was an enormous white tent filled with sky blue linen draped tables and white chairs, large urns of multi-colored flowers surrounded the front of the tent and a string quartet was seated in the far corner.

A resplendent circular buffet table held center stage with gleaming silver serving trays and bowls around a large topiary of potted herbs. It was designed as the showpiece of the tent. Guest tables held centerpieces of candles in varying heights, their lights flattering every face, and small packages wrapped in floral fabric sat next to each plate. People mingled as they found their chairs and commented on the elegantly staged tables. Waiters in starched white uniforms served guests from the buffet as Mary Lawson oversaw each detail and ensured everything was perfect. Dinner was outstanding with perfectly roasted lamb chops, whole green beans tied-up with fresh chives and herbed small potatoes. Leslie looked up to see Mrs. Conlan take Mary's arm and lead her toward the house. She knew something had gone wrong by the look on Diane's face. Heads turned as guests heard voices from inside. Diane berated Mary because she had misspelled someone's name. Mr. Conlan stood and scurried toward the musicians to play louder as Diane returned to her guests, smiling as if nothing had happened, unaware her guests had heard her outburst.

Following dessert, Leslie excused herself from the table as she heard thunder and lightning. She saw the approaching storm as an excuse to leave as soon as she had the opportunity. Mary Lawson reassured everyone there was no danger in the tent if a storm began but some still took refuge in the house. Leslie saw Mr. Anders say his goodbyes to Diane and took it as her cue. She thanked Mr. and Mrs. Conlan for a wonderful evening and explained she needed to get home before the storm. She drove away, relieved to be free of another couple of hours of small talk. She thought about how humiliated Diane would be when her husband told her the guests heard her yelling at Mary Lawson. She laughed. If he knew what was good for him, he wouldn't tell her.

The incident at the Conlan party was fodder for several jokes at work. Bill Lawrence warned Tom Morrison to watch his step. "Your office is next door to hers, I'm glad mine is at the opposite end of the hall. She scares me." Arthur talked with George Cater about what happened. "Keep your ears open George. I want to hear about any problems. Diane has quite a reputation for her temper."

CHAPTER SIX

David stalled calling Barbara for over a week. "I've been busy Barbara. The West Side project is having problems that take priority right now. I have deposited some funds for you; take a vacation or a shopping trip. I will call you when things calm down." He literally bought himself more time.

David flew to New York the afternoon of Friday the thirteenth, not an omen he hoped. He met with his financial advisors and joined an old friend for dinner at a favorite haunt in Greenwich Village. The next day Martin met David at his hotel and they rode to the club together. The others were seated in the dining room when they arrived and stood as David and Martin appeared. David took a seat opposite Isabelle where he could watch her. Martin got the conversations going about Isabelle's background in Connecticut and his friendship with her father. David watched as she spoke, she had such poise and elegance. "I moved to Manhattan just two years ago and am still learning my way around.

My father often talked about a restaurant in SoHo where they serve amazing seafood but I have forgotten the name. Are you familiar with SoHo Mr. Siegel?"

"Please, call me David. Yes, SoHo is charming and has several fine restaurants. If you are free for lunch tomorrow, we could try to find the one your father liked. Shall I call for you at noon?" Isabelle felt a little pushed but agreed and thanked David. "Noon it is." She made a point of asking the others at the table about their families and he noticed how intently she listened and remembered names and events. The evening passed quickly and soon the others began to depart. David and Martin walked Isabelle to the door. She handed David her business card with the address. "You work on Sunday?" She rarely gave out her home address. "Our offices aren't open but I like to catch up on paperwork without distractions." She thanked Martin for dinner and turned to David. "Good night, I will see you tomorrow."

Martin congratulated David on the ride back to the hotel. "You're pretty good at this for an old guy. A lunch date tomorrow, I'm impressed."

Martin knew he could get away with an age joke since he had been a friend of David's father and was easily twenty-five years older. David laughed. "She did ask my advice and that's something we old guys have plenty of. Thanks for the lift Martin, I'll keep in touch."

Isabelle was in the reception area when David arrived the next day. She looked at her watch. "Mr. Siegel, David, how good to see you. I didn't realize it was noon already." He shook her hand. "It's good to see you too." She walked with him to her office to get her purse. "This is my home away from home, what do you think?" David walked to the windows and looked out at the view. "Not bad for a young doctor but I hope you don't spend all of your time here." Isabelle stood beside him. "I worked very long hours as an intern and I am still acquiring new patients here. I'm fortunate to be part of the practice and I love what I do." She reached for her purse and they walked to the elevator.

Their car stopped in front of a seafood restaurant on Spring Street as Isabelle looked out the window.

"Gregory's, this is it! Now I remember! This is the spot my father loved so much. But how in the world did you know?" David opened the car door for her. "I talked with the concierge at my hotel and we narrowed it down to three restaurants. I phoned to ask if they remembered Marvin Sachs and the owner of Gregory's said your father was a regular customer for many years." Isabelle shook her head in disbelief. "You, David Siegel, are a most resourceful man." They were seated in a quiet corner of the room and David's full attention was on Isabelle. They talked about New York and David told stories about growing up in Manhattan and why he moved to Chicago. He learned Isabelle was from Connecticut, had studied for two years at the Sorbonne in Paris and graduated from Harvard where her father had studied. She spoke of her father in endearing terms and David could tell she had obviously adored him. "So, now here I am, out on my own in the big city with an exciting new career." David was mesmerized with her. They talked and talked, no awkward pauses, totally as ease with one another.

Isabelle looked around the restaurant. "Everyone has gone. They will think we're staying for dinner." She looked at her watch. "It's three-fifteen." David reached for her hand. "I hope I haven't kept you too long. I had fun talking with you." Isabelle looked into his eyes. "Not at all David, I had fun too and totally lost track of time." David stood. "I'll take that as a compliment. I am staying in the city for a couple of days and would like to see a play while I'm here, any suggestions?" Isabelle smiled and shook her head. "You won't believe this but I have tickets for Monday night, the opening night of "Envelope Three" and my friend cancelled this morning. Would you like to join me?"
"I look forward to it. We can have dinner after the show." They returned to her office and David agreed to come for her at seven o'clock the next day.

David didn't want to go back to his hotel. He was elated from their lunch and thrilled at the prospect of seeing Isabelle again. He told the driver to take him to Fifth Avenue.

Isabelle sat at her desk, looked out the window and thought about the afternoon with David.

He was the most charming man she had ever met; worldly, sophisticated, a powerful businessman, yet he was easy to talk with and interesting without being boorish. She thought he must be in his early fifties yet he was in excellent shape and attractive. He had a kindness about him and a gentle persuasion she found appealing.

Monday's schedule was full and she saw her last patient at four-thirty. She sat at her desk at the end of the day and went over the records. Her intercom rang. "Mr. Siegel is here to see you." Isabelle checked her watch, seven o'clock on the dot. "Please tell him I will be right out." Isabelle took a quick look in the mirror, grabbed her bag and met David in the reception area. "David, it's good to see you." He stood and watched as she walked toward him. "Isabelle, hello." He kissed her on the hand and noticed the faint aroma of a fabulous perfume. She was dressed in a steel blue dress with a matching jacket that brought out the color of her eyes. "You look wonderful."

They chatted on the way to the theater and sat enchanted at the performance. The production was a tongue-in-cheek musical about Wall Street that had them both laughing.

"The music was wonderful and I loved the character of Henry." David agreed, he thought they had done a good job of poking fun at the investment firms. The restaurant was lively with the after-theater crowd and everyone buzzed about the play. David reached in his jacket and held out a small package. "For you, as a thank you for the theater tickets." Isabelle blushed. "David, I should be thanking you for such a wonderful time." She opened the gift, a small white gold charm in the shape of a theater ticket with a blue sapphire stone. He had noticed at lunch she wore a tasteful white gold bracelet with one small charm, a star. Her eyes filled with tears as she looked at David and held out her arm. "My father gave me this bracelet and charm when I graduated from Harvard. He said I was his star. I will add the theater ticket charm to remember our evening. Thank you." It was a small gesture but one that meant David paid attention to her. He noticed things most men didn't and took the time to want to please her.

David returned to Chicago and made the decision to end his relationship with Barbara. He had not spoken with her or seen her for over a month. He phoned and told her he would be at her condo the next evening, not for dinner, just for a drink. He knew he was in for a scene. He thought of taking flowers but decided against it not wanting to encourage her in any way. He arrived at seven-thirty and could see she already had a couple of drinks. Barbara met him at the door. "Hello? Do I know you?" David walked past her into the room. "Not funny Barbara. I have been swamped. What have you been up to?" She told him she had flown to Dallas for a shopping trip with her friend Sally. "Wait until you see the shoes I found; they are fantastic. Dallas has such better shopping than Chicago and it doesn't rain there constantly." He noticed the negativity in her voice, always, about everything. He poured a drink and sat on the sofa. "Barbara, come here. I want to talk with you." She sat beside him on the couch and kissed him. "Okay, what do we need to discuss?" David took a breath.

"I am going to be blunt Barbara. I am ending our relationship.

I do not want to lead you on that this will develop into anything more than it is now. I have my hands full with my business, I need to concentrate on my work and you need to plan for your future." He had taken her completely by surprise. She dropped her glass and stood. "You are ending our relationship? You? You make all of the decisions? You are too busy? You want this, you want that. What about what I want? What about me? I have been here for you, whenever you decide you have the time to see me. I have been available to you. I have been the one waiting for you to call. Obviously, I have been the fool!" David had expected this reaction. He let her rant, let her vent her anger. He stood. "I will have an agreement drawn-up legally spelling out the separation of our relationship. I will compensate you to find your own condo and make your own life. I will have my attorney contact you. Goodnight Barbara." As he walked to the door she picked-up her glass and threw it at him. It missed and hit the wall. David closed the door behind him, went to his car and drove home.

The next morning David met with an attorney in Chicago, a college friend he felt he could trust. He didn't want Martin to be involved with this, even though he knew he could trust him, he wanted no trace of it where Isabelle might know. He was totally honest with the attorney, described Barbara's personality and anger and explained he wanted to provide her with a financial settlement hopefully to keep her quiet. The attorney assured David they would make sure she agreed to discretion or would receive no money. The agreement was ready for David the next week. He took it home to study the contents. It spelled out the length of the relationship between David Siegel and Barbara Orenstein. It detailed the separation of the relationship, at once and forever. The agreement provided monetary compensation to Barbara Orenstein for a term of three years. The funds would be held in an escrow account with monthly allotments transferred into her account. She was to vacate the condominium owned by David Siegel within thirty days. She would retain title to her car and all personal belongings.

By signing the agreement Barbara Orenstein agreed to complete confidentiality of the relationship with David Siegel. Any attempt by Barbara Orenstein to contact David Siegel in any manner would nullify the agreement and the escrow funding would be returned to Mr. Siegel. David was pleased. The agreement seemed to cover all of his bases. David gave the attorney the go-ahead to approach Barbara with the agreement. She was to be in his office the following Monday morning.

David had instructed his personal secretary to screen all of his calls. When he was home, he checked caller ID to avoid talking to Barbara. He had severed all ties and refused to be drawn into another scene with her.

The attorney phoned David Monday afternoon. "Barbara came in today and you're right, she is angry. I went over the agreement with her and she blew a fuse. She is insisting on more money, she wants the terms for five years." David was angry. "No. That's as far as I go. Make that clear to her. It's that or nothing."

The attorney contacted Barbara and it was another week before she replied.

She agreed to the terms and would be in his office to sign the agreement the next day.

The attorney called. "She was in today and signed it. I need your signature to make it complete, then you're done with her." David signed the papers that afternoon. Finally, it was over. Barbara vacated the condo at the end of the month and took all of the furnishings. David sold the unit.

CHAPTER SEVEN

Ann and Arthur Barrington arrived at the "Set Sail on the Magnificent Mile" fundraiser and it was everything Arthur had described from his lunch with Beathe. It was over the top in design and dimension, the performing arts center outfitted as a replica of the QE2. Arthur often wondered if these events actually made money after all of the expenses were paid. Beathe Billingsly was extravagant as always, dressed in a jeweled caftan straight from the Milan runway. Jordan Banks gave a welcome speech and thanked everyone for attending. He acknowledged the major contributors to the event and cited the importance of their generosity to the community foundation. Arthur and Ann stood with the others to a round of applause as the spotlight turned to their table. People were looking at the stunning brunette with David Siegel. She was the talk of the evening. David was extremely protective of Isabelle, stayed by her side the entire evening and devoted his every moment to her attention.

He enjoyed watching people's reactions to Isabelle. She and Ann Barrington hit it off immediately. Ann invited her to join her for lunch at the club and a game of tennis. "I fly back to New York Sunday but I will call you when I return to Chicago." Ann quietly told David to hang onto Isabelle. "She is wonderful."

David took her to the club for a late lunch when she arrived on Saturday, the charity event that night and met her for brunch the next day at her hotel. "What a wonderful weekend David, I enjoyed every moment." David didn't want his time with her to end. "It was a whirlwind weekend I know. Hopefully next time you can stay longer. I will be in the city next week. How about a Mets game and dinner?" Isabelle smiled. "I adore going to the Mets games but dinner is on me, at my place, okay?"

"Sounds even better, but can you cook?" Isabelle lightly pinched his arm. "You will be the judge of that Mr. Siegel."

David took the invitation to her home seriously. She must trust him to want to open her home to him. He wanted to see the art she liked, the books she read, the music she listened to, her surroundings, her home.

He flew in Friday evening, went to his hotel and phoned her. "I'll pick you up at ten o'clock for a light lunch before the game, okay?" "Okay, but there's one problem David, you don't know where I live."

"Touché Isabelle."

"I just like to torment you David. I'm on Eighty-Fifth and Lexington, in the Excelsior building, number 534."

"I'll be there at ten. Good night Isabelle."

David always had a driver as it was much easier to navigate New York than driving himself. He arrived at Isabelle's precisely at ten o'clock and announced himself to the lobby attendant. In two minutes, the elevator doors opened and Isabelle stepped out. "That was fast."

"I like to be prompt and I'm so happy to see you!" They stopped in a deli for an early lunch and rode to the ball park where David had arranged box seats. It was a close game with the Mets winning five to four. "We had better be going. I need to impress a certain someone with my culinary skills tonight." They returned to Isabelle's home and went inside. Isabelle poured them each a glass of wine and turned on some music.

"You're on your own while I get dinner going."
David looked around the living room. The
artwork was classical, mostly prints but he did
spot one Renoir, original and beautifully framed.
The music was Schubert, playing softly. He went
to the bookshelves lined with leather bound
volumes of Keats, Faulkner, Thoreau and Stein.
He would have imagined her home exactly like
this; classical, tasteful, refined and sophisticated,
just like her. The furnishings were cream-colored
fabrics against mahogany woods with an antique
Persian rug and polished wood floors. Her sense
of style permeated the home with elegance. He
joined her in the kitchen for a peek at what she
was preparing. "Something does smell good, are
you sure you know what you're doing?" David
sat down and placed a small package on the
countertop. Isabelle turned. "David, is this for
me?" He laughed. "Probably. Take a look." She
opened the wrappings and found another small
white gold charm, this one in the shape of a
baseball. "To remember our day."
"You are the most thoughtful man! I love it
David and it will go right here next to the theater
ticket." She held out her arm to show him.

Isabelle placed a tray of stuffed mushrooms on the counter in front of him. "Here, try these." David took a bite and was pleasantly surprised. The filling was a combination of spinach and cream cheese that melted in his mouth. "Bravo, delicious!" Isabelle walked over to him. "See, I told you I knew what I was doing." David pulled her closer and kissed her. "Isabelle, I love everything about you. You are beautiful, charming, intelligent, fun to be with and I just learned you can cook too. I think I'm in love." She pulled away from him for an instant and looked into his eyes. "I have been feeling the same way but the analytical side of me tells me to take some time to know more about you." David took her hand and led her to the sofa. He sat up straight and became very serious. "I, David Siegel, am fifty-one years old, five feet eleven inches tall, one hundred seventy-six pounds. I eat healthy most of the time, I work out twice a week at home and my internist says I'm in great shape. I was born in New York to Jewish parents, both of whom are deceased, and I have one brother who lives in St. Louis with his wife and two children. I have had two long-term relationships in the past but never found the right girl.

I began my business career after graduating from Columbia with rather mediocre grades and have been solely devoted to building my business. I like ice cream, steak and potatoes and spinach stuffed mushrooms. I detest broccoli, tuna and liver. I am hardworking, honest, loyal, and kind. I want to find the perfect woman with whom to share my life, have a gaggle of children and live happily ever after. Do you have any questions Ms. Sachs?"

Isabelle sat stunned listening to him. She loved his humor, his directness and his candor. She took a deep breath and spoke. "Yes, I need to know if this means I have to give up broccoli." He put his arms around her. "You can have all the broccoli you want. Now it's your turn. Are you prepared to divulge your personal information?" Isabelle sat up straight and looked him in the eyes. "I, Isabelle Sachs, am thirty-four years of age, five feet seven inches tall and weigh between one hundred ten and one hundred twenty pounds, depending upon who is asking. I was born in New Canaan, Connecticut, to Jewish parents, Marvin and Rebecca, both deceased.

I have a sister, five years younger than I, who lives in Massachusetts in a private residential facility for the mentally challenged. I am her only family and intend to take care of her every wish for her entire life. I am one hundred percent committed to her well-being." She paused and took a deep breath. "I fell madly in love with my first French professor who turned out to be a bore. I studied at the Sorbonne for two years and graduated with honors from my father's alma mater, Harvard. I practice medicine delivering beautiful little babies. I enjoy horseback riding, snow skiing and tennis. I work out three times a week at the athletic club and passed my last physical with flying colors. I like broccoli, salmon and lamb chops. I do not care for rare meat, pickles or Brussels sprouts. I am hard working, compassionate, honest and loyal. I want world peace and an end to hunger on our planet. Are there any further questions Mr. Siegel?"

"Just one. Do you think you could learn to like pickles?" They both began to laugh. David took a sip of wine. "How long has your sister lived in Massachusetts?"

"Since she was ten years old. She is now twenty-nine."

"Do you see her often?"

"Yes. I visit at least once each month and she comes to New York to stay with me. David…"

He stopped her, holding up his hand. "You do not need to tell me anything more than you want. You are obviously devoted to your sister, as you should be, and I am sure she adores you."

Isabelle appreciated his understanding that she did not want to go into details about her sister.

"Your analytical side is very wise in cautioning you to be wary of gray-haired men bearing promises. I would like to see you as often as possible and will wait until you feel comfortable, or six months, whichever comes first. Fair?"

Isabelle laughed and kissed his cheek. "Fair."

CHAPTER SEVEN

Arthur, John Douglas, Bill Lawrence and a team of advisors flew to Washington to appear before the Senate Committee on Banking. Arthur had consulted with David Siegel about how to deflect any attacks on his character. They had rehearsed their responses to arguments expected to be raised at the meeting. They filed into the room and took their seats before the committee, an imposing group. The Chairman called the session to order and welcomed the team from Barrington Bank. "I would like to start by thanking the witnesses for appearing before the panel today. I recognize all of you are very busy people with a number of other responsibilities, so I appreciate you taking time to travel here and help us with our oversight responsibilities." Arthur thanked the committee for the invitation to participate in the discussions on banking reform.

Senator Jennings was the first to question Arthur. "Mr. Barrington, what was your total income last year including bonuses and options?"

Arthur replied. "Senator, salary information is in our annual report."
"Yes, but it does not include bonuses, does it? You and your contemporaries stash away millions of dollars every year while your bank increases fees to your customers. This insatiable greed has gone too far." Senator Polk spoke up. "Isn't it customary to receive bonuses of restricted stock and generous compensation on top of annual salaries? Especially when these bonuses are not public information? The committee members broke into laughter. "Is this true Mr. Barrington?" Arthur was seething. "I am certain Senator Polk has documentation to that effect." Bill Lawrence cupped his hand over Arthur's microphone and whispered to him. "Why don't you ask Senator Polk why he doesn't offer proof of his documentation." Arthur smiled and shuffled his notes. Senator Nash spoke out. "Mr. Barrington, I would like to know how you can justify charging excessive interest rates on your credit cards. Rates have risen ten, fifteen percent on cards held by your customers.

Your credit card company hikes interest rates even on consumers who pay on time and consistently meet the terms of their credit card agreements. You change the terms of the agreement, including the interest rate, at any time, for any reason. These practices can mean mountains of debt for families and financial ruin for too many. Our young sons and daughters are faced with an onslaught of credit card offers as soon as they set foot onto a college campus. I have here a copy of your credit card agreement." He held up a corner of the paper as it unfolded nearly two feet long. "Have you, Mr. Barrington, read this agreement? Do you actually expect your customers to read this entire agreement?" John Douglas whispered in Arthur's ear. "Yes, Senator, I do expect our customers to read the information we provide as our agreement." The Senator laughed loudly. "I'd like to see a poll on those numbers! I understand you flew to Washington today on your corporate jet. How many aircraft does Barrington Bank own?" Arthur clinched his fist under the table. "We have three Gulfstream jets. These are our mobile offices allowing us to save time and money conducting business across the country."

Senator Nash continued. "I'm sure your stockholders will appreciate that as they read about the $20 million in losses last year. Mr. Barrington there is a deep and legitimate distrust in America for power and privilege enjoyed at the expense of the public. Your customers are keys to your success yet they are also victims of your success. The time has come for the government to step in and place controls on the banking industry."

The senators continued to question Arthur on various allegations as the meeting wore on for hours. The Chairman of the committee pounded his gavel and spoke. "Mr. Barrington, we feel reform is needed in the banking industry to protect consumers. This is the time for us to look forward, not backward. We need to work proactively to resolve problems. The industry and regulators must work together to identify the scope of the problems. We want to place a cap on interest rates, simplify credit card agreements and institute stricter lending requirements. We are considering new limitations on the fees you charge merchants for swiping debit cards, fees resulting in billions of dollars annually.

This committee urges you to reconsider your bonus structures in the wake of the economic slowdown as a sign of leadership. We want to work together with the leaders in the financial industry on this reform. We are scheduled to meet with the other major banks within the next month to formulate a timeline to enact these changes. Do you have anything further to say?"

"Yes, Senator, I do. Barrington Bank is committed to improvements in the financial sector and we are open to discussions with the committee. Thank you for meeting with us today and we look forward to working together on the reform."

On the flight back to Chicago the team congratulated Arthur on the way he remained calm and collected before the committee. "It would defeat our position to lose control with them." Bill Lawrence agreed. "We all know how slow politicians work; it will be at least another year before they can agree on what to do. Many expect the next two years will be heavy on rhetoric but light on legislative achievements. Arthur is absolutely right to play along and let them think we agree with their ideas.

It may sound good to them but let them try to institute it throughout the industry. However, Clark Barnett was clearly out of line and revengeful in his attack. His Chicago constituency may need a reminder of Clark's ethical ineptitude." Arthur told John Douglas to meet with their corporate governance committee. "I want to step-up our lobbying campaigns on the financial reform legislation. The other banks will join us in meetings with regulators and staffers at the Federal Reserve, the Federal Deposit Insurance Corporation, the Comptroller of the Currency and the Securities and Exchange Commission to hash out details of proposed legislation. Together we provide a formidable presence."

Despite his good-guy image Arthur was as aggressive as any banker when it came to finding ways to generate fees from credit cards and consumer banking products. He was motivated with a clear-eyed focus on getting bigger and bigger with larger and larger worth. He decided to stop free checking accounts for new customers and set-up a service fee of twelve dollars per month.

He argued that less than half of their customers reconciled their statements on a monthly basis. "They are busy with jobs and families and most won't even notice a twelve-dollar charge. We have an opportunity to increase revenue before any legislation is passed and I intend to do just that."

CHAPTER EIGHT

First thing Monday morning David asked his secretary to get the number of a florist on Lexington Avenue in New York. He made the call himself and placed a standing order for two dozen red roses to be delivered to Isabelle Sachs every Saturday morning at ten a.m. She could enjoy them over the weekend and he would never embarrass her by sending them to her office. He told them there need be no message on the card.

David met with his executive team at nine. They went around the table reporting on each division and their projections for the coming month. Business was going well with revenues up and expenses down due to a corporate-wide push to cut back on unnecessary expenditures.

David had saved the big news and stood to announce the zoning board had approved the final request for the West Side project. There was a round of applause and congratulations. "We have jumped the final hurdle. With the zoning approval we are positioned to launch the full construction schedule.

I want monthly updates on the progress. Jack, you keep an eye on the leasing contracts, I don't want anyone pulling out on me now. How are you coming with the theater?" Jack assured him he had commitments in writing and was scheduled to attend a meeting the following week to finalize the deal.

The plans for his project were in full operation and he should start seeing physical progress soon. The scale model of the project sat on a large conference table and was updated with each new leasing commitment. He had not talked about the project with Isabelle but was waiting until she could see the complexity of his plans. Since meeting her everything seemed to be going his way. She was his good luck charm, he knew.

He dictated a letter of appreciation to the head of the board of zoning and made a note to invite him to lunch within the next week. David was meticulous in protocol and always thought in advance of favors he may need in the future.

He phoned Isabelle at least twice a week usually in the evening when they could talk without interruptions. She looked forward to his calls and found herself looking at the clock as soon as she got home.

It had been two weeks since she had seen him and she thought about him constantly. She kept busy at work and knew David was running an empire in Chicago, she would not allow herself to get caught up in doubts about his feelings. The phone rang and she answered on the second ring. "David, hi, it's good to hear your voice." David leaned back in his chair. It was good to hear her voice. "I've been thinking, could you arrange to take a long weekend from work, Friday through Sunday?" She looked at her calendar. "I'm sure I can work it out. What do you have in mind?" "What I have on my mind is seeing you, as always. How would you like a short trip to Nantucket? We could relax, walk the beach and eat all the fresh seafood we want." An internal alarm went off in her mind; a weekend in Nantucket with David. She wasn't sure she was ready for a weekend. Her pause alerted him. "Don't worry. You will have your own room. I have the use of a beach house that belongs to a friend of mine. There are four bedrooms, so you can have your choice." She had to laugh. He could read her mind. "It sounds wonderful David. I could use some sea air and I miss your smiling face."

"Good, I like hearing you miss me. We can fly over Friday morning and be there in time for lunch. I'll send a car for you and you can meet me at the airfield if you don't mind." She assured him she did not mind at all. "I'll see you Friday, thank you David. Goodnight."

The car arrived with Isabelle and they boarded his plane. It was luxurious, outfitted with mahogany cabinetry and plush leather seating. He offered her coffee and they arrived in Nantucket by ten thirty. The beach house was charming, covered in gray wooden shingles with slate roof tiles and a row of white shuttered windows along the front. "What a delightful house David, it's lovely." The key was under the doormat. David opened the door and stood back for Isabelle to enter. The house was fresh and bright with three sets of French doors that opened onto an expansive covered porch lined with Adirondack chairs. The main room was done in sage green upholstered furnishings that gave the room a cool feel, with a white fireplace, polished wood floors and a magnificent view of the beach. David opened two of the windows to let in the cooling summer breeze. Isabelle took a deep breath. "Ah, nothing smells as fresh as that.

I already feel relaxed." David put his arm around her. "Good, now follow me for your room selection, Madam." She followed him up the stairs to four well-appointed bedrooms each with its own bath. Isabelle stood in the doorway of one of the rooms. The décor was cream, rose and pale-yellow fabrics with a seating area by a large window that looked toward the sea. "This is the one for me. Look at the view, its spectacular!" David set down her bag and opened a window. "You can freshen up while I get organized. I'll see you downstairs." He dropped off his bag and went downstairs to check his phone for messages. Isabelle came into the kitchen and noticed the large vase of roses on the table. "Did you arrange for these?" David took off his glasses. "Yes Madam, as you will not be home this weekend, I did not want you to go without your roses." Isabelle kissed him on the cheek and looked out toward the beach. "I can't wait to take a walk, are you interested?" David looked at his watch. "I skipped breakfast this morning and I'm starved. Let's have something to eat first, okay with you?" He opened the refrigerator and stood back for her to see. "Jason's caretaker stocked some things for us.

Do you see anything you'd like?" Isabelle stood beside him looking at the contents. She handed David a carton of blueberries and two plastic containers he set on the counter. "Cobb salads, how nice and here is a loaf of nut bread. Is this okay with you?" David set dishes on the table and Isabelle held up a bottle of wine. "David, you had them bring the Riesling I like. You scare me sometimes with the things you notice." He held out two wine glasses. "How can I not notice everything about you? I have looked for you all of my life." They ate lunch, stacked the dishes in the sink and went for a walk along the shore. Isabelle picked-up seashells and examined each one as if it was a rare gem. They watched children flying kites with their parents and the seabirds as they soared playfully along the wind currents. "Tell me about your work David. You mentioned you were having a problem with some zoning approvals last time we talked. Has it been resolved?" He smiled. "Yes, just this week. The last obstacles were approved and we can get going on construction." He described the scope of the project to her, the entertainment venues, performing arts theater and restaurants.

He explained it would take two, maybe three years to completion. "It will be a unique center of interest that will bring people in from around the country. There is no other experience like it." Isabelle shook her head. "I don't know how you do it all David. A project of that size must take so much of your time and energy. You are so committed to your business and have done so well with it over the years. You must be very proud." He stopped, reached down for a shell and handed it to her. "I am going to be blunt with you Isabelle. I am proud of what I have built. I must warn you that I do often work long hours. I have put all of my thought, all of my time and all of my energy into my business for almost twenty years to make it what it is today. However, I also want you to know that meeting you made me realize what I do not have. I am a wealthy man Isabelle and I want to share my life with you. I want to see you every morning and every night, I want to have our children and I want to make you happy." Isabelle took a shaky breath. "You, Mr. Siegel, have already made me very happy." He took her in his arms and kissed her. "That's a good start and every day it will be my goal to keep you happy."

They held hands and walked along the beach back to the house. They sat on the porch, looked toward the sea and relaxed. "Isabelle, I would like to know more about your sister." She folded her hands in her lap and looked toward the sky. "Allison is a very special person. When she was born, she was a beautiful child and I was so excited to have a baby sister. I was five and I remember what fun we had taking her for walks and playing. She was slow learning to crawl, walk and talk. I remember going to the doctor with mother and the tests he did on Allison. Mother was worried and talked with my dad about her development. We worked at home with her, read to her, played games with her, but year by year she slowly drifted away. My parents tried local schools, psychiatrists, therapists and caregivers but Allison was off in her own world. When I was eight, I remember finding my mother in her room crying. I asked why and she told me Allison was going away to a special school. I remember visiting different schools with my parents and how my mother would come home withdrawn and depressed. She blamed herself for Allison's condition.

She was sure she had done something during pregnancy to cause it; ate the wrong foods, didn't get enough rest, she tortured herself with guilt. She finally conceded and agreed to give up her little girl when she was ten, sending her to live in a residential care facility. It was the worst decision of my parents' lives and my mother never recovered. She died four years later. Now that my father is gone, I am the only family Allison has. She is my little sister and I will be there for her, always, whatever else my life may bring. We come as a pair David." He stood, went inside, turned on some music and returned with two drinks. "Isabelle, I would expect nothing less than for you to take care of your sister. You are the woman I love and your family is part of you. Would you consider taking me to meet Allison? I don't want to intrude but I would like to know her." She looked up at David and smiled. "You are in for a treat, Mr. Siegel. Allison will adore you." David kissed her on the cheek. "Then it's a date. I'm going to get a shower and make some calls. We have dinner reservations at seven-thirty." Isabelle reached for his hand. "I'm going to sit here a while longer and relax."

She stared at the ocean and thought about David. She had dated several men over the years but they had all be too self-absorbed, not ready for a commitment and no one who took the time to understand her as much as did David. He wasn't threatened by her devotion to her sister. He loved her; she was sure. She loved him; she was sure. At first, she had been hesitant to become involved with him because she did not want to be part of a casual fling. But now he was asking her to spend her life with him, marry him. He was attractive, thoughtful, caring, generous and fun to be with. A successful businessman, one of the wealthiest men in the country and highly respected, all of the things she could ever want. She took off her sunglasses and placed them on top of her head. She paused as she started to go inside and looked down at their shoes side by side by the door. She smiled. She knew David was the one.

She went upstairs, took a shower and changed for dinner. It was six o'clock when she found David sitting in the living room watching the news. "He stood when he saw her. "You look refreshed. Are you ready to leave?"

The restaurant had a spectacular view of Nantucket harbor from the outdoor terrace and the aromas of lavender and hydrangea were alluring but they sat inside as there was a chill in the air with the setting sun. They watched as the sky turned a brilliant orange with pink layers of light as the sun set over the water. Isabelle told David how she had come to Nantucket with her parents one summer when she was twelve and fell in love with it then. "I thought it must surely be the most romantic place on earth and now I know I was right." David reached for her hand. "Anywhere we are as long as we are together will be romantic, always." She told him how her love of horses began when she was a young girl. She took riding lessons when she was ten and had adored horses ever since. She spent her summers at the stables down the road from their house, grooming the horses and riding for hours. "I still go riding when I have the chance which isn't as often as I would like."

They returned to the house at ten and sat on the porch talking. David looked at his watch. "I'm turning in for the night. Will you be okay out here alone?"

She stood. "No, I'm afraid of the dark, I'm going in too." David kissed her. "I will see you in the morning." She turned out the lights and went to her room where she drifted off to sleep listening to the sound of the ocean outside her window.

CHAPTER NINE

They played golf Saturday morning on a scenic course near the ocean, had lunch in town, strolled through galleries and window shopped. They stopped for ice cream cones and headed back to the beach house at four. "There is a gala at the Art Museum of Chicago on the fourteenth that I really must attend since I'm on the Board, and I would love for you to go with me." Isabelle checked her phone where she kept a date book. "I would love to go. A gala? I'll need to bring something appropriate." David asked if she would mind flying in by herself. "I'll have a driver pick you up and take you to the plane and I'll be waiting for you when you arrive." Isabelle assured him she did not mind. David stood. "I am going in to shower and change for dinner. Would you like a glass of wine?"
"No, thank you. I want to read for a little while."
Their driver stopped in front of a charming restaurant and they walked along the curving stone pathway.

The ivy-covered structure was a typically quaint Nantucket style with high ceilings, exposed white painted beams and table linens in shades of pale greens and blues, soft lighting and garden walkways for after dinner strolls. They both decided on seared salmon fillets with the most delicious avocado sauce and fresh corn soufflé. David couldn't take his eyes from her. She talked about one of her patients, the unmarried daughter of a New York politician, seventeen years old and frightened. Her parents were devastated that she had become pregnant and forbid her to see the boy ever again. They convinced her to give up the baby for adoption at birth and planned to send her to a private school in Rhode Island. David watched as she described the girl and her situation. He could see she was clearly concerned for the girl's future and the future of the unborn child. "I'm sorry, David. I did not intend to spoil our evening with such a depressing story." He touched her hand. "You must be a wonderful doctor. You are so compassionate and caring." David changed the subject and told her a funny story that made her laugh.

The next morning Isabelle came down the stairs and onto the porch where David was engrossed in the newspaper. "Good morning." He removed his reading glasses and stood. "Good afternoon to you Ms. Sachs. I presume you slept well?" She laughed. "I never sleep past seven o'clock but this is so restful with the sound of the ocean and the fresh air. I'm getting lazy." David never slept past six a.m. He liked the early hours to get a jump on the day. He read the newspapers, checked the markets, read his schedule for the day and caught up on reports before he headed for his office. He went into the kitchen and brought a cup of coffee for her. "Thank you. What time do we leave?" David looked at his watch. "I thought we would have brunch in town and fly out around two o'clock. Okay with you?" It was only nine o'clock so she had plenty of time. "Yes, I will miss this David, I had a wonderful time." He folded the paper and set it aside. "I am glad you had a chance to relax. We will come back again." Isabelle finished her coffee and went inside to tidy-up the house. She noticed a small familiar looking blue box on the kitchen table. She picked it up as David came through the door.

"Is this for me?" He nodded and smiled. She removed the white ribbon, took off the lid and her mouth fell open. She stared at the contents, looked up at David and back at the box. "David!" She was trembling. He reached for the box, removed the ring and placed it on her finger. "Isabelle Sachs, will you marry me?" She stared at the ring on her finger, speechless. He waited, nervously watching her. She touched the ring and looked in his eyes. "Yes, David, I love you." He took her in his arms and kissed her gently. "Come here and sit down, you are pale as a ghost." He led her to the living room sofa. She held his hand with one hand and looked at the ring on her other hand. "David, it is magnificent." The ring was a bold ten carat emerald faceted center diamond with tapered baguettes on either side, set on a platinum band. "You are magnificent Isabelle. I have carried this around in my pocket for two months waiting for the right moment. I do not want to risk losing you." She put her arms around his shoulders and kissed him. "You will never lose me."

David placed an envelope on the kitchen table with the name "Tom" written on the front for the caretaker.

They closed up the house and went to a restaurant by the bay where they sat on the veranda for brunch. David teased her about her reaction when she saw the engagement ring. "Did you think I bought you another charm?" She took a drink of juice. "Yes, I did. You surprised me. I certainly did not expect this!" He watched as she looked at the ring, holding her hand to the side as the sunlight glistened from the diamonds. He knew she was thrilled.

They landed in New York and rode to her apartment. He carried her bag inside and Isabelle poured them each a glass of iced tea. "I've been thinking, now that we are engaged, we really do need to go see Allison. She will be very surprised." David checked his watch. "How about next weekend? I will fly in Saturday morning and we can take a car to Berkshire Sunday morning to spend the day." Isabelle hugged him. "Thank you, David. It will mean so much to me."

Isabelle prepared David for meeting Allison on their drive to Berkshire.

"She is the main reason I chose to specialize in obstetrics, to ask the genetic questions that need to be asked, to insist on diagnostic testing and to council prospective parents on the possibilities of Downs Syndrome. It changes the lives of the entire family."

They arrived at Lakeside Village and went to Allison's room. Isabelle knocked. "Allison? It's Isabelle." The door swung open and a young girl flew into Isabelle's arms. "You're here! I have been waiting all morning!" She stepped back and looked at David. "I have brought someone to meet you. This is David." Allison released Isabelle and turned to David. "How nice of you to come. What is your last name?" He kissed her hand. "My name is David Siegel and I am charmed to meet you." Allison blushed and pulled back her hand. "What a nice man. Are you dating my sister?" Isabelle interrupted. "Let's not ask so many questions or you will scare him. Let's go outside for a walk." She walked arm in arm with Allison down the hallway and turned to wink at David. He watched them walk ahead of him, true sisters, worlds apart yet held together by their family bond.

The only similarity between them was the blueness of their eyes. Allison was small, only about four feet five or six inches tall and just slightly plump. Her light brown hair was held to one side with a barrette in a rather childish way. She was dressed in a navy pleated skirt, white blouse and a pink cardigan sweater that reminded David of a school uniform, odd for a woman of twenty-nine. Allison waved to a woman passing by. "Mrs. Sims, look, Isabelle is here." They stopped and chatted with Allison's teacher. "Allison, have you told your sister about your award at the art show?"

"Not yet, she just got here. We're going down to the lake to feed the birds." They walked on to a gazebo encircled with climbing roses of orange and pink blooms. Allison let go of Isabelle's hand and ran toward the water. "Oh, look Isabelle, there's a family of ducks, the father, mother and three babies. Aren't they cute? Look at how the babies follow close behind their mother just like we used to do. I miss mother." She turned to David. "You won't really be scared if I ask you a question, will you?"

"No Allison, what do you want to know?"

"Okay, good. I think you are very handsome and I can tell my sister likes you. She has never brought a boyfriend to meet me before. What do you do for work?" David looked at Isabelle, slightly stunned at the directness of the question. "I buy office buildings and condominiums and lease them to large companies."

"How nice, it must keep you very busy. Look, the ducks walked up on the bank to rest." Isabelle asked her about the art show. "What is this award you won?"

"Oh, it was great, Isabelle! I was so surprised when they called my name. I painted a picture of flowers, pink flowers, pink is my favorite color. It is on display in the art center with my name on it. Everyone likes it."

"That is very special Allison. Congratulations. I want to see it after lunch. Come, we should be going inside, I'm hungry."

They walked back to the main building, Allison in the middle holding both of their hands. "The dining room is this way, come on." She led them to a table by a window that overlooked the courtyard. "I like to sit here where I can see outside. Usually I have lunch with Millie but she's sick today."

David looked around the room at the other tables with people of all ages; some teenagers, some in their thirties and forties, some talked wildly and some sat quietly staring off into space. "Oh good, look, we're having fish for lunch. Do you like fish David?"

"Yes, I do. It's very healthy for you."

"Oh, I know and good for my waistline. Isabelle is so skinny. She must eat a lot of fish."

"Allison, how would you like to come to New York for your birthday? We could have lunch, go to the zoo and do some shopping."

"Oh, I already told them I would be gone. We always spend my birthday together, remember? We will have cake and ice cream and presents, right? David, will you come to my party?"

"I would be honored. What is your favorite kind of cake?"

"Chocolate, of course, with lots of frosting!"

"Me too. What would you like for your birthday?" Allison thought for a moment. "I would like to dance with you. I haven't danced for a long time."

"Then a dance we shall have. Okay with you Isabelle?" Isabelle smiled. "It sounds like fun."

She listened to the way David talked with Allison. He was not condescending toward her but listened and treated her like a woman not as a child.

"Allison, David and I have something special to tell you. We are going to be married." Allison covered her mouth with her hand and looked at Isabelle then David. "You are? When?" Isabelle laughed. "We have only been engaged for a week." She held out her hand to show Allison her ring. "Oh, my, it is beautiful! It that a diamond? Did it cost lots of money?" Isabelle held her hand. "Yes, it is a beautiful ring."

"Will that make you my brother when you marry Isabelle?" "Actually, I will be your brother-in-law. What do you think?" Allison took a deep breath and looked back at Isabelle. "Does this mean you won't come to see me anymore?" "No, absolutely not. David and I will both come to see you as often as possible. I love you Allison, nothing will ever change that." She smiled. "Okay, then I think it's a good idea for you to get married."

They finished lunch and went to the art center where Allison's painting was set on an easel in the main gallery with a blue ribbon attached. "See, I told you so. I won first prize." "I am so proud of you, this is wonderful. You must keep painting Allison. You are very talented."

"I know. Let's go back to my room. I want to show you something new."

Allison went to her closet and brought out a photo album she handed to Isabelle. She sat down beside her and turned to the first page. "Look, here is a picture of us when we were little." She turned the page. "Here is one of mother and me, I was two years old." Isabelle watched as she turned each page and pointed to the family pictures of her childhood. Isabelle had given her the album years before as a keepsake and they had viewed the album together many times. It frightened her that Allison did not remember the times they shared and became alarmed. It was not uncommon for young adults with Downs to develop a number of health issues; heart disease, epilepsy or dementia. She changed the conversation and asked Allison some memory questions to test her level of awareness.

"You sound like Mrs. Sims. She asks me questions like that all the time." Isabelle laughed. "I just want David to see how smart you are." David hugged Allison and Isabelle kissed her on the cheek. "I will call you in a couple of days so we can plan your trip to the city. I love you."

Isabelle talked about Allison on the drive back to the city. "I am concerned about her David. Today was the first time I have seen any hint of dementia in her. For all of these years she has received such excellent care and has been relatively healthy."

"Is there any treatment for it?"

"Dementia isn't a specific disease. It describes a group of symptoms that affect intellectual and social abilities severely enough to interfere with daily functioning. It's caused by conditions or changes in the brain. Dementia can lead to confusion and the inability to remember people and names. I want Allison to undergo some medical tests. I will call Mrs. Montgomery tomorrow."

CHAPTER TEN

Diane Conlan sat on the Board of Arcoe, a national electronic manufacturer, with her long-time friend Chip Harwood. They had known each other since college and traded favors as part of the Ivy League tradition. Diane hired Chip as a consultant to help re-organize her corporate structure and improve financial performance. She mentioned it nonchalantly in her monthly meeting with Arthur. "I must admit, Diane, I am surprised you feel you need help. What is the consulting fee?"

"We agreed on a four-day session for one hundred sixty thousand." Arthur made a note. "I presume your budget can accommodate the expense. I want a report next month on the results and from now on I want to approve expenditures exceeding one hundred thousand." Diane dug her nails into the back of her portfolio. "Of course, Arthur, I am sure you will be pleased with the recommendations."

"What else do you have?"

"I flew to Wisconsin and met with Tim a few days ago. His numbers have not improved and I told him his time was up. He has had two months to come up with new accounts and he has every excuse in the book but no accounts. Tim finally understands I mean business; get your numbers up or you're out. I want to replace him with Joe Reagan." Arthur listened carefully to her. "Diane, I told you I wanted to know before you let Tim go. He has been with me for a number of years and has always performed. Do you have his reports for me?" She handed a folder to Arthur. "Of course, here they are." Arthur scanned the numbers for the past quarter. "I will talk with him. I want him to explain this to me." Diane stood. "Fine, let me know what you think. I have Joe Reagan ready to take over." They concluded their meeting and Diane left. Arthur added notes to her folder and sat back in his chair. It irritated him that she was bringing in her friend for a consulting session. Chip Harwood must need a new car or tuition for his son in Harvard. Arthur knew the game; you scratch my back and I'll scratch yours. Diane's report on the consulting should be interesting reading.

Arthur picked up the phone and called Tim. "Arthur here, Tim. I just talked with Diane Conlan and she gave me your quarterly report. What's the problem?"

"The problem is Diane Conlan, Arthur. What you do not see in the report are the five leasing accounts I had a chance to nail down with a local medical group. Mrs. Conlan told me to back off because she didn't feel they fit our 'business model'. Plain and simple Arthur, she wants me out, why I don't know." Arthur made notes. "What is the name of the medical group?" Tim told him. "What was the potential revenue?" Tim told him. "Okay. Sit tight Tim until I get back with you."

Arthur did a little background check on Joe Reagan and found out he had gone to school with Diane's husband. So, Arthur thought, she wants to do a favor for a friend at the expense of Tim; big mistake.

Arthur told Lillian to schedule a breakfast meeting with Diane Conlan at the Ambassador Club the next morning. He was waiting when she arrived. "Good morning Arthur, how nice of you to invite me." Arthur motioned for her to take a seat and poured a cup of coffee for her.

"Diane, I talked with Tim and I also did a little background check on Joe Reagan. Tim tells me he had a contract nailed down that would net five and a half million in one year. He tells me you told him not to go forward." Diane put down her coffee. "It was a start-up medical group Arthur, a group of struggling doctors hoping to develop their practice, a far shot from a guarantee." Arthur made notes in the folder. "They had backing and collateral Diane." She smirked. "Tim is overstating his case." Arthur closed his folder. "I am not yet convinced of that. Diane, the cornerstone of my career has been taking care of my people, the people I trust. Tim is a good man and has performed well for ten years. I am not ready to let him go. Furthermore, I believe you may have a conflict of interest with Joe Reagan in the fact that he is a friend of your husband." He watched her expression. He had surprised her. "Joe Reagan has an impressive background in leasing Arthur. Yes, he did go to school with Richard but that has nothing to do with his skill set." She was far too defensive. "As I told you before Diane, I do not want you to let Tim go before I say so, understood?" She backed away from the table and stood.

"Understood." She walked out of the room.

Arthur was angry. Diane had pushed this too far. He would not tolerate her rudeness and insubordination. He finished his breakfast and returned to the office. His resentment toward her was growing. He didn't like her business approach, always defiant toward her direct reports and more recently toward Arthur. She basically did not understand being part of a team. Her idea of conversation was a one-sided oration of what she demanded, unyielding and uninterested in what the other person was saying. Arthur had built his executive team with people who were the best in their field, cooperative and rational. Diane was too brash which impeded the progress of the holding company figures. Her staff was afraid of her rage and held back on key issues needing attention for fear of her wrath. More and more he doubted her value to lead the holding companies.

"Lillian, I want to see George Cater this morning." Lillian knew from the tone in his voice that something was wrong after his breakfast with Diane Conlan.

George came up the back stairs and into Arthur's office within ten minutes. "Good morning Arthur. You wanted to see me?"

"Come in George, have a seat. I have an issue and need your advice." He told George about his concern with Diane Conlan. "She is a maverick George. Thinks she can make her own decisions without my approval. This morning she was insubordinate and rude. I want to know my options as far as her employment is concerned."

"I will have to check, but I think she came on board about four years ago. After three years, she is eligible for her compensation package, stock options and severance. I do suggest you have something tangible to go with, someone to collaborate her behavior or something in writing to prove insubordination, otherwise, you could face a lawsuit. Have there been other issues before today?"

"Yes, but nothing like this. I want a record of her calls to Joe Reagan. Pull her employment contract and get back to me today." Arthur phoned Tim. "Two calls from the boss in one day. Either I'm in big trouble or you miss me."

Arthur laughed. "I do miss you Tim. But the reason for the call is that I want you to go ahead with the medical group lease if you still have a chance. If you have any problems with Mrs. Conlan, I want you to call me."

"Thanks Arthur. I appreciate your confidence."

CHAPTER ELEVEN

David phoned Isabelle Thursday evening as usual and she told him about the reactions at work when she announced their engagement. "Everyone was surprised. They all asked when we are being married. I explained we have not yet set a date. I assured them I will keep my patients in mind and give them plenty of time to hire another doctor. How about you? Have you told your associates?" David admitted he had. "Talk about surprised. I'm sure they thought I would never find a woman who would have me. They all want to meet you." Isabelle laughed. "Ah, yes, the inspection to see if I am worthy. David, I have been thinking that it is too time consuming for you to come here to get me on the fourteenth. I can fly to Chicago and save you a trip." David appreciated her thoughtfulness. "If you are sure you don't mind. I will have a car drive you to the airfield and you can fly over alone. I will be there to meet you and bring you home." She smiled at the thought of 'bring you home'.

He was waiting when the plane landed and Isabelle looked radiant as always as she waved to David. He gave her a kiss and helped her into the car. She told him how smooth the flight had been and how luxurious she felt having the plane all to herself.

She was a little apprehensive about seeing David's home. As they approached the house, she caught her first glimpse of the enormous fieldstone structure surrounded by acres and acres of grounds all lined with black iron fencing. "David, this is immense, the grounds go on and on."

"The house is surrounded by thirty acres of privacy as well as security." The winding drive was lined with rows of gracefully shaped white pines, manicured beds of azaleas and rhododendrons all in abundant bloom. "David it is lovely." He squeezed her hand. "I hope you love it as much as I." The entry was framed with a wide, two-story portico and large, heavily carved mahogany doors worthy of a fortress. He unlocked the door and held it open as Isabelle entered the foyer, a large area with travertine floors and silk wall coverings.

A round mahogany table in the center of the room held a large authentic Ming vase with an enormous bouquet of fresh flowers. He walked with her through the rooms and pointed out features she would readily appreciate as well as the surprises he relished. The kitchen was equipped with dual German manufactured stoves in stainless steel, two refrigerators, two dishwashers, Italian marble countertops, microwave oven drawers that opened with the touch of a button and imported walnut cabinetry. French doors led to a veranda with an ivy-covered pagoda overlooking the herb garden. The living room was massive with three seating areas of the finest furnishings. French bombe chests flanked the stone fireplace, down-stuffed sofas covered in silk fabrics, authentic Louis XVI chairs and a sideboard from the Orient. She was surprised to see his large art collection. He had a montage of Renoir, Monet and Matisse paintings that lined the walls. Large windows allowed in the northern light but minimized sun damage to the room. The dining room was an elegant space with a table capable of seating thirty people and large crystal-adorned wall sconce lighting.

Upstairs there were six bedroom suites, each furnished with fine antiques and exquisite bed linens. The master suite was a space of grandeur with an elevated platform bed and polished side tables. A recessed tray ceiling above the bed glowed with indirect lighting and the walls were covered with muted hand-painted silk murals. David crossed the room and opened the doors of his and hers closets. "This is something I know you will love." Isabelle walked into the space, larger than most bedrooms, and gasped at the elegant customized cabinetry. There were felt-lined drawers for lingerie, cantilevered shelving for shoes and specific sections for hanging pants, suits and long gowns. He pointed out the safe built into the wall for valuables. "This is every woman's dream." He went to the bookcase, opened an obscure piece of molding, turned a lever and the entire bookcase glided to one side revealing an elevator. "This goes all the way to the lower level, between the gym and the safe room." They went on to the mirrored master bath done in travertine and stone with platinum fixtures, an eight-foot walk-in shower and a large window by the whirlpool.

Isabelle was pleasantly surprised with the attention to detail he had insisted upon in the house. They continued to the lower level, a state-of-the-art gymnasium with flat screen televisions and a sauna that seated six people. David took her to the safe room. I have twenty-four-seven security around the house but this is for any unanticipated problems should they occur. He explained the design and safety precautions. "The room is built with concrete and steel re-enforced walls and ceilings. There are security cameras at the door and inside the room where we can see the entire house, inside and out. There is a wireless command center, backed-up by a massive battery system, with the ability to contact the police department as well as trusted friends. It is equipped with food, water and a ventilation system good for thirty days." He showed her the toilet facilities, the beds and supplies. "You are to come here in an emergency, with or without me, understood?" She looked at him seriously. "Understood."

"Here is a box of Krugerrand gold coins that will always be of value as tender for anything we might need. There are two people who know the access code to enter, you and I.

My security team does not know it. The code is SOHO2 for our first date. I do not want to frighten you but it is better to be prepared than not." Isabelle repeated the code. "SOHO2." He hugged her. "I don't ever want you to be in harm's way." They returned to the kitchen where he poured them each a glass of wine and led the way outside to the veranda. Isabelle spoke first. "David, you have a beautiful home and I love how you have brought out the detail of each space. The windows let in the soft filtered light allowing every room to feel bright and airy. The artwork was a surprise. I didn't know you collected."

"I have saved a spot for your Renoir." He reached for her hand. "Isabelle, one thing I want you to know, no woman has ever spent the night in this house. I have lived here alone. Now, this house is ours to share. You are free to make any changes you want." Isabelle set down her glass. "There is nothing I would change here. I feel at home as long as you are with me." She looked down at her ring and back to David. "I have been thinking about our getting married. Has Martin suggested a pre-nuptial agreement?"

David set down his glass. "I will admit my advisors have recommended one, however, I know you Isabelle. I would risk my life for you. I have complete faith in you and I do not want a piece of paper to come between us with any doubts whatsoever. Are you sure you can trust me?" She smiled. "I have an inheritance from my father that I entrust you with completely." He laughed. "It is yours to do with as you wish, Isabelle. We can discuss all of this some other time. Come with me, we need to get dressed for the party." He led her upstairs to the bedroom next to his where he had placed her luggage. "Please let me know if there is anything you need. I will see you downstairs."

David dressed in his tuxedo, draped his jacket over a chair in the living room and poured a glass of wine. He looked up as she entered the room, dressed in a floor-length gown of navy-blue satin with a u-shaped neckline and a fitted waist. She looked like a queen. He stood, went to her and gently kissed her cheek. "You look wonderful. Every man will be jealous of me as they should. Here, turn for just a moment." He reached in his pocket and fastened a necklace around her.

She reached up and turned to look in a mirror. It was a sapphire and diamond necklace that fell just below her collarbone. "David, it's beautiful. You are spoiling me, you know." He set the box on the table. "I adore spoiling you."

They arrived at the museum and David led her into the room toward friends to whom he introduced her simply as Isabelle. He tried to keep a low profile for both of them. They mingled with acquaintances of David's and finally were seated at their table for dinner. The master of ceremonies stood and thanked everyone for their support of the museum. He talked about the latest acquisitions and plans for future expansion. He thanked Mr. David Siegel for founding the Siegel Foundation the year before with the formation of an endowment to provide funds to secure future works of old masters for the museum. There was a round of applause and David stood in acknowledgement. Isabelle watched the others at their table as they also stood in congratulations for David. The speaker turned to upcoming events for the museum and soon dinner was served. Isabelle reached for David's hand. "I didn't realize you were to be recognized tonight."

"Neither did I." There was much conversation around the room about David and his date. 'Who was he with?' 'Do you know who she is?' 'What a beauty.'

Following dinner, a band began to play. David took Isabelle's hand. "I would like to get away from here, what do you think?" She squeezed his hand. "I think it's a good idea." They quietly walked away from the table as if they were going to dance and headed for the exit. David called the valet on his cell phone as they waited outside. "I hope you didn't mind all of that. I didn't want you to feel uncomfortable." She held his hand. "No, David. I could tell you were surprised too. Let's go home." They stepped into the car and headed home. "I am going to get into something more comfortable. I'll be down in a minute." Isabelle went up the stairs as David removed his jacket and went into the study for a glass of brandy. Isabelle soon joined him, wearing a long sleeve tee shirt dress. "This is how I feel comfortable. Do you mind?" He poured her a brandy and handed it to her. "You were beautiful tonight, the star of the party, but to me, you look more beautiful now."

He sat on the sofa and Isabelle joined him as she set her drink on the coffee table. "David, you must be very proud to have endowed the museum with funds to acquire works of art." He turned to her. "It is an investment in the future of Chicago. We need to ensure the museum continues to grow with acquisitions to become a premier center of the arts." He picked up his glass and continued. "Sorry, that sounded like a speech, but it is true. Without the support of the community the museum cannot survive." Isabelle took a sip of brandy and looked into the glass. "You are absolutely right. Now, I have an announcement. You have been a very patient man with me, allowing me to take the time to feel comfortable in our relationship. After careful consideration, I would love for you to hold me in your arms tonight." David stood and reached for her hand. "Come with me, Isabelle. Let's go upstairs."

CHAPTER TWELVE

Isabelle awoke, sat up and looked around the room. The aroma of pancakes let her know breakfast was in the making. She got up, brushed her teeth and went downstairs to the kitchen. David was there engrossed at the stovetop over a griddle of blueberry pancakes. She walked up behind him, put her arms around his waist and kissed him on the back of his neck. "What is going on here? You know how to cook and you have been hiding it from me?" He turned, kissed her and stood back with the spatula in his hand. "You should be careful sneaking up on a man with a weapon." He kissed her again, led her to the breakfast table and poured a cup of coffee. "You are about to experience the best pancakes in the city of Chicago; airy, plump pancakes filled with a mélange of fresh blueberries and raspberries, with grilled sausages and freshly squeezed orange juice. Truly a breakfast fit for a queen." He stacked the food on a platter and set it before her. "I cannot give away all of my secrets at once.

How do you think I have survived for all of these years on my own?" She took a deep breath of the aromas and placed her napkin on her lap. "I think I am in love." David sat beside her and they ate the entire platter of food. "Happiness breeds hunger", someone famous once said. "How did you sleep?"

"Like a baby. I feel like a princess." He touched her hand. "You know, these two-day visits are not enough time to show you all of the things I want you to see. I would like for you to come for a week or two when you can make arrangements." She carried the dishes to the sink. "I would love to David. I will see what I can work out when I get back and let you know. I'm going to dress and I would like to take a walk around the property for some fresh air, interested?" He gently nudged her away from the sink. "I'll take care of this. You get dressed and we'll go for that walk."

Isabelle went upstairs, showered, dressed and packed her things. She joined David and they went outside together, holding hands. They walked toward the back of the property along a pathway that curved along hundreds of white rhododendron, hydrangea and azaleas.

The lawns were lush with gardens of colorful perennials and dozens of white dogwoods, cherry trees and massive oaks that balanced the size of the house. Isabelle looked toward the back of the house in the distance. The large windows gave a strong, architectural look to the three stories of stone. There was a long, arched loggia of white columns, surrounded by a manicured boxwood hedge. They continued toward the side of the property along a clear stream of water that cascaded into a pond filled with koi and water lilies. "This is charming David. You must keep a crew of landscapers busy taking care of it all." "They are here every day. They have to remove the fish in the winter months and bring them back in the spring but I like coming here to feed them, it's very relaxing. Come with me, I want you to see this." They walked to the side of the house to a covered veranda made of enormous blocks of stone set into the ground and along the sides forming a low continuous wall. There was a summer kitchen complete with cabinets, appliances, granite counters and wrought iron tables for dining. Ceiling fans, recessed lighting and long canvas drapes gave it an airy feeling of casual ambiance.

"What a wonderful place for a quiet dinner. You put a lot of thought and planning into the house David and it shows. She turned as she heard a vehicle on the back of the property. "That's Andy. He patrols the property along with Brad. They keep an eye on things for me. Don't worry, it is actually very secure here, I just like to take precautions." They had circled the house and returned to the front drive. Isabelle looked up to take in the scope of it all. The size of the property and the large stately trees gave the impression the imposing house had been there for years, years beyond the time it took to complete. "It's nearly two o'clock, we should probably be leaving." Isabelle agreed and they went inside to gather her things. "I would like to keep this here." She handed David the box containing the sapphire necklace. "It will be safe here I know." He set it on the table. "It will be here for your return, hopefully soon." They rode to the airport and David walked with her up the steps into the plane. "Safe trip, call me when you get home."

Isabelle talked with the other doctors about her schedule. "I have made a chart of the pregnancy timelines of each of my mothers.

I have four due to deliver in the next two weeks and the others are all four to six months out. I would like to take two weeks to fly to Chicago and spend time with David. What do you think?" They promised to cover for her. "Isabelle, you are a good doctor, you actually care about your patients and all of their apprehensions. We are going to miss you as are they. However, we understand. You must go on with your life with David Siegel. You will have the opportunity to fulfill your dreams of helping others. You have a wonderful life ahead of you Isabelle. Take whatever time you want to be with him, we will take care of things here." She told David she would fly to Chicago at the end of the month for two weeks. He was elated. "Great. We will have time to work in some of the things I want you to see. This time, I am coming for you. I don't like the idea of you flying alone."

Isabelle became more comfortable with the house as she found her way around and learned how to operate the intricate electronic systems. David took her to his offices and showed her through the building as he explained the various departments and capabilities.

It was impressive. He took her to his office on the second floor of the building, a corner office of enormous proportions, contemporary in décor; it was a light, bright space with intricately sculpted carpets, a massive mahogany desk and furnishings done all in the signature gray color scheme. "What a commanding space. This is the most luxurious office I have ever seen. It's no wonder you spend so much time here David." He sat behind the desk. "This has been my home away from home but that is all soon to change. I never had a reason to go home. There was never anyone I wanted to go home to. This was my refuge, my work, my life, until now."

They played golf, attended a reception at the university, an opening night ballet and dined at David's club where he introduced Isabelle to several friends. Everyone was most impressed with her and David beamed with pride with her beside him.

They took turns making breakfast for one another. Isabelle chose fruit and cereal over eggs and bacon to keep them in shape and healthy. They read the Sunday papers and relaxed is his study, totally comfortable with each other. David handed the travel section to her.

"Here, have a look at this. I know how much you like France, what do you think of spending our honeymoon there?" Her eyes sparkled as she looked at the article about Paris. "I do adore France." She thought for a moment. "But not Paris, not for our honeymoon, it's too crowded. I visited a lovely town in the Provence region of southern France years ago, Avignon. It would be perfect. There are cultural activities, it is picturesque, quiet and near the sea. We could rent a house." David watched her expression as she described Avignon and he could see how much she loved it. "It sounds perfect. Avignon it is. I will have my travel assistant look into rentals for, two weeks?" Isabelle hugged him. "Oh David, two weeks with you in France, it will be heaven." He jotted a note to himself. "Now we have a problem." She looked at him in surprise. "What is it?" He took her hand. "We cannot plan the honeymoon until we set a date for our wedding." She laughed aloud. "Yes, I guess that would be a good idea. The best time to visit France is in early June before tourist season gets in full swing. The temperature will be mild and flowers will be in bloom." She checked her calendar.

"June first falls on a Saturday, what do you think?" David removed his glasses and looked at her. "Sounds like a slightly clinical way to set a date but if you're okay with the selection, so am I. June the first it will be." They talked about what kind of ceremony they wanted. David admitted he was not in favor of a large wedding and asked Isabelle if she would mind. She was relieved. "I totally agree. I was concerned you might want a big wedding but frankly I do not want to share our day with a crowd of people I barely know." They decided upon a small Jewish ceremony in the New York synagogue Isabelle attended. David's brother would be his best man and witness and Isabelle's friend Joan would stand with her. "Allison will be my bridesmaid. She will be so excited."

"I like the way you think Isabelle. We have planned our wedding and our honeymoon is less than an hour."

"We do think alike, don't we? There are just a few other things to be taken care of you know, but I can handle the minor details. I am so excited David. It will be wonderful." He kissed her.

Isabelle returned to New York at the end of their two weeks totally rested. She wandered around her condo and thought about the move to Chicago. She would always have a fondness for New York but now Chicago held a special charm to her.

She contacted the rabbi at her synagogue and reserved the date of June first, the coming spring. She met her friend Joan for lunch and told her about the plans she and David had made. "I would like you to stand with me at our wedding and help take care of Allison." Joan was thrilled. "I will be honored Isabelle. I cannot wait to meet David and I am so happy for you." Isabelle told her how they were planning their honeymoon in France. "Two weeks in the French countryside with this man who adores you? You are a very lucky girl, Isabelle." She smiled. "I know."

Isabelle ordered engraved announcements and hired a photographer who had taken pictures at a friend's wedding. She liked the candid photos he did, not the staid, posed portraits she felt were boring. She met with a florist and described in detail the flowers she wanted at the synagogue as well as in her bouquet.

She gave them a sample of fabric from her gown to use as a guide. She told David about it all when he called. "I guess I left those things in your lap." David told her he had mailed information on two chateaus in France he wanted her to look over. "We can discuss it when I am in New York next week." Isabelle suggested they invite Martin to the wedding. "Martin has been important in each of our lives and I know he would want to be with us." David agreed. "Absolutely, thank you for thinking to include him Isabelle."

Mrs. Morrison phoned Isabelle with the results of Allison's medical tests. "They found absolutely no sign of any changes in her M.R.I. readings. We have not noticed any further signs of dementia, perhaps she just had an off day." Isabelle talked with Allison twice each week and had to agree. Allison told her about events at school and stories about her friend Millie and Isabelle was relieved to hear that she remembered things she had done during the week.

The package of information about the rentals in Avignon arrived and Isabelle read everything about them.

One was a private, luxurious home that had been photographed in major design magazines. It was a contemporary house with a high-tech kitchen, marble bathrooms, eight rooms furnished in chrome and leather. It did not appeal to her in the least, too much like New York. The other was an eighteenth-century stone chateau, twenty minutes north of Avignon, a bed and breakfast owned by a young French couple. There was a cottage next to the main house that provided an independent stay on the grounds with all of the amenities. The photographs showed the exterior of the cottage with its own private pool and gardens. It had two bedroom suites with baths, a living room with fireplace, a sun-lit kitchen and a porch along the back of the house. The main chateau was in true Provence style, an elegant home with a long tree-lined drive that wound toward the house. Topiary trees framed the entry behind a large iron gate and lushly planted gardens. It looked like a Van Gogh painting. That was the one, the cottage.

David arrived on Friday night about seven o'clock. Isabelle had prepared dinner for them at home. They had a drink, ate dinner and sat to talk.

She told him she had read the literature he sent about the houses in France. "What do you think? Which is your favorite?" She told him the chateau with the guest cottage was the one she favored. "It is lovely David and we will have our privacy." David agreed. "Then the cottage it is. I will contact them Monday morning to reserve it." They discussed their plans and Isabelle told him she had talked with Martin. "He is thrilled for both of us and pleased to be included in the wedding."

David's brother and sister-in-law would fly in on Friday, the day before the wedding, and stay at the Plaza in Manhattan. David said he would fly in Friday afternoon and join them at the hotel. "After all, I do realize I am not to see you the morning of the ceremony." Joan agreed that Allison would stay with her and ride with Isabelle to the synagogue. They would all meet at Martin's club following the ceremony. "I know this sounds silly David, but I have to admit I am a little nervous."

"Brides are supposed to be nervous, but I will be at your side."

The next morning they rode into Greenwich Village for breakfast and went for a walk. They stopped in a bookstore where Isabelle bought a book on Provence for David. "Wait till you see the photographs, it is beautiful." They returned to the condo early afternoon and sat in the living room. David talked about his project and the construction schedule. "So far we haven't hit any snags. I'm sure we will but right now things are going as planned. I brought the plans to show you." He went to his briefcase and spread the blueprints out on the coffee table. As he explained the scope of the project Isabelle was astounded. "David this is enormous, it's beautiful. How long until it's completed?" David explained to her it would take four years, barring any major problems. "The hotel is the priceless gem of the entire plan. It will be in colonial revival architecture with a four-story central atrium and a coffered glass sky-lit ceiling. I placed it here, away from the activities, on five acres that will be surrounded with lush landscaping and total privacy. I want it to be the most luxurious destination west of Manhattan."

He went on to point out features difficult to see on a blueprint; the signage, the landscaping, the easy access from airports and interstate highways. "It is a landmark project that will attract people from across the country."

"You must be so proud. This is quite remarkable."

"I am proud of it, Isabelle. It is the culmination of years of hard work."

The next few weeks flew by and June arrived the next weekend. David flew to New York, met his brother and sister-in-law at the hotel and drove with them to pick-up Isabelle for dinner. "Where are we going?"

"It's a surprise Isabelle." The car stopped in front of the Gregory restaurant in SoHo where they had their first date. "David, this is perfect." Joan was waiting for them with Isabelle's sister and they enjoyed a quiet dinner together, celebrating and reminiscing. They talked about how they met and the honeymoon they planned in France. After dinner Allison and Joan left together, Daniel and his wife returned to their hotel and David took Isabelle home. He placed a gift on the coffee table as she went to her bedroom to change.

She returned with a small package and handed it to David. "I guess we do think alike." They sat on the sofa and opened their gifts, David first. It was a solid gold Swiss watch. "It belonged to my father David." He kissed her. "Thank you. It is a gift I will treasure always." Isabelle opened her gift of emerald-cut diamond earrings. "David, they are fabulous. I will wear them tomorrow. Thank you my dear." They kissed and David stood. "Until tomorrow, good night Isabelle."

David was up early Saturday morning and met his brother for breakfast. Daniel questioned David about the decision to have such a small ceremony. "We both agreed. Neither of us wanted to share our day with a crowd of people, just the ones important to us. Isabelle has only one sister and her parents are both deceased. Her uncle will walk her down the aisle."

They arrived at the synagogue at two-thirty. David and his brother took their positions at the altar and the rabbi signaled the music to begin. Isabelle hugged Allison. "You are the prettiest bride I ever saw." Joan took Allison's hand and they walked to the front of the chapel. Isabelle followed, walking slowly toward David, smiling radiantly.

She wore a below the knee column of cream-colored satin accented with small pleating around the bust line, the diamond earrings from David and carried a bouquet of cream-colored roses, the stems tied with satin ribbon. She was a vision of elegant simplicity David would remember always. They stood beneath the wedding canopy as the rabbi conducted the ceremony, exchanged their vows and kissed as the guests applauded Mr. and Mrs. David Siegel. They walked out of the synagogue arm in arm as the photographer snapped pictures of the smiling couple.

They met up with their guests at Martin's club in a private dining room with one large round table covered in cream satin to the floor with a centerpiece of the same creamy roses. Allison sat on one side of Isabelle, David on the other. Isabelle had put on the short beaded jacket that matched her gown, perfect for their celebration dinner.

Daniel led the first toast to the bride and groom. "May you live a long and happy marriage." Martin followed. "I take great pride in the fact that I introduced David and Isabelle to one another. I toast to great happiness for my two favorite clients and friends."

Allison stood and nervously began to speak. "My sister is the most beautiful bride I have ever seen and I now have a new brother, David." She began to cry and Isabelle stood beside her. "Thank you, Allison. We both love you very much."

CHAPTER THIRTEEN

Tom Morrison came into Arthur's office promptly at ten-thirty. Few people kept Arthur waiting, especially his senior staff. "The presentation on the card reader was outstanding, Art. This is going to improve our position immensely across the board."

"The big hit is being the first to come out with it. We'll grab the accounts from the savvy consumers who want the latest and greatest technology. Cell phones and computers will seem passé against this. I can't wait to see the market response. What do you have for me?"

Tom handed an annual report to Arthur. "I'm looking at a regional bank headquartered in Missouri. Twenty-five offices, strong assets, solid earnings, a clean track record as far as I can see and a compatible culture as a merger candidate. I'd like to take a closer look if you agree." Arthur glanced through the report.

"Tom, a month ago I would have told you we couldn't even think about a merger but your timing is good.

The rollout of the card reader will put us in an aggressive posture to consider looking at expansion."

"It may be a good fit for us. We could use a presence in St. Louis and southern Missouri as well as their other offices in Columbia, Branson, Farmington and Jefferson City."

"I agree and I like the idea of a regional bank next door. My first priority is to get the card reader project off the ground and growing. Hopefully in two to three months we'll know how successful it is. Look into it quietly. Any due diligence proposals will have to wait. I'll take a look at the report and get back to you. What have you been up to for fun?" Tom laughed. "Mary and I rode with the bicycle club over the weekend to Indianapolis, overnight, and back on Sunday. The weather was great."

"Most people I ask tell me they went to a new restaurant or saw a play. Only you would ride a bicycle hundreds of miles for fun."

"It is fun Art. You should try it."

"They would have to life-flight me to the nearest hospital. I'm impressed Tom, you're going to live forever."

"I plan to enjoy myself while I'm here." Tom stood. "Thanks Art, I'll let you know what I find on the merger idea."

The press release for the thumbprint credit card went out the first of the month and the media campaign hit ten states the first week. The response was instantaneous with requests pouring in for the new card. The branch offices were inundated with customers who wanted to update their cards and new customers from competing banks. Lillian's phone rang constantly for four days with reporters calling for an interview with Arthur. She took messages and showed them to Arthur. "I guess I'm pretty popular these days." He was elated with the interest and the response. He agreed to an interview with the Chicago paper and one New York reporter. Burt Williams and Doug Swan would accompany him to New York.

Barrington's earnings rose significantly during the first month of the credit card release and he expected it to continue until other banks could launch their competing cards.

Doug Swan met with Arthur twice a week with detailed reporting on the numbers. "My projections were conservative Arthur. We have already issued five hundred thousand cards."

"Great. Keep an eye on these two markets. Their numbers should be higher." Arthur closed the report. "Deborah did a good job on this and I want you to give her a bonus, five thousand, I don't want to lose her."

Arthur was in the dining room having lunch with Bill Lawrence when Jordan Banks called. "Lillian, its Jordan. Is Arthur in? I need to see him today."
"Yes Mr. Banks, he is in. I will have him call you." As soon as Arthur came out from lunch Lillian told him about Jordan Banks phone call. "He sounded urgent." Arthur closed his door and returned the call. "Arthur, do you have some time this afternoon? I need to talk with you." Arthur told him to come right over.

"My friend at the SEC called me this morning with some information. He warned me to keep my distance from endorsing Clark Barnett's senate race because they found an illegal campaign fund, two and a half million. He will have a tough time squirming out of this one. But the piece de resistance is that the fund was traced to Bartel. Your suspicions were right." Arthur hit the desk with his hand. "Great!

He finally got what he deserved. Jordan, this is just what I need to get him off the Board and Bartel off my back. I can't tell you what this means to me." Arthur paced around the room elated with the news. "What about his senate campaign?" He sat down beside Jordan. "The story will hit the morning papers and you can be sure his opponents will be as happy as you. His response will be the key factor. He can't deny the findings. He could deny knowledge of where the money came from and blame one of his advisors but he would have to pay back the money and I'm not sure he can do that." Arthur shook his head. "He wasn't very smart. He tried to sell out my bank to become a senator. Imagine what he would do in Washington." Jordan stood and shook Arthur's hand. "I have to go. We're breaking ground later today for the new technical school. Congratulations, Art. Keep me posted." Arthur thanked Jordan again. "Lillian, ask John Douglas to come in if he has a moment." Mr. Douglas appeared at Arthur's door. "Come in John, have a seat." Arthur closed the door, sat beside John and told him about the news. "What are the legal guidelines to get Barnett off the Board?"

"When this story breaks Art, we have every right to vote him out. He mentioned Bartel in front of the entire Board at the last meeting. My suggestion is that you ask for his resignation. If he is smart, he will go willingly to save face. If not, I'm sure the Board will side with you." Arthur went to his desk and checked his calendar. "I want to take care of this as soon as possible. The news will hit the papers tomorrow. I will set up a meeting with him here for Thursday or Friday and I want you to sit in as my witness." "You've got it Art. I will draw-up the resignation letter."

Arthur asked Lillian to come to his office. "Please cancel my four o'clock meeting with Bill. I have some things to take care of and am leaving for the day. I'll see you in the morning."

The next morning, he read the papers. 'Barnett Senate Campaign Bites the Dust.' The story went on to detail findings of illegal campaign funds tied to Bartel Corporation. Barnett's campaign opponents were calling for him to step out of the senate race and Bartel had so far refused to comment on the allegations.

David Siegel stopped in to see Arthur and congratulate him on the news. "I suspected something after Barnett's actions at the last meeting. He showed his hand, Art."

Arthur stopped by Lillian's desk when he arrived at work. "Good morning Lillian, beautiful day isn't it?" She had the newspaper on her desk and held it up. "It is indeed, Mr. Barrington." She followed him to his office and they talked about the news. "I want a meeting with Barnett scheduled as soon as possible. Clear my schedule for whatever works for him and let John know so that he can join me." Lillian handed him his mail and phone messages. "Yes Mr. Barrington. Have a good day."

The meeting was scheduled for Friday morning at nine o'clock. John went to Arthur's office at eight-thirty and they reviewed the resignation letter. Lillian announced Mr. Barnett had arrived and showed him to Arthur's office. "Good morning, Clark, please have a seat. I asked John to join us this morning." Clark looked at John Douglas and knew immediately he was on the hook. The chief legal counsel was only summoned when there was trouble.

162

"Clark, we have read the news articles about your illegal campaign funds and your ties to Bartel Corporation. You failed to disclose your conflict of interest, you breached your confidentiality agreement as a Director and you attempted to sell out my bank." Barnett grinned. "Come on Art, you know you can't believe everything you read. I don't know where every dollar comes from. I have a staff in charge of keeping those records. I have requested an audit to determine who is at fault and believe me I will find out. It is a hit to my campaign but I do not intend to back out of the race. As far as Barrington goes, I have been on this Board for six years and for the most part, have supported your decisions. I only suggested we consider a buy-out to protect our shareholders." Arthur watched him as he talked. Ever the politician, he evaded any responsibility or guilt and glossed over the facts like a schoolboy caught cheating. Arthur spoke calmly. "Clark, this publicity is not good for my bank. I will not have a director who is under suspicion of illegal activities sit on the Board. MY shareholders are legally protected by a Board of Directors ethically above reproach.

I offer you a choice. The next Board meeting is on the twelfth where I will call for a vote for your dismissal, or, you can tender your resignation here and now." Arthur opened the folder containing the resignation letter and turned it toward Barnett. His smile slipped. "John, are you in agreement with Art?"

"I am. Your seat on the Board is terminated." Barnett picked-up the letter and read. "I am resigning for 'personal reasons'? Is that how it will be announced?" Arthur told him yes. Barnett picked-up a pen and signed the letter. Arthur and John both signed and John left to make copies for each of them. Barnett stood and reached out to shake Arthur's hand. "No hard feelings, I hope. You know I still want your vote on Election Day, Art."

"Goodbye Clark." John returned and handed a copy of the letter to Barnett. They shook hands and John walked him to the door.

John and Arthur talked about the meeting. "He thought he could talk his way out of resigning, unbelievable." Arthur agreed. "When you told him his seat on the Board was terminated, he finally knew we had him. Thanks John."

CHAPTER FOURTEEN

David and Isabelle rode to the airport the next afternoon, boarded their plane and flew off to France. They rented a car and drove south toward Provence. Isabelle opened her window and inhaled the aromas of the countryside. They chatted about their wedding the day before. "Allison was rather quiet, didn't you think? I told her I would be gone two weeks and I think she was worried."

"We'll be back before she can miss you. We'll find something special to take back to her." They heard the blaring horn of a French police car behind them and David pulled to the side of the road and stopped. The policeman came to the window and in French asked David for his driving license. Isabelle leaned forward. "May I speak to him?" She spoke French to the policeman and explained they had just flown in from New York and were unfamiliar with the rental car and the roadways. Je suis désolé." The policeman smiled at Isabelle and tipped his hat to her.

"Faire attention. Bon jour Madame, Monsieur."
They watched as the policeman drove away and
David looked at her shaking his head. "You did
not tell me you spoke fluent French but I am very
glad you do. You charmed us out of a ticket,
Madame. What did he say?" She smiled. "He
told us to be careful."

They drove on past the terraced fields of
southern France planted with precise rows of
grapevines, groves of olive trees, lush green
hillsides and valleys of lavender with the
beautiful scent that seemed to go on forever.
Rows of pink oleander lined the roadway, profuse
with blooms, regal chestnut trees, pines and white
birch, true to Provence dotted the hillsides. "We
are almost there. The drive should be on our
left." David saw a sign, 'Chateau Bouchard'.
They drove along the long grass-lined gravel lane
to the chateau and parked the car in front of the
house. As they stepped from their car the owners
came to the door to greet them. "Mr. and Mrs.
Siegel? Hello, I am Renee and this is my wife
Michelle." He held out his hand to David and
kissed Isabelle on her hand. Michelle told them
how happy she was to meet them. "Welcome to
our home."

They invited David and Isabelle inside and offered them a glass of wine. They were a charming couple. Renee, quite outgoing, was dressed in a white shirt and navy blazer. Michelle, a petite blond, had a contagious smile and a delightful personality. Renee stood. "I am sure you would like to see your cottage and get settled. Please come with me." He led them through the chateau, outside and along a stone pathway to the cottage. Isabelle commented on the beautiful gardens. "Merci. We love flowers." He opened the door and stood back for them to enter. "Welcome. We are at your service to make your stay with us perfect in every way. I will bring your luggage while you look around." David and Isabelle smiled at each other when he left. "Merci", David mocked. "Now I understand your love of this area. You are right, it is charming in every way." They walked through the rooms and noticed everything was in perfect order with a bouquet of roses on a table in the living room. "Did you arrange for these?" David shook his head. "I wish I could take credit for them but I think you owe your gratitude to our hosts." Renee returned with their luggage and handed them a packet of information.

"We have taken the liberty of leaving dinner for you in the oven. We understand what a long journey you have had today. As you wished Mr. Siegel, we have no other guests during your stay and we are a phone call away from anything you may want. Bon soir and bon appetite." David began to reach in his pocket but Isabelle touched his arm as a sign not to offer a tip. When Renee had gone, she explained. "The French are easily offended. We will leave an envelope when we go. David, did you reserve the entire chateau?" He walked toward the kitchen. "Yes, I did. I did not want to share you with any tourists. We have the services of Renee and Michelle for two weeks." There was a basket of cheese, grapes and crackers on the sideboard in the living room with napkins and wine glasses. David found a bottle of champagne in the refrigerator that he uncorked and poured for them. "A toast to Mrs. Siegel. Welcome to France."

They relaxed from their trip and took a nap. When they woke they were starving. Isabelle went to the kitchen and found a casserole of beef bourguignon in the oven with parsley potatoes. There was a handmade apple tart on the counter with a loaf of fresh bread.

She set the table while David opened a bottle of red wine. They sat at the table and enjoyed the food. The beef was accented with pearl onions and whole mushrooms in a buttery brown wine sauce. They ate nearly all of the beef and half of the apple tart. "I need some exercise tomorrow or I am going to get fat with this food." They sat outside after dinner and talked about their trip.

The next morning David was up early as usual and made breakfast for them. There was a bowl of farm eggs in the refrigerator with a bottle of milk and a basket of berries. He lit the stove and began to cook the eggs. "Good morning. Do you realize we slept ten hours?" Just then they both noticed a burning smell. David turned to the stove and the pan with the eggs was charred and smoking. "I guess the stoves are different here, I have ruined breakfast." Isabelle laughed at him. "I will clean this up. Why don't we call Renee and tell them we will come for breakfast?" She phoned the house and Michelle answered. "Good morning." Isabelle told her they would like to come for breakfast. "But of course, come whenever you are ready." They showered and dressed and walked along the path to the chateau where they saw Michelle in the herb garden.

"Hello, please, come with me." She led them to a shaded area in the garden with an iron table and chairs. "I will be right back." She returned with a platter of sausages, an oven-baked omelet and a bowl of fresh fruit. "Renee will be right here with your coffee and rolls. Enjoy." Renee appeared with the coffee and a basket of lovely cinnamon-scented croissants. "Please let me know if you need anything." David told him they would like to drive into town. "But of course, it is only twenty minutes. Turn left at the end of the lane, you cannot miss it."

They walked along the narrow streets of Avignon and took in the sights including a bookstore where they found a guide on the Provence region. They wandered through antique stores and looked at the finely crafted furniture. Isabelle found a cut glass powder jar with a sterling silver lid. The lid was engraved with the initials JB. "David, look at this. These are Joan's initials. This will be the perfect gift for her." As the owner of the shop wrapped the gift David saw something that caught his eye. "And this is the perfect gift for Mrs. Siegel." He pointed in the case to a small silver fleur-de-lis charm. "I love it, it is perfect David."

The shopkeeper attached it to her bracelet while they looked through the shop. "Merci." Isabelle held out her arm admiring the addition to her bracelet.

They sat at a sidewalk cafe for an iced coffee and read the guidebook. "This entire area is a wine enthusiast's paradise. I'll read more about the different wineries when we go back to the house. I want to ship some wine home." Isabelle looked at a map she picked up in the bookstore. "Look, here is Aix en Provence, the city of a thousand fountains, just an hour from here. Can we drive there later in the week?" They decided to walk to the famous bridge in Avignon, the Pont Benazet, a beautiful arched bridge built in the twelfth century. It was magnificent. They passed the outdoor markets filled with fruits, vegetables and flowers and watched as the French housewives took meticulous care in selecting only the most perfect produce to take home for their families. The aromas from a bakery, or patisserie as they called it, lured them inside. The cases were filled with the most delectable looking pastries and cakes. They each decided on a glazed fruit tart, tender and flaky and delicious.

David looked at the women on the street. "Why aren't they fat with all of this great food?" Isabelle laughed. "I know, the French women must have a distinct metabolism that keeps them thin. Plus, if you notice, everyone walks instead of driving. I always liked that about France, the leisurely pace and the love of the outdoors. Are you enjoying it here David?" He held her hand. "I enjoy every moment being with you."

"Mr. Siegel, hello." David turned to see Renee stepping from his car. "Mrs. Siegel." He kissed her hand. "I come to the markets every day as Michelle demands the freshest of everything. She is preparing the most fabulous bouillabaisse for dinner tonight. I don't know your plans but I will give you a hint that no restaurant in Provence can surpass her succulent seafood stew." David looked at Isabelle. "Renee has convinced me. It sounds too good to miss." Isabelle agreed. "We would love to join you." Renee smiled. "Magnifique! Michelle will be delighted. Au revoir!" He hurried down the street with a list in his hand. David looked back at Renee's car, a nineteen seventy-five red convertible, a Jensen Healey roadster.

He walked over to the car and looked inside. "What a car. It is in perfect condition. Maybe Renee will let us take it for a drive." Isabelle laughed at David. "Men and cars; a match made in heaven."

They returned to the cottage and relaxed in the living room with a glass of wine. "David, that was a wonderful day. I love it here, merci my darling." They changed for dinner and walked the pathway to the chateau. Renee greeted them in the foyer dressed in white slacks and shirt with a light blue blazer. He always looked impcccable. "Welcome, please come have a seat." He showed them to the living room and offered them a glass of wine. He explained the different grape varieties and suggested a Rhone wine he produced there at the chateau. David asked him about his vineyard and the history of the house and Renee offered to give them a tour the next morning. Michelle joined them, dressed in a lightweight floral dress in shades of blue. "I hope Renee is treating you well. We are so happy to have you join us for dinner. Did you have a pleasant day?" David and Isabelle felt comfortable,
as though they had known them for years.

Dinner was outstanding. The bouillabaisse was everything Renee had promised, rich with mussels, clams, lobster and fish in an herbed broth perfectly seasoned. They talked for hours, David interested in the history of the chateau and the surrounding region and Isabelle asked advice on nearby places they should visit. They said their goodbyes at midnight and returned to their cottage. "That was a delightful evening." Isabelle agreed. "They are wonderful, so gracious and unassuming. I enjoy talking with them."

They joined Michelle and Renee for breakfast in the garden the next morning then went for a walk through the vineyard. "Here is my winery. Please, come in." Renee explained the winemaking process he used and tapped one of the barrels to give them a taste of his red variety. David was impressed with Renee's knowledge of wine and admired the fact he had continued his family traditions at the chateau. "We are the third generation to take care of the property and it is our life. We are happy here."

David and Isabelle left at eleven to drive to Aix-en-Provence for the afternoon.

They drove through the narrow labyrinth streets of the city's old town, parked the car and walked by the city's famous decorated fountains. They sat in the park beneath rows of sycamores where Cezanne had found inspiration and visited his studio where he created some of his most immortal works. It was a much more intimate view of his life than a museum. They strolled through the town square with its stately fountain and a bustling flower market filled with row after row of colorful flowers and the aromas of jasmine, lavender, anemone, lilies and roses. "Ah, the scents in the air, no wonder they create some of the most prized perfumes in the world." David couldn't resist buying a bundle of roses for Isabelle. They toured the Saint Sauveur Cathedral built in the twelfth century with its amazing architectural influences. They came upon another town square with a stretch of outdoor restaurants and stopped for a rest. "I am exhausted." Isabelle slumped in her chair. David ordered soft drinks and salads and they relaxed as they watched the people pass by.

They returned to the chateau at six o'clock and decided to eat in the cottage. The lateness of the previous night and a day of walking had tired them both. Isabelle phoned Michelle and explained what all they had done that day. "You relax with some wine. Renee will bring some food to you about eight."

"That will be perfect. Thank you so much." David kicked off his shoes, opened a bottle of wine and joined Isabelle in the living room where she curled up next to him on the sofa. "I think we need to slow down a little. I apologize for dragging you around Provence all day and I thank you for being so patient with me."

They joined Michelle and Renee for breakfast the next morning. "We enjoyed the delicious food last night and turned in early. We were exhausted." Michelle smiled at Isabelle. "We understand. The first few days here everyone wants to see the region and there is so much to do." Isabelle explained they had decided to take the day to relax by the pool and enjoy the grounds of the chateau. After breakfast Michelle asked David and Isabelle, "We may drive to the seashore today if you wouldn't mind being on your own for the afternoon."

Isabelle assured her they did not mind. "I have prepared a niçoise salad with fresh tuna and vegetables for lunch. It is in the refrigerator with sliced fruit and croissants. Our home is your home. Please help yourselves to anything you want. We will return at five o'clock. Enjoy your day."

David and Isabelle returned to the cottage, changed into swim suits and went to the large outdoor pool. "David, I think they decided we need some time alone, some privacy. They are so very thoughtful." They stretched out on pool chaises, read and relaxed in the warm gentle breeze and bright sunshine. They swam playfully in the crystal blue water, ate lunch by the pool and returned to their cottage for an afternoon nap. They awoke at six o'clock, rested, refreshed and renewed. David hugged her. "I am now ready for whatever you have in mind; touring, walking, sightseeing, whatever." She hugged him back. "This day would be pretty hard to top." The phone rang and David answered it. Isabelle heard him talking. "Sounds good to me. We will be there in thirty minutes." He set down the phone. "It was Renee. They are back and he is grilling steaks for dinner. I'm hungry."

Isabelle hugged him. "I remember steak is on your list of favorites. Let's get dressed."

They met Renee and Michelle on the patio where they sat together and talked about the day. "You and Isabelle should try to go to Marseille one day. The beach is fabulous and the sea air invigorating." They had dinner of grilled steaks, salad and a wonderful rice pilaf. Isabelle asked Michelle where she gained her cooking skills. "Cooking is my passion. As a girl I would beg my mother to allow me to prepare dinner for our family. Of course, I wanted to cook something quite exotic, not our usual meals. My poor parents and brother suffered through numerous nights of heavy pasta dishes and spicy curries. I finally realized the Provence foods were the most flavorful and healthy. I studied at Cordon Blue with some wonderful chefs who taught me how to use herbs and to prepare light sauces, not the typical heavy cream-based sauces associated most commonly with French cuisine." Renee smiled and touched her hand. "Thank goodness. I would weigh a ton by now." Renee asked about their lives in the states and where they lived. Isabelle listened as David talked about Chicago and about his business.

He was usually reluctant to open-up about his work and she had not heard him talk about his new project in such detail. She could see he felt as ease with Renee and that he trusted the two of them.

CHAPTER FIFTEEN

Burt wrote the press release that Clark Barnett had resigned from the Board of Directors of Barrington Bank for personal reasons. It hit the papers the next day after he signed the resignation letter. Barnett's senate campaign was going as strong as ever. He dismissed the allegations against him and vowed to find who knew of the illegal campaign contributions. Opponents were doing their best to discredit him and called for him to end his candidacy.

The Barrington Board was scheduled to meet within the week and they would begin the search for a replacement for Barnett. Arthur met with his senior staff and asked for their recommendations. Tom Morrison said he thought Howard Driscoll, owner of Bio-source would be a good fit. "He runs a multi-billion chemical corporation that he built from the ground up." Bill Lawrence mentioned Walter Morris, senior partner of the largest law firm in Chicago. "With all due respect to you John, we could use an independent legal opinion on the Board."

Doug Swan and John Douglas offered nothing. "Those are both good men, and I'm sure the Board members will have some names in mind. I want to get this before our shareholder meeting for a vote. Arthur noticed Doug Swan looked thin and drawn. He asked him to stay after the meeting. "Doug, is everything okay? You look like you have lost weight." Doug smoothed the crease in his pants, a nervous habit. "Sure, Arthur, everything's great. I'm thrilled with the new credit card numbers. We have surpassed all estimates with its success." Arthur pressed him. "The reports look good. I don't mean to pry Doug and stop me if I am, but you don't look well." Doug broke down and his eyes filled with tears. Arthur stood and closed his office door. "I'm sorry Arthur. I didn't mean to become emotional." Arthur gave him time to regain his composure. "It's Kay. We have separated. She has gone to Maryland to stay with her sister for a while. I still want to work things out but I don't know if I can." Arthur watched as he talked, he was a defeated man. "I'm sorry Doug. I hope it works out the way you want. Let me know if there's anything I can do." Doug stood. "Thank you, Arthur. Let's keep this between us."

Arthur sat in his office and thought about Doug. He picked-up the phone and called Ann. "Hi there, I was thinking we should get away for a few days. How would you like to go fishing?" "I can be ready in an hour." Arthur laughed. "You are too easy. How about Friday morning? We can be in Canada by ten o'clock." "A weekend away with you sounds great. Love you."

Arthur buzzed Lillian. "Do you have a minute?" "Yes, Mr. Barrington, I will be right there." Arthur asked her to schedule the plane for Friday morning. "Ann and I are going fishing. We will leave at seven in the morning and come back Tuesday afternoon." Lillian made notes as he spoke. "Sounds like fun." Arthur leaned back in his chair. "Now that this thing with Clark Barnett is finished, I could use a break."

Arthur phoned the fishing lodge near their cabin and arranged to have food and supplies delivered for their visit. The plane dropped them off in Ontario and they took the bush plane for the thirty-minute flight to the remote lake. They unpacked their bags and sat outside on the porch to enjoy the scenery.

"I am always surprised at how rejuvenated I feel as soon as we get here." Ann took a deep breath. "Fresh, clean air, it smells great." The cabin was set in a clearing surrounded by wilderness a short walk to the lake. They were in northwest Ontario on a pristine lake they had fished for fifteen years. "Best investment we ever made, buying the cabin." Ann went inside and came back wearing her fishing vest and hat. "Come on, let's go for a ride." Arthur grabbed a cooler, his fishing vest, tackle box and rods while Ann filled a bag with her camera and binoculars.

They idled quietly through the water as families of ducks swam by and wound their way to a favorite tree-shaded cove. Arthur cast his line and sat back relaxed with Ann. She reached in her bag, "How about a cold beer?"
"You read my mind, sounds good." She opened the bottle of beer and handed it to him. He was always amazed at her adaptability; she could look elegant in a formal gown at a black-tie charity event and equally attractive in khaki pants and a fishing hat. "Would you like a sandwich?"
"You are a magician, when did you make these?"
"I wish I could take the credit, but they were in the refrigerator along with the beer."

Arthur felt a tug on his line and stood to reel in his catch, a four-pound lake trout he held up for Ann's approval. She reached for her camera and took a picture. "My hero, we have dinner for tonight." He removed the hook and placed the fish in the cooler. They ate their sandwiches as a flock of loons watched, hungry for a crumb of food. Arthur caught a second trout and they decided to return to the cabin. He cleaned the fish, placed them in the refrigerator and he and Ann sat in the living room to talk. "You have had quite a time the last few weeks. This was a great idea to get away for a few days of rest and relaxation." Arthur agreed. "This is just what I needed, time alone with you without phones ringing."

Ann prepared dinner of pan-seared trout, oven-roasted potatoes and glazed carrots while Arthur poured them each a glass of white wine. They sat at the kitchen table and looked outside as the sun flickered through a forest of trees. "The best seat in the house and the best trout in the world, who could ask for more?"

Arthur built a fire after dinner and they sat on the couch to watch the flames.

"Do you think you could be happy living here full-time once we are too old to do anything else?" Ann smiled and hugged him. "I will be happy anywhere as long as I am with you." They fell asleep next to each other by the warmth of the fire.

They fished the next three days. Ann reeled in two walleye, one five pounds, and Arthur three walleye and a six-pound northern pike that put up quite a fight. They hiked along the north side of the lake and took pictures of a moose as he munched on a bush of berries.

Tuesday morning, they packed-up their things and boarded the bush plane to Ontario. Paul was waiting for them at the airfield and they were back in Chicago by four o'clock. As they descended into Chicago Ann held onto Arthur's arm. "Let's do this more often."

CHAPTER SIXTEEN

David slept until nine o'clock with Isabelle beside him. He felt more relaxed than he had in years. They met in the kitchen, had breakfast and sat on the porch. "I think I will call Renee and ask him about what wineries we should visit." Isabelle looked up from her book. "David, he is a vintner. It may be insulting to him to ask about other wineries in the area." Just then the phone rang and David answered. "Yes, I do. Yes, it sounds great. I will be there in fifteen minutes." David hung up the phone and told Isabelle he was invited to a round of golf by Renee. "You don't mind, do you?"
"Of course not David, it will be good for you." David changed, kissed her and promised they would go to dinner that night, just the two of them. Isabelle did not mind him going. She showered, read the travel guide and went for a walk on the grounds. She met up with Michelle in the rose garden. "So, the men are off playing golf, would you like to join me in the house?"

Isabelle followed her to the kitchen and took a seat at the table as Michelle clipped the rose stems and placed them in a vase. Isabelle talked about how she studied in Paris when she was young and how she had always wanted to return to France. I feel a sense of belonging when I am here, the language, the food and the countryside all seem so familiar to me. "Parlez vous Francais?" Isabelle smiled. "Oui." They spoke French and it all came back to Isabelle in an instant. She told Michelle how she met David and about their wedding in New York. "David invited you and Renee to visit us and we both would like that very much. You have shown us such wonderful hospitality during our stay and we would like to return the favor." Michelle blushed. "Je vous en prie." The pleasure is mine. Michelle gave Isabelle a cookbook she received when studying in Paris, "My gift to you. May you enjoy it as much as I."

David and Renee returned at two o'clock from their golf game. "Renee won but I did okay." Renee handed David a glass of wine. "David was exceptional on a course with which he was unfamiliar." David kissed Isabelle. "And what have you been up to this afternoon?"

She put on a sullen look. "Oh, I have pined away the entire day waiting for my husband to return." She laughed. "I am joking. Actually, I have had the most enjoyable day. Michelle gave me a gift I shall treasure always." She held up the cookbook, "From Cordon Blue, signed and with the appropriate look of a well-used volume." She opened the book to a stained page. "She also, most graciously, allowed me to assist her in preparing our dinner for tonight. I now know how to present a proper potato Lyonnaise, perfectly seasoned and browned to perfection. I cannot wait for you to taste it." They moved to the patio for appetizers of cheese, small shrimp-filled turnovers and wine.

Renee had seen David's enthusiasm for his car and the next morning he insisted they take it for a drive. They drove the car into town. "Where did you learn to drive sports cars?" He explained to Isabelle his first car in college had been a used Austin Healey. He sold it when he began his business and needed the money. He regretted selling the car ever since. "Cars do not mean much to me now but I have always wished I had kept that one."

Isabelle saw something in a shop window. "Look in the window, at the pink sweater. I hope they have Allison's size. It will be perfect for her. I'll be right back."

Their days in Provence passed all too quickly and it was soon time to leave. The night before leaving they invited Michelle and Renee to join them for dinner at a restaurant in St. Remy. "A night off for you both." They left at noon and drove south to a winery Renee had suggested in the village of Beaumes de Venise. Renee told them they had begun making wine at the start of the nineteenth century. It had been tended by five generations of the same family and they made two reds as well as a rose. The four of them toured the wine cellar for a tasting and were served foie gras and camembert on baguettes to enhance the bouquet of the wines. They drove on, south to St. Remy the birthplace of Vincent Van Gogh. They passed fragrant fields of wild flowers, Cyprus and olive trees. Renee explained that while living there Van Gogh painted more than one hundred fifty works of the surrounding countryside, including the well-known 'vase with irises'.

They walked along the narrow cobblestone streets, stopped in antique shops and flower stalls and had their photo taken by a friendly Frenchman in the town square. They decided upon a restaurant named The Bellards for dinner. They were served a first course of goat cheese wrapped in chestnut leaves that was wonderful. David and Renee both ordered lamb with roasted potatoes while Isabelle and Michelle chose grilled fish. The food was plausible, nothing memorable. On the drive home David proclaimed that certainly the best food in Provence was to be found at Chateau Bouchard. They sat in the garden with Michelle and Renee until midnight, then said their goodnights and went to their cottage.

The morning of their departure Isabelle and David joined Michelle and Renee for breakfast in the chateau. They talked about what a wonderful stay they had enjoyed and how they hoped to see the Bouchards in Chicago within the year. Renee helped with their luggage and once the car was packed, they drove down the lane and waved out the windows. They talked all the way to the airport about how fond they were of Michelle and Renee.

"Did you think to leave an envelope in the cottage David?" He assured her he had. "I genuinely enjoyed both of them as I know you did." David's car was waiting when they arrived in Chicago and they were anxious to get home. It was ten-thirty and they were so tired they went to bed without even opening their luggage. The next morning they were both awake by eight o'clock. David made coffee while Isabelle phoned Allison to tell her they were back. "Allison says hello to her new brother-in-law. She wants to come see us. I told her I would come for her week after next, okay with you?" "Of course, Allison is welcome anytime, you know that."

David had a mountain of mail waiting for him stacked on his desk with a note on top of the neatly bundled pile. 'Look in the dining room'. He went into the dining room and called for Isabelle. "Come here, we have a surprise." She came to the door beside David and they looked at the boxes stacked along the wall. "Where did all of this come from?" He walked over and looked at one of the boxes. "They are wedding gifts Isabelle." There must have been nearly a hundred of them.

"I can't believe it. I didn't think this many people knew we were married." David laughed. "Word travels fast especially when it concerns a beautiful bride." They decided to unpack and get organized before opening the packages. Isabelle went upstairs to unpack her bags while David opened his mail. She came downstairs with her French cookbook and placed it in one of the kitchen drawers. The thought occurred to her that she would need an office space of her own, but decided that could wait, there were so many other things to take care of first. David had given his housekeeper, Marian, a month-long vacation. It was time off she deserved and he wanted to be alone with Isabelle. She had stocked the freezer and pantry with food before leaving to be sure they would have everything they would need.

Isabelle puttered around the house all afternoon. David found her sitting in the living room with music playing softly. "Are you okay?" She looked up. "Yes, I'm fine. Here, come sit with me."
"Do I sense some melancholy?"
"No. I was just thinking about our wedding, our wonderful time in France and you. I am sure I am the happiest girl in the world."

"Then come with me, the happiest man in the world. Let's see what's in the packages." She followed him to the dining room and sat down. He handed her a box. "Wait, I am going to need something to write on." David brought a tablet from his desk. Isabelle opened the first box to find an exquisite sterling silver bowl engraved with her initials. David looked at it inquisitively. "It is customary to engrave with the bride's initials, David. It's from your brother and his wife." She made a note for herself. David opened the next box which contained eight hand-cut crystal wine glasses from Martin and another from Renee and Michelle, a dozen bottles of wine from their chateau and a copy of the photograph taken in St. Remy of the four of them. "Look at this Isabelle, our picture with the two of them in St. Remy."

"What a wonderful photo. I will find a frame for it and a special spot in the house." They opened boxes for an hour as Isabelle noted which gifts were from whom. "David, I am in awe. What an outpouring of generosity. It will take a week to open all of these gifts."

"I am as surprised as you. Can we take a break? I'm hungry."

They went to the kitchen and prepared broiled salmon fillets and a salad for dinner. Isabelle admitted she was still catching up from the long flight home. "Let's clean up the kitchen and go watch a movie."

Isabelle turned one of the guest rooms into an office where she spent a couple of hours each morning writing thank you notes, caught up on correspondence and household records. She received invitations to luncheons, charity fashion shows and the docent program at the art museum, but chose to become actively involved in a charity benefiting the children of Chicago and neighboring communities. They were thrilled to have her and asked if she would accept the role of chairperson of the fundraising committee. She accepted and scheduled visits to the corporate offices of hospitals, financial institutions, law firms and private businesses to solicit contributions. Within the first year she had raised over one million dollars to provide the immediate needs of food, clothing and shelter for thousands of children. She visited homeless shelters, food kitchens, day care centers and schools where she informed all who would listen of the help available to them.

She reveled in the success stories of parents and children who were able to improve their lives with the help of the charity and agonized over each story of abuse, neglect and mal-nourished children. She shared the stories with David and although he admired her commitment he also worried about her safety. "We always go on our visits with three people and I have never felt threatened. However, I did have a bit of a shock the other day. We left the food kitchen and discovered Beth's car had been vandalized. The driver's side window was broken and they had taken her purse and bricfcase." David became angry for the first time since she had known him. "That does it! I have worried about your safety in those areas. If you insist on continuing your volunteer work, I want you to have a driver who will stay with you. I will make the arrangements." He went to his study and picked-up the phone. "Bob, it's David Siegel. I want a security officer and car devoted solely to the use of Mrs. Siegel starting tomorrow morning. I want him five days a week, Monday through Friday, and on call as necessary. Can you take care of that for me?" Isabelle sat quietly as she listened to David speaking.

He hung up the phone and came back into the room. "Isabelle, I apologize for my temper but I will not have you placed in dangerous situations. I will feel much better knowing you are protected." She looked into his eyes. "I know. I didn't want to worry you. I do intend to continue my volunteer work but I promise I will try to limit it to corporate contributions." He put his arms around her and held her tightly. "Let's go out for dinner tonight. Where would you like to go?" She smiled and squeezed his hand. "Ann told me about a new restaurant downtown, Baruccio's. She says the food and the service are wonderful."

"Baruccio's it will be. Shall I call for reservations?" Isabelle stood. "I will call, I have their number."

The next day Isabelle had a pleasant surprise, a call from Michelle in France. "We have been thinking of coming for a visit as we have missed you both. The chateau is booked for the Easter holiday of April twelfth but we could fly over anytime between the fifteenth of April and the middle of May. The temperatures here are still in the fifties so we have until the middle of May before more reservations."

Isabelle was thrilled to hear from her and knew David would be happy they could come to Chicago. "Michelle, we would be honored to have you both visit. I will check with David's schedule and call you tomorrow. We have missed you both. Give our love to Renee, au revoir."

Isabelle told David about the call from Michelle. "Wonderful, it will be great seeing them again." He checked his calendar. "Let's suggest the last week of April or anytime the first two weeks of May, what works best for them. This will be fun showing them around Chicago and returning their hospitality." Isabelle called Michelle the next day and they agreed on April twenty-sixth through May second. "Wonderful, we look forward to seeing you both. Please send your itinerary and we will be there to meet you."

They met Renee and Michelle at the airport to rounds of hugs and kisses. "How good to see you here." The driver took care of their luggage and they rode to the house as David pointed out Chicago landmarks. Renee had been to New York twice but this was Michelle's first visit to the states.

"It is very busy, no? So many cars all speeding along." Isabelle agreed. "Yes, everyone seems to be in such a hurry here, a totally different pace than in Provence." They arrived at the house, showed Renee and Michelle to their room to refresh and met up in the living room. David poured the wine and Isabelle set a basket of crackers and cheese on the coffee table. "Isabelle, you are not having wine?" David reached for her hand. "Mrs. Siegel is not having wine because we recently learned we are expecting a child." Renee stood and proposed a toast. "Magnifique! Congratulations to the happy couple. When shall we expect this child?" Isabelle told them the baby was due the end of November. Michelle held out her hand to Isabelle. "You will be the most wonderful mother, congratulations to you both."

"We are so happy to see you two. I must warn you, I told our housekeeper Marian what a talented chef you are and she can't wait to impress you with her cooking." David took them for a drive the next afternoon while Isabelle rested, per his suggestion.

He drove them through the Brighton project under construction, past the elegant Victorian glass conservatory by the lake and down the cobblestone main street pointing out the entertainment venues and restaurants. Renee was astounded by the scope of it all. "You have created a city, David, with enormous charm and character. I never dreamed it would be such a big project." David gave them details of the number of acres the project covered, the miles of sidewalk and roadways. "There are four thousand street lights on the property, the electric company loves me."

They drove on to his offices for a quick tour. "This is where the idea for Brighton was born nearly eight years ago." David led them down the hallway toward his office and held the door as they entered. They walked to the wall of windows looking out over the campus surrounding the building. "How many acres do you have here?"

"Fifteen, and the location is ideal, near the freeway and only ten minutes from the city."

They drove along Lake Shore Boulevard and Michigan Avenue as David pointed out the architecture of Chicago, Navy Pier, the art museum and the El Trains traversing high above the city streets. "Chicago is a city of surprises. It has twenty-four miles of lakefront and thirty-one beaches, quite rare for a cosmopolitan city. We'll bring Isabelle later in the week, have lunch and do some shopping."

They returned to the house and found Isabelle in the library reading. "You're back, thank goodness. I was beginning to feel like a neglected child. Did you have fun?"
"David drove us through Brighton and we're still stunned. It is magnificent!" Marian served cocktails and hors d'oeuvres on the veranda then returned to her kitchen to watch over the meal she had worked on all afternoon. Isabelle winked at Michelle. "You are in for a treat tonight. Marian has come up with a French menu of salmon and vegetables. I hope you're hungry."

They lingered over the meal of wine-poached salmon in a creamy truffle sauce, roasted vegetable ratatouille of eggplant, zucchini, bell peppers, tomatoes, garlic and herbs, and crusty homemade bread.

Michelle congratulated Marian. "Your salmon was tender, light and flavorful with just the right number of truffles and you have mastered the classic ratatouille by roasting the vegetables. Tres bien!" Marian beamed with pride. She cleared the table and returned with a warm apple tarte tatin, golden brown and glistening with a dusting of sugar. "Marian, I am most impressed. You must show me some of your recipes." Marian had to laugh. "They are all in the cookbook you gave to Mrs. Siegel."

"We thought we might have lunch downtown tomorrow and do some window shopping. Are you up to it?"
"David, that's a great idea and it will give us a chance to show Michelle and Renee around the city. There is an area of smart boutiques and antique shops you will enjoy." David suggested another idea for later in the week. "I know of a charming restaurant I would like to show you on Friday. We should leave about nine a.m. as it is a bit of a hike but well worth the effort." He shared his surprise that night with Isabelle. "They will love that David." They left the house Friday morning and drove south of the city.
Renee looked out the window of the car.

"Chicago Aviation, they have a restaurant?"
David laughed. "Not exactly, I thought we would
fly to New York for lunch. Michelle cannot come
to the states and not see Manhattan." Michelle
was stunned. "What a wonderful surprise!
David, you are the most thoughtful man!"
Isabelle smiled toward David. She had told him
that many times.

They landed in New York, took a car to
Central Park and had a leisurely lunch at a
charming restaurant by the lake. After lunch they
drove through the park, Times Square, past the
New York Stock Exchange, the Empire State
Building and parked on Fifth Avenue. "Here you
are ladies, the shopping mecca of the world."
Isabelle stepped out of the car. "Come Michelle,
there is a fabulous boutique just there and you
must see Tiffany's." They strolled through the
shops as Michelle purchased items to take to her
friends at home. "The linens are fabulous. I must
have some for the chateau." Renee shook his
head. "Do you see why I love her so? She comes
to New York and what does she want, sheets!"
David and Renee followed along, carried
packages and watched the girls have fun together.
They ducked into a favorite shop of David's.

"You must see their ties. They are the best in New York." Renee chose a navy and gold silk ascot. "Remember, Avignon is more casual than New York. I will wear this often." They met up with the ladies and David looked at his watch. "Okay, if you have spent enough money, may we get going? We're having cocktails at the Plaza Palm Court, Isabelle's favorite."

They boarded David's plane and were back in Chicago by ten that night. Michelle talked all the way to the house. "This was the most fabulous day, thank you both so much. I will always remember seeing New York as if I was a princess."

CAPTER NINETEEN

Diane Conlan was scheduled to meet with Arthur Wednesday morning. The reason for the meeting was to discuss the security corporation. She arrived promptly at ten o'clock, restrained with a simple, 'good morning'. Arthur got right down to business. "I want to see the second quarter numbers on Securities Corp Diane." She handed a folder to him. Arthur looked over the figures and compared them to her last report he had on his desk. "I see little improvement from last month. What is the problem?" She straightened her posture and glanced out the window before answering. "Our mutual funds are doing well as you can see in the report, with a thirty percent rise in the past three weeks, but we lost fifteen percent in returns with large cap funds. I told you last time, market conditions have had a direct impact on our performance." She had come in with an attitude and was not offering the information he wanted.

Arthur closed both of the folders. "Diane, what is your problem?

You were totally out of line the last time we met and today you come here with a chip on your shoulder. I do not have time for this. I want results, not excuses." She slammed her red portfolio loudly on his desk and leaned forward. "I am tired of being scrutinized for every decision I make. I am not accustomed to being second guessed and micro-managed. I am Chairman of six holding companies and I can handle a couple of men who aren't doing what I tell them to do!" She was screaming at Arthur. Bill Lawrence walked down the hall and heard her voice. He tapped on Arthur's door. "Everything okay in here?" Diane stood with her hands on her hips. "This is a private meeting Bill. Do not interrupt." Arthur stood. "Come in Bill. Diane was just telling me she feels I am second-guessing her decisions." She picked-up her portfolio. "I don't feel that, I put up with it every day. I am in charge of the holding companies and I need to be able to direct the activities without intervention." Arthur answered. "Diane, you are dismissed, please leave my office." Bill stood by as she stormed out of Arthur's office.

He looked at Arthur and grinned. "You certainly have a way with the ladies Art." Arthur sank into his chair. "She has a problem, Bill. When her temper flares up, she is irrational. She pulled this once on the plane with Paul. She pulled it once before with me and again today." Bill sat down. "So? What are you waiting for? Kick her out. You don't need to put up with her." Arthur told him he had already talked with George Cater about her. "You need a witness, right? Well, I guess I happened by at just the right time. Of course, everyone else on the floor heard her too."

Arthur scheduled another breakfast meeting with Diane for the next morning. George would be there as well as Bill Lawrence. When Diane arrived and saw George, she knew what was about to happen. George spoke first. "Mrs. Conlan, your position at Barrington Bank has been terminated, effective today. Mr. Barrington and I will go over your employment contract with you and answer any questions you may have." Diane smiled at Arthur. "I guess we have different expectations of how to manage our business." Arthur handed a file to her containing her contract.

"Let's go over this." They explained her severance agreement and stock option allotment. George closed his file. "You are not to return to the bank. Any personal belongings will be sent to your home. We will provide job placement assistance for six months. Do you have any questions?" She stood and shook hands with Arthur. "I do not. Good day gentlemen."

George Cater returned to the bank with Bill and Arthur. "I will talk with Leslie and explain why Mrs. Conlan will not be returning to the bank." Arthur nodded. "Reassure her that she has not done anything wrong. Tell her we will find a position for her within the bank."

Leslie answered her phone and agreed to meet George Cater in his office. She took a note pad and rode the elevator to the fourth floor wondering why he wanted to see her. It couldn't be good news for the head of human relations to call you to his office. Was she going to be fired? George greeted her and offered her a seat. "Leslie, Mrs. Conlan has resigned from Barrington as of today and will not be returning to the bank." Leslie was shocked. "However, we do not want you to be concerned about your job. I will watch for an opening at Barrington for you.

We ask that you respond to questions about Diane simply by telling callers she has resigned. We also ask that you continue your work as usual, collect her mail and phone messages, box up her personal files and belongings." Leslie's mind was reeling. She wondered what had happened. At least it wasn't she who was fired. "Of course, yes I can do that."

"Please don't hesitate to call me with any questions or concerns. We want you to stay at Barrington." She stood. "Thank you, George. I'm sure I will have some questions once I get over the shock." He walked her to the door. "Call me any time."

Leslie returned to her desk, sat down and took a deep breath. She looked at Mrs. Conlan's calendar on her desk, closed it and smiled to herself. Lillian came to her desk. "Are you okay?" Leslie nodded. "Oh, yes, I'm fine, just surprised."

"I think you should go home early today. I will explain if there are any questions."

"Thank you, Lillian. I think I will."

Arthur stopped by Lillian's desk on his way out and handed some folders to her. "I brought you some presents." One of the folders contained Diane Conlan's severance agreement signed that morning. Lillian read the details and took a deep breath as she filed it away. She stared at her computer screen thinking about the inequalities of the working world. In just five years with the bank Mrs. Conlan's biggest accomplishment was failure to perform and now she was walking away with a package of cash, stock options and company-paid taxes worth over three million dollars. Her peers would applaud her financial windfall, not pity the loss of her job. She would move on to another corporation with the help of friends, members in a secret brotherhood, a Skull and Bones society. They served as Directors on one another's Boards and doled out favors for consulting contracts, club memberships and Ivy League college admissions. Lillian had seen talented employees who would never be considered for an executive position because they had no one to open the iron-clad door of opportunity to them. They struggled to get ahead and earned less in an entire year than an executive earned in one workday.

Lillian placed her glasses on the desk and rubbed her eyes. Glass ceilings, fraternal guilds and the good-ole-boy mentality would go on forever. There was no equality.

The next few weeks at work were interesting to say the least. Mrs. Conlan would phone Leslie a couple of times each week and ask her to bring her mail to the alley behind the bank building. She would drive by and pick it up. The first time Leslie went to meet her, she felt like she was in a spy film passing documents to a car in an alley. She stood outside with the package of mail, waiting. Soon a car pulled up, stopped and the window went down. Mrs. Conlan leaned over. "Hello Leslie, how are you?" Leslie handed her the package. "I'm fine Mrs. Conlan. Here you are, there are also some phone messages. I packed some things from your office and Dan will bring them to your house later in the week." Diane nodded. "That will be fine. Thank you." The car window closed and she drove away. Leslie stood there watching as the car turned onto First Street. How humiliating that must be for her, she isn't allowed to come inside the bank. Leslie returned to her desk silently enjoying the turn of events.

CHAPTER TWENTY

Isabelle watched her diet carefully. She ate only fresh fruits, vegetables and occasionally grilled fish or chicken. She gave up wine, drank only water, fruit juice and milk, and for the first time in her life developed a strong craving for pickles. David teased her about it. "The baby is teaching you to appreciate the finer things in life." He pampered her and watched as she became larger each week, concerned that her stomach was getting so big. She laughed at him. "This is what happens to pregnant women. Yes, it is uncomfortable but when the baby arrives, we will forget all of this and have a beautiful child to share always." An ultrasound test determined the unborn child was a boy. David was elated, an heir to continue his name, a son. They interviewed and hired a nanny, Nell, to help and decided the nursery would be in the guest room nearest their room. The nanny would have plenty of space and her own bath. They hired a designer to help with the details.

Isabelle wanted a sophisticated nursery that would grow with the baby and was thrilled with the ideas the designer suggested. They selected a solid cherry crib that would convert to a full-size bed when needed, matching nightstands, a bachelor chest, a rocking chair and changing table completed the room. Isabelle chose colors of sky blue and khaki and once the room was finished, she and David were both pleased.

Allison came the next week and was totally confused in the house. Isabelle had to go everywhere with her as she forgot where the kitchen was or how to get to her room. "I know the house is big, it took me a while to get used to it too." Isabelle told her they were expecting a child and showed her the nursery. Allison looked around, touched the crib, the changing table and sat down in the rocking chair. "It's pretty but I wish you had made it pink." Isabelle laughed. "Oh, Allison, you do love pink. Come with me, let's go for a walk." Allison talked non-stop about her school and her friends and Isabelle realized that she missed it all. She had lived there nineteen years and it had become home to her where she was comfortable. Isabelle took her back on Sunday afternoon.

They had dinner with her friend Millie who wanted to know all about Chicago. "It's a busy place with lots of traffic and noise. I'm glad to be home." Isabelle told her she would call on Sunday and said goodbye.

Joan called to check in on Isabelle and was thrilled to learn they were expecting a child. "Isabelle, what wonderful news."
"I am so excited, Joan. We know the baby is a boy and David and I are thrilled."

Isabelle's doctor confined her to bed the last two weeks of her pregnancy as a precautionary measure. David curtailed all travel and worked out of the house three days a week. Marian was as nervous as they about the birth and checked in on Isabelle regularly. She was a motherly figure, a little plump with graying hair and a cheerful personality and she adored Isabelle. She took hot tea to her each afternoon at four o'clock and dinner on a tray with a single red rose. Isabelle treated Marian with respect and appreciated her kindness during the difficult weeks leading up to having the baby. David insisted on joining Isabelle for dinner in their room. "I feel like such an invalid lying here all day. Tell me what is going on in the world."

"Here, look at this and tell me what you think. It is an updated drawing of the Brighton project. Wait until you see the pavilion, it absolutely sparkles in the reflection of the lake. Construction is falling behind by about five months but that's not uncommon." Isabelle looked at the drawing and asked questions about the restaurants and theater. "It is fabulous David. People are going to want to spend days here taking in all there is to do." She sat up straight, took a deep breath and clinched her teeth in pain. David stood. "Isabelle, are you okay?" She reached for his hand. "I'm fine, but I think we should go to the hospital now. Our son is ready to see you." David kissed her. "It will be all right, sit still." He ran to the top of the stairway and yelled for the housekeeper. "Marian, come quickly, we need you." He went back to Isabelle who was sitting on the side of the bed holding her stomach. Marian came running. "Is it time?" David shook his head. Marian went to the closet where Isabelle's bag had been packed for a month. "I will take this down to the car. Is there anything else I can do?"

David helped Isabelle stand. "Yes. Get Brad. I need him to drive us to the hospital." He helped Isabelle into her robe and they went down the stairs and outside to the waiting car. Brad drove them to the emergency entrance of the hospital where a nurse whisked them down the hall and into a birthing room. Isabelle was concerned about David. He was pale as a ghost. "David, bring a chair here and sit with me. The nurses know what they are doing and they will take good care of me. Try not to worry." The doctor told them the baby was coming and it was too late for anesthesia to ease the pain. David watched the monitors and held Isabelle's hand as the contractions mounted. He couldn't bear the look on her face. He wished he could make it all stop. The doctor asked him to move to the head of the bed and he watched helplessly as they told Isabelle to push. He closed his eyes, prayed, and soon heard a cry. He opened his eyes to see the nurse holding a red-faced crying baby. "Congratulations, you have a son." Isabelle began to cry. David went to her side and kissed her, tears ran down his face and his throat too constricted to speak. Isabelle sank back on the bed and smiled at him. "I did it."

David took a handkerchief from his pocket and wiped her tears, then his own. "You were wonderful Isabelle. Are you okay?" The nurse handed the baby to Isabelle. She gently lifted the blanket so they could look at him. "David, look. He's beautiful, he's perfect." They counted his tiny fingers and toes and lightly touched his head covered in black hair. The nurse told them they needed to draw blood from the baby's foot and get him cleaned up. She picked-up the baby and told David to follow her. "Let's give mother a minute to catch her breath." David followed her and watched as they stuck a needle in his son's little foot and bathed him. He nearly stopped them a couple of times as he thought they were being too rough. They shampooed his hair, put a shirt and hat on him and wrapped him in a blanket. David watched his son as he opened his eyes. They were blue, as blue as Isabelle's eyes, and he looked directly at David. The nurse wheeled him to the nursery with the other babies and David returned to Isabelle. She was sitting up in bed. "Where is our son?" David went to her and kissed her. "He just had a bath and is sleeping quietly in the nursery. He has been through quite a lot as have you.

"I am a little tired but I am also so excited. I want to hold him David." David rang for the nurse and asked if they could have the baby in the room with them. "Of course, I will bring him right in." The nurse handed the baby to Isabelle and she cradled him in her arms. David looked at the two of them and thought his heart might burst with happiness. "He looks like a Benjamin to me, what do you think?" Isabelle touched the baby's cheek and he smiled. "I think he likes the name. Benjamin Siegel. It's perfect. David, you should call Marian and tell her our child is here. She has worried so."

They took Ben home to the smiling faces of Marian and Nell who waited by the door. Marian cried when she saw him. "He is such a little prince." Isabelle hugged her. "He's wonderful, isn't he?" David insisted Isabelle get some rest and helped her to their room. There were two dozen red roses on the table beside the bed. "David, my roses. They're beautiful." She sat on the side of the bed and David pulled up a chair. He handed her a box. "This, my dear, is for you, my love and my life." Isabelle leaned forward to kiss him.

She looked down at the box, untied the ribbon and opened the lid. Lying inside was a white gold and diamond necklace. "David, it's beautiful. Thank you my dear."

"You have given me happiness I didn't know existed and now you have given me a son. My life is devoted to making you smile. I love you Isabelle." He kissed her and set the box on the table. "You really must rest for a while. The nanny is with Ben who is sleeping. I am going to change and will be back in an hour." Isabelle sank into the pillows and fell sound asleep.

Nell adored Benjamin and took wonderful care of him. She bathed and dressed him each morning before taking him to Isabelle. She rocked him to sleep, sang lullabies and got up with him in the middle of the night to change his diaper. Marian went upstairs every chance she had to check on him and Isabelle.

Isabelle was up and around within a week and took Ben with her to her office to sleep while she caught up on her correspondence. Gifts poured into the house for Ben; silver cups, rattles and banks, hand-knit blankets, sweaters and caps. Toys of all description arrived; toy trucks, boats and cars to life-sized stuffed animals.

David and Isabelle played with Ben, rolled balls toward him and bounced him on their knees. He smiled as they talked and they were certain he understood what they said. Isabelle was happy with Nell. She listened as she got up with him in the middle of the night and watched as she wrapped him in soft blankets to keep him warm. But she had feelings of jealously with another woman taking care of her son. She heard Ben giggle when Nell tickled him and saw him fall asleep in her arms while she rocked him. Isabelle couldn't fight the feelings. She called her friend Joan in New York to ask her advice. "I can't believe you're asking me about babies - you're the doctor!" Isabelle laughed. "Yes, but it is all very different when one is the mother. What shall I do?" Joan suggested a diversion for Nell. "Ask her to help you with a project or one of your charities, maybe some work on the computer. While she is 'helping' you can spend time with Ben."

"You are a genius! I do need some files set-up, mailing lists and household folders."

"When do I get to come see Ben?"

"Anytime, you know that." Isabelle checked her calendar. "I have nothing scheduled for the next two weeks. Can you fly in next Tuesday or Wednesday?"

"Let's make it Tuesday. I'm closing the gallery next week to have new flooring installed and a fresh coat of paint. It is perfect timing. I will fly back here Thursday afternoon to help put things back together for the weekend."

"Great! Let me know your arrival time and I'll have the car waiting for you. See you Tuesday." Isabelle made a note on her calendar, 'Joan, Tuesday & Wednesday'. She waited until Ben went down for his afternoon nap and went to talk with Nell. "Do you use a computer Nell? I could use some help setting-up some files of addresses and organizing some reports."

"Yes, I used to work on my computer a lot. I would be glad to help, maybe when Ben is sleeping." Isabelle picked him up. "I will entertain this little fellow while you're in the office. Thank you, Nell. This will be a big help."

Joan arrived at the house Tuesday afternoon and Isabelle greeted her at the door with a big hug.

"How good it is to see you." She led Joan to the porch where they could relax. Joan followed Isabelle and complimented her on how good she looked for a new mother. "Thank you, I have been working on getting back my shape." Joan was intrigued with the house, its size and opulence. "Good grief, Isabelle, you are living in a mansion! My friend, the lady of the manor, is living the American dream in her own country estate. The house is larger than many hotels! Would you and David consider adopting me?" "You can't fool me, Joan. You wouldn't trade your life in New York, your gallery and the pace of the city."

"Touché. Now, where is the baby? I can't wait to see him." Isabelle beamed. "He's napping, but come upstairs with me and we'll look in on him." Isabelle opened the door of the nursery and tiptoed over to the crib. Joan whispered. "Isabelle, he is perfectly adorable. Look at all of his black curls." She hugged Isabelle. "I am so happy for you."

"This is what I've always wanted, Joan. Now here I am with a wonderful husband and a beautiful child.

I *want* to be a mother. I want to read bedtime stories, bake cookies, kiss skinned knees and help with homework. I want it all to be perfect."

"You want what to be perfect?" Isabelle looked up to see David standing in the doorway. "David, you startled me. Come join us." David went to Isabelle and kissed her on the cheek. "I come home to find my two favorite girls in the nursery engrossed in a philosophical discussion. I hope it wasn't about me." He gave Joan a hug. "Welcome, what do you think of Ben?" Joan hugged him. "He is the cutest baby in the world, of course. You two look so happy I can hardly stand it." Isabelle took Joan's arm. "Let's go downstairs. I know you must be dying for a glass of wine."

"David, you should give Joan a tour of your art collection. She is an expert on renaissance art." They walked through the house as David pointed out the paintings and described when he had acquired each one with precise dates. "This is an impressive collection, David. There are many galleries in Manhattan that would love to have such a display "Isabelle has told me how perceptive you are in finding emerging artists."

"I'm excited about the Santos showing, he is wildly popular in Brazil and I know New York will love his work. It is impressionistic yet modern."

Isabelle looked at her watch. "Ben should be waking from his nap by now. By the way, I took your suggestion and asked Nell to help out in my office. She has been busy organizing files and setting-up a filing system for me while I take care of Ben." Joan smiled. "Glad to be of help. Isabelle, you really do look radiant, happiness is most appealing on you. You are like Cinderella without the wicked stepmother and all of those mice." Isabelle went to check on Ben while David poured the wine. "Joan, please meet our son, Benjamin."

"Hello Ben. What a handsome boy you are. I am Aunt Joan and I am very pleased to meet you." Ben smiled at Joan and giggled as David tickled his cheek. "Oh, and quite the little charmer I see. He is absolutely beautiful. Look at those eyes and all of his curls. I feel a slight tug on my maternal instinct."

"He does have that effect. Careful, it's very easy to fall in love with him." Joan placed a gift on the table.

"This is for you, Ben." Isabelle untied the blue ribbon and opened the box. Inside was an antique silver rattle shaped like a lollipop with his name engraved on the handle. "Joan, where did you find this, it is fabulous."

"I came across it at an estate sale at Chadwick's last month and I couldn't resist. It is eighteenth century, crafted in England and belonged to the Earl of Sussex or so I'm told. Something special for a very special boy."

"Thank you, Joan." She put it in Ben's hand. "He likes it."

Isabelle took Joan downtown the next day for lunch at one of Chicago's premier hotels. The lobby of the hotel had sky-high ceilings, floral carpeting and buttery walls in shades of gold and cream. Sunlight streamed in through the floor to ceiling windows. It was a decidedly European ambiance, the perfect setting for what they billed their Royal Tea. They were served a selection of beautifully stacked sandwiches of smoked salmon with cucumber and caviar, a divine lobster egg salad and a vegetarian crustade. Desserts were served on mirrored trays; Parisian macaroons, raspberry tarts and layered chocolate mousse.

"I should know you would seek out an elegant Parisian spot like this, it's so refined, like you." Isabelle laughed. "I brought Allison here for lunch and she ate six of the macaroons." Joan popped one into her mouth. "Good for her, they're wonderful. Do you miss New York?" Isabelle smiled. "A little, but I like Chicago. It is a cosmopolitan city, sophisticated yet not overpowering and I'm finding my way around." Joan asked if there was a men's store nearby. "I would like to get a little gift for someone special." Isabelle looked at her suspiciously. "Someone special? Are you seeing someone new? Don't answer that, I have seen this look before. Who is he?"

"His name is Alex, Alex Marteau. He came into the gallery and swept me off my feet. He is gorgeous, tall, dark, handsome and charming." Isabelle listened as Joan gushed on about him. "He gave me his card and I checked out his website. He is a well-known photographer, mostly fashion shots for the major magazines but he has also photographed some celebrities and politicians. He came to the gallery that night with his publicist who is a big fan of my art.

The attraction was immediate, the moment he kissed my hand I was intrigued. He phoned the next morning and invited me to lunch. I liked that. You know lunch is such a non-threatening date." Isabelle smiled. "Yes, I remember. Has he invited you up to see his work?"

"Isabelle, please don't be so facetious."

"Have you spent the night together?"

"Isabelle, I am thirty-six years old, not exactly a teenager, and I know what I'm doing."

"Joan, please promise me you will be careful. What else do you know about him? Where is he from? Does he have family in New York? Have you met his friends? It sounds as though he travels in some pretty fast circles and you know they can be dangerous. You are an intelligent and highly successful woman and you deserve someone who appreciates you. I love you and I don't want to see you get hurt." Joan gave her a hug. "I love you too, even when you are skeptical. I promise to be careful." They had been friends since the third grade. They grew up together, went to the same summer camp, the same debutante ball and flew off to study at the Sorbonne when they were eighteen.

They had seen each other through their first teenage crush, the flirtatious Frenchmen they met in Paris and a two-year relationship Joan had with a man she later learned was married. She had been devastated when it ended and mourned for six months. Isabelle didn't want to see her go through another broken heart.

They played with Ben the next afternoon and Joan marveled as she watched Isabelle take care of him. It was a non-stop job of bathing him, feeding him and changing diapers. Joan watched in amazement as Isabelle tended to his every need, patiently and lovingly, enjoying every moment.

David made breakfast the next morning as Marian had gone to church. Joan insisted on taking a cab to the airport to save them the trip. "You two stay here with Ben. Thank you for a lovely weekend. I'll call you later in the week."

Isabelle sat with David and told him about the man Joan had met. "I'm concerned about her. Joan is impetuous and sometimes far too daring. She owns one of the most acclaimed galleries in Manhattan with art worth hundreds of thousands of dollars on display.

She has fallen head over heels for a man she knows nothing about, who has charmed his way into her home and her gallery. I'm worried about her." David had never heard Isabelle be so suspicious of anyone. "Joan is a big girl, very savvy and I'm sure she will be fine."

Isabelle called Joan a couple of weeks later. She had flown to Bali with Alex on a photo shoot he did for a major fashion house. Joan fell in love with Bali and its people but wasn't as thrilled with the Alex she saw on the job. "He was like a different man, obsessed with the angle of the sun and the shadows it cast. He exploded several times on the set, upset with models who didn't follow his direction and became moody and sullen over delays he couldn't control. The local people who had been hired as extras were so gentle and kind yet he had no patience with them and became verbally abusive on several occasions. I couldn't wait to get back to New York."

"Joan, I'm sorry, but it is best you discovered these things before it went any further."

"I told him I needed some time on my own to prepare for an exhibit scheduled for the end of the month.

228

He seemed okay with that but kept calling and left messages all hours of the day and night. I avoided them and I think he finally took the hint. He hasn't called for over a week."

"Good. Now, what is this big exhibit?"

"It's not your style, Isabelle. The artist is from Santa Fe and works in desert landscapes with incredible scope and movement. I've been trying to book him for a year, it should be a hit."

Isabelle was glad to hear Joan excited about work again. "Congratulations, I know it will be a success. Send me a brochure, even if it's not my style."

Two days later Isabelle had a call from Joan's assistant. "Mrs. Siegel, it's Paul Hobbs, Miss Bernstein asked me to call you. There was a terrible incident at the gallery last night and she is in the hospital."

"Joan? Is she okay? What happened?"

"There was an intruder. He stabbed her, but she is going to be okay. I had started home but returned to get my cell phone, and found her on the floor. The police said he ran when he heard me." Isabelle held her hand to her throat, shaking. "How awful. Where is she, what hospital?"

"She is in Manhattan General, room six-forty-two." Isabelle wrote down the room number. "Thank you for calling, Paul. Tell Joan I will be there as soon as possible." Isabelle phoned the hospital and asked for Joan's condition. She was listed as guarded.

Isabelle phoned David and told him what had happened. "David, I must go to New York to see her."

"Of course, but I think you should wait until morning. I'll have the pilot ready first thing. Do you want me to go with you?"

"Thank you, but I don't know how long she will need me. I'd better go alone. Nell and Marian will be here with Ben."

"We'll be fine. Call me as soon as you know anything."

Isabelle opened the door of Joan's room and quietly went inside. She walked to the bed and grimaced as she looked at her friend lying there with her eyes closed. Joan's face was bruised, her left eye black and blue and swollen and there were stitches in her lip. Her right arm was in a cast and her left shoulder heavily bandaged.

Isabelle took a shaky breath and gently touched Joan's hand. She opened her eyes, saw Isabelle and began to cry. "It's okay, I'm here." She dabbed Joan's tears with a tissue. "Here, take a drink of water." Isabelle pulled a chair next to the bed and Joan managed a weak smile. "I bet I'm a pretty sight."

"You are always a pretty sight to me. How do you feel?"

"Like I've been run over by a train. Oh, Isabelle, it was awful." She described what had happened. "Paul and I were putting the finishing touches on the new exhibit. It was nearly ten o'clock and I told him to go on home. I was in my office when I heard a noise from the center gallery. I started through the hall and a man grabbed me from behind, jerked my arm behind my back and covered my mouth with his hand. I could smell alcohol on his breath. He pushed me against the wall, covered my mouth with tape and turned me around to face him. I couldn't believe it, it was Alex." Isabelle frowned. "Alex?" She couldn't believe what she was hearing. Joan shook her head. "Yes.

He was drunk and out of control, he yelled and called me names, said I thought I was too good for him, then hit me in the face with his fist." She began shaking. "Slow down, take your time." "He had a knife in his hand and dragged me by my hair through the hallway. He slashed paintings and said he would ruin me. I heard Paul's voice calling my name, he had come back for some reason. Alex shoved me into my office and came toward me with the knife. I tried to push him away but he stabbed me, here." She touched her shoulder. "He ran out the back door and said he would be back to show me who was boss." Isabelle felt sick to her stomach hearing the horror Joan had been through. "Thank God Paul came back." She bent over and kissed Joan on the forehead. "Is Alex in jail?"

"Yes. He threw the knife in a dumpster behind the gallery. The police found it and matched his fingerprints."

"Do they know how he got in? What about the alarm system?"

"The police said the back door was pried open and I don't set the alarm until I leave at night." Joan began to cry. "Isabelle, I thought he was going to kill me."

Isabelle felt so angry that someone Joan had trusted could do something so horrible. "You are going to be okay. No one is going to hurt you again." The nurse came in and suggested Joan get some rest. "I'll be back in a couple of hours."

Isabelle followed the nurse into the hallway. "Is her doctor due in this morning? I would like to talk with him." The nurse checked her watch. "Yes, Dr. Farr should be here soon. There is a lounge at the end of the hall."

"Dr. Siegel? Hello, I am Dr. Farr. I understand you are a friend of Joan Bernstein. How can I help you?" Isabelle shook his hand. "Please call me Isabelle." She asked about Joan's condition. "She is a very lucky lady. The stab wound is in the subscapularis muscle of the shoulder. I operated and sutured the muscle and the skin puncture. The arm was a clean break that is set and immobilized. She may need some physical therapy for her shoulder and counseling to deal with the emotional trauma. I understand she lives alone?" Isabelle explained she and Joan had been close friends since childhood. "I don't want her to be alone just now. I would like to take her home with me to Chicago as soon as she can travel.

I am a physician, not currently practicing, but can assure you she will have the best care."

"She can use a good friend right now. She should be able to travel in a couple of days."

Isabelle called David and told him Joan's condition. "I talked with her doctor and I want to bring her home with me to recuperate. He said she will be released in a couple of days. David, it was Alex, the man I told you about. He is the one who did this to her." David was as shocked as Isabelle. "Joan must be a wreck. Of course, bring her home where we can help her. Isabelle, I am going to send a photographer to the hospital to take pictures of Joan. She may need them if this thing goes to trial. Call me tomorrow and let me know when you can leave and I'll send the plane. Are you okay?"

"I'm fine. Give Ben a kiss for me. I love you."

Isabelle brought Joan home. Marian had placed a bouquet of fresh flowers in her room and several books. David was shocked when he saw her, the cast on her arm and the bandaged shoulder looked as though she had been in a horrible accident.

"It's good to see you, Joan. Our home is your home, always."

Dr. Farr referred Joan to a doctor in Chicago who monitored her progress and Isabelle arranged for a physical therapist to come to the house twice each week to work with Joan on her shoulder and arm. Joan felt secure knowing Alex was behind bars. The police found he had a prior record of sexual battery on a woman he had beaten in a jealous rage and left paralyzed. David and Isabelle accompanied her to New York where Martin had negotiated with the judge for one day of testimony from Joan. She refused to look at him during her testimony and the defense attorney was brief in his cross examination. The three of them returned to Chicago relieved to be home. The court sentenced Alex Marteau ten to fifteen years for breaking and entering, assault and battery and attempted murder with a lethal weapon.

Joan recuperated and at the end of three months and insisted on returning to New York and her gallery. "David, you and Isabelle have been wonderful to me and I will never forget your generosity and love. You know, you are the last of the true gentlemen of the world, kind, thoughtful, gentle and charming."

CHAPTER TWENTY-ONE

Isabelle became pregnant when Ben was one year old and they were thrilled at the prospect of another child. Ben was the joy of their lives, a dark-haired beautiful boy with an exuberant personality and the energy of two children. He walked and ran through the house, up and down stairs as he played peek-a-boo with Isabelle. He was the joy of her life and she treasured every moment with him.

They talked about buying a home in Palm Beach and flew to Florida with Ben to look at the ones the realtor suggested. Isabelle fell in love with the first house they toured. A tree-lined drive led to the entrance of a Mediterranean-inspired two-story house in white stucco with a terracotta tile roof. The manicured lawn was large and beautifully landscaped with neatly pruned hedges, flowering shrubs and palm trees. The back of the house opened onto a large stone patio that terraced down to a rectangular pool with rows of queen palms on either side.

There was a cabana beyond the swimming pool with a fully equipped kitchen, a fireplace and a lounge area for a retreat from the sun. The house had four bedroom suites, a study for David and a large gathering room off of the kitchen. A formal living room and dining room each had rows of sliding glass doors that opened out of sight providing an open-air island-like atmosphere. "It is perfect David, I love it. I do not need to look at any others." He hugged her. "I agree." He went inside to talk with the realtor. "Mrs. Siegel likes it. We will take the house."

Isabelle and David met with a designer the next afternoon to tell her how they wanted the house furnished and gave her a budget with which to complete the house. She would keep them updated with photographs and samples of fabrics and paint. They returned to Chicago four days later.

Isabelle was determined to take better care of herself and hopefully not be confined to bed with this pregnancy. She gained weight quickly this time and unlike Ben, this time it was all around her. The ultrasound test in her fifth month determined she was having a girl.

Isabelle and David were delighted, a boy and a girl, how perfect. Isabelle thought and thought about a name. "David, what do you think of naming the baby Catherine?"

"It is beautiful, just as I know she will be, just like her mother." Isabelle had the second bedroom across the hall from them redecorated for Ben's new room. She chose hand-painted large zoo animals for the walls in the colors of blue and tan and Ben was excited to move to his big boy room. She readied the nursery for a baby girl. The walls were painted pale celery green with white trim. She found a large, round, soft pink rug for the floor and had plantation shutters installed at the windows. This time she chose the same type of crib but in a glossy white finish with matching tables. The room was airy and bright and feminine. Isabelle played with Ben, read stories to him and watched him sleep. He was her little prince and she had never imagined being so happy.

Their daughter came two weeks early weighing only six pounds two ounces. The doctor assured them she was fine, "just a tiny little girl."

The baby was in an incubator for a week and Isabelle stayed at the hospital to be near her. Once she gained six ounces, they allowed David and Isabelle to take her home. Isabelle phoned Nell and asked her to have Ben near the front door as they pulled into the driveway. "David will carry the baby into the house and I want to be able to hug Ben immediately." Ben cried when he saw her and wrapped his arms around her neck so tightly she thought she would fall. She sat with him on her lap and David handed the baby to her. "Ben, we want you to meet your baby sister. Her name is Catherine. She is very small so we need to be careful with her but one of these days she will be able to play with you, her big brother." He looked at the tiny bundle in his mother's arms. "She isn't very pretty mama." David couldn't help but laugh. Ben was right, she was wrinkled and red skinned. "She will be pretty when she gets bigger." Ben wanted to play in his room and ran up the stairs in front of Nell. Isabelle shook her head. "I guess he is not easily impressed."

"His vision of beauty is his mother and not many can compete with her."

Marian had been standing by quietly but walked over to Isabelle to see the baby. "Oh, my, she is beautiful and so small. Welcome home Mrs. Siegel."

They carried Catherine to the nursery and placed her in the bassinet. They stood looking down as she slept peacefully. "You know, you once told me you wanted a gaggle of children. Just how many are in a gaggle?" David threw back his head laughing. "You remember everything. A gaggle, my dear, is a flock of at least seven, but now that I have witnessed the two a.m. feedings and the mountains of diapers we may want to reconsider." He took her by the arm. "Come with me. You should sit down and rest." He led her to the sofa in their room and sat down beside her. "This is for you in celebration of our daughter." She untied the ribbon from the package and opened the box. "David, it is beautiful. Thank you." He placed the blue sapphire and diamond ring on her finger. "I love you Isabelle."

Nell was wonderful with the baby and Ben and Isabelle knew she could not do it all without her. "David, is it okay with you if I give Nell a raise in salary?"

"Whatever you think is okay with me. Ben adores her and she is a big help." David stayed close to home for the next few weeks to help out with Ben and make sure Isabelle rested when the baby slept. Marian prepared their meals, kept the house spotless and baked animal-shaped cookies for Ben.

Isabelle joined Ann Barrington once a week for lunch and tennis at the club. They became good friends and shared many of the same interests; they both volunteered for children's charities, enjoyed fashion, good books and travel. Ann invited Isabelle to society fashion shows and introduced her to a private shopper who arranged previews of favorite designer collections. "Ann, how would you like to join me on a trip to New York for some shopping? I need to update my wardrobe after my pregnancy. We could stay at our condo and my friend in the garment district will get us into some of the showrooms." Ann was thrilled. "How fun, I would love to go. Let me know when you have a date." Isabelle mentioned the idea to David. "What do you think of Arthur and me going too? You and Ann can shop and we will play golf."

"That's a great idea, when?"

"I'll give Arthur a call tomorrow and work out some dates."

The four of them flew to New York and had reservations at the Plaza as the condo was a little small for two couples. They had dinner in Central Park the first evening and planned to go to the theater the next night. Arthur and David left early for their golf game. Ann and Isabelle met in the lobby and took a car to the Upper East Side where boutiques and restaurants lined the streets. They shopped, had lunch and went to the garment district at two o'clock. Isabelle had a pass for the Paraganto showroom, an Italian designer famous for exquisite detailing on his dresses and suits. Ann could hardly hold in her enthusiasm as she saw the line. She ordered a dress of tissue thin gabardine in taupe with finely stitched tucks in asymmetrical rows across the bodice and a red cashmere winter coat. Isabelle selected a cocktail suit in a silk blend boucle of deep sapphire blue with a slight hint of silver thread in the fabric and a white silk evening gown and matching jacket that wrapped at the waist with a heavily stitched band of matching fabric.

They returned to the hotel at four-thirty and sat in the Palm Court for a glass of wine to celebrate their purchases. "The clothes were fabulous Isabelle. The blue suit you ordered is stunning and I cannot wait to receive my dress. Arthur will not believe I chose a red coat but it was so gorgeous I couldn't resist." Isabelle agreed. "It will look great on you Ann." She called home to check on the children and Nell told her they were fine. "We took Catherine for a walk this afternoon and they are both napping now."

They flew back to Chicago the next morning talking about what a fun weekend they had. Arthur shook David's hand when they landed. "You two are invited to join us in Montana this winter for a ski trip. The scenery is fabulous. Thanks again."

The hotel near Brighton was completed and exceeded even David's expectations. It featured thirty individually designed guest rooms filled with luxurious linens, classic furnishings and private terraces. A striking art deco cocktail lounge and restaurant overlooked the grounds of meticulous landscaping and beautiful garden spaces.

The breathtaking interior was designed with incredible attention to detail featuring deep crown moldings, thickly sculpted carpets, an ornate black iron staircase, sconce pendant lights and furnishings in the finest fabrics. David insisted upon a creed of unfaltering service reminiscent of bygone eras to welcome each and every guest and each associate was required to attend week-long on-site training sessions where they were schooled in the protocol of the Bingham Hotel. He secretly sent members of his corporate staff to stay at the hotel and report back to him with their reviews, a practice he found provided excellent inside information. The hotel was to be a destination of its own but was conveniently located just a quarter of a mile from Brighton. Uniformed escorts would drive guests along cobblestone paths to the entertainment venue.

The final landscaping and signage were installed at Brighton and plans were underway for the private preview party. Invitations were mailed in the signature silver envelopes, die-cut replicas of the entrance, a silver pass card inside, along with the date and time.

Four hundred invitations went out to business leaders, politicians, developers and the zoning board members. David felt fortunate the entire project came together just six months off schedule. The years of planning, design and headaches had been worth it as he toured the facilities on the final inspection. He pointed out things he wanted changed, everything from a sign with the wrong color paint to a missing light bulb and a row of trees he wanted removed. He was meticulous and demanded everything be in order. He met with his staff to congratulate them on their efforts and to remind them to inspect the property daily for repair and maintenance.

The day of the preview guests arrived in droves. Valet parking attendants were stationed at three locations and guides dressed in gray uniforms handed out programs with the night's activities listed. The performing arts center was host to a live production of synchronized dancers with a shadowed background of the cityscape. Guests were welcomed to the virtual theater that showed a three hundred sixty-degree experience of a white-water rafting adventure with the sound of waterfalls and a slight mist of water.

The outdoor areas were filled with piped-in music, white swans swam in the lakes and servers passed chilled champagne. A wide tiered courtyard featured outdoor fireplaces on either side with comfortable seating and protective awnings. It was meant to attract people during all seasons to relax and watch the glowing embers while enjoying a flavored coffee or a cool gelato. All of the restaurants were open serving small plates of their menu selections and a large white tent was set-up in the main square as a French bakery with uniformed servers who offered trays of cakes, tarts, pastries and chocolate truffles to the guests.

David and Isabelle walked down the main street, arm in arm, and stopped to chat with their guests. They complimented David on the innovative concept of bringing his luxurious hotel, entertainment venues and dining options together in a new fresh approach. David held on to Isabelle and his bodyguard stayed beside them asking people to wait their turn. The evening ended with a pyrotechnic finale complete with customized music that was met with rounds of applause from the guests. David was thrilled at the turnout and the compliments he heard.

Isabelle squeezed his hand. "Whew, that must be what life is like for a rock star."

"Pretty exciting wasn't it? I think people were impressed."

"Of course, they were. It is so beautifully done and so charming with all of the flowers, trees and fountains. I heard people talking about the dance show and the excitement of the virtual theater film. I think you have a big hit on your hands."

Brighton opened to the public two days later, time enough to correct some minor flaws. A full-page ad in local papers announced the grand opening and helicopters hovered over the complex reporting on the crowds. The number of visitors was counted by an electronic eye at each entrance, surveillance cameras monitored the entire complex and plain-clothed security personnel mingled with the crowds. The gate count for the first seven days was in the tens of thousands. David shared the reports with his staff to a round of applause. "We could double the numbers during peak holiday periods."

The performing arts center changed productions every other month and the virtual theater rotated among eight adventures.

There were outdoor concerts, art festivals and family entertainment. The news media raved about it. "Brighton is an idyllic atmosphere for a weekend get-away, an afternoon stroll with friends, or an evening of elegant dining. There is something for everyone." Travelers to Chicago from all over the world headed to Brighton directly from the airport, only twelve miles away and Chicagoans loved that it was only thirty minutes from downtown. It was the perfect location and quickly became a vacation destination in nationwide publications.

The year-end revenues were higher than David had thought possible. Isabelle was happy for him that the project was so successful. "You should sit back and enjoy the rewards David. Let's take the children to Palm Beach the first of the year when things quiet down a little." He agreed. "Sounds good. A week or two lying by the pool will be good for us both."

Nell went with them to help with Ben and Catherine. They played in the pool, walked on the beach and ran around the house. David and Isabelle went into the city one afternoon for some gifts for them and a quiet lunch.

Isabelle declined to join David with a glass of wine. "I will pass on the wine for now, since I am expecting."

"Isabelle, that's wonderful news. How long have you known?"

"I was pretty sure but I went to the doctor two weeks ago and he confirmed it.

David was thrilled, "When?" Isabelle laughed. "In about seven months. I didn't want to mention it until after the grand opening of Brighton. So, any vacations we want to take had better be soon. We are going to be busy." David poured a glass of water from the pitcher and handed it to her. "Isabelle, what wonderful news but please promise me you will never keep something from me because of business."

Isabelle was tired, a result of the pregnancy, and was happy to relax by the pool as she watched Nell play with the children. David brought some magazines for her to read. He opened one to a picture of a boat. "Look at this Isabelle. What do you think?"

She looked at the color photographs of the interior of the boat, it was luxuriously appointed resembling a home more than a boat with large living and dining areas, four bedrooms and a full kitchen. "It's beautiful, such a large boat." David sat down beside her. "It isn't a boat. It is categorized as a yacht."

"Oh, I beg your pardon. It is such a large *yacht*. Are you thinking of buying a *yacht*?" She was poking fun at him. "Actually yes, I have been reading about them. We could travel up the coast to Chesapeake Bay or south to the Keys and the Bahamas. The children will love it as they get older." Isabelle looked at the pictures again. "It would be a great getaway as a family." David reached for the magazine. "I am going to make some calls. Maybe we can look at some while we're here."

David immersed himself into thoughts of owning a yacht as he read about the dimensions and specifications and talked with brokers. He and Isabelle met the broker and walked along the pier to see two yachts brought in for their inspection. The first yacht was breathtakingly beautiful, bright white with silver trim and fittings.

He described the yacht in detail to David while Isabelle looked around the main deck. They caught up with her in the galley, a kitchen equipped as well as her home with hundreds of custom fit compartments and cabinets. They went to the dining room, the living room, or salon as the broker called it, and the forward owners' suite and study. They went downstairs to the lower deck where there were four guest cabins with baths, an exterior swimming platform and the engine room. Isabelle felt claustrophobic and went back upstairs for a breath of fresh air. They climbed to the upper deck to the captain's quarters, a gymnasium and the bridge. The array of instruments on the bridge was impressive with satellite communications and large wrap around windows. Isabelle chose to stay behind while David and the broker climbed up to the sun deck. She realized David was completely taken with the idea of a yacht. It was luxurious and beautifully appointed but she wasn't so sure she had the stomach for being on water. David came down the stairs and took one look at her. "Isabelle, here sit down. You are white as a ghost." He got a drink of water for her and a damp towel. "Are you okay?"

She smiled, "Just a little woozy today." David helped her stand. "Come with me, I think you need some fresh air and some solid ground." He helped her off the boat and onto the pier to a shaded bench. He returned to the broker to thank him for the tour. "I will be in contact with you."

They drove back to the house and Isabelle stretched out on the bed. "I'm sorry David. I guess the motion got to me."

"I am sorry for dragging you to look at a boat when you are carrying our baby." She looked up at him. "Boat?"

"Yes, as far as you and I are concerned it is a boat."

They returned to Chicago five days later and Isabelle was happy to be home. She had consoled patients through the first few months of pregnancy, explained that they would be nauseated and tired but that it would pass. Her other pregnancies had gone so smoothly, this caught her by complete surprise. David phoned her doctor in concern. "David, Isabelle is thirty-eight years old, a little past her prime for pregnancy, but she is an active, healthy woman and just needs to take things a little slower now. There is nothing to be worried about."

David relaxed somewhat but talked with Nell and Marian to ask them to help out as much as possible with the children. They turned down an invitation from Arthur and Ann to go to Montana and decided to stay close to home for the remainder of the pregnancy. As the time drew nearer David worked out of the house three days each week as he wanted to there if Isabelle needed him. He brought Ben and Catherine into her room in the afternoons where she read books to them and the three of them fell asleep together. He watched them sleep, his heart bursting at the sight of his wife and children who he loved with all of his heart.

On the fourth day David woke to an empty bed. He jumped up and went to the nursery where Catherine slept peacefully. He went to Ben's room only to find his empty bed. He ran down the stairs and into the kitchen where Isabelle sat at the breakfast table with Ben. "Good morning David. We are having breakfast. Would you like to join us?" He leaned against the countertop with a sigh of relief. "What are you doing up so early?"

"I have been in bed for three days. Ben and I decided it was time for me to get up and he said he was hungry." David poured a cup of coffee and joined them. "Daddy, do you want some cereal?" David put his arm around Ben. "Yes, I would love to have some cereal, thank you." Ben passed a bowl to him and handed him a spoon. "Do you want what mommy is having?" David looked at Isabelle and smiled. "Yes, I definitely want the same thing mommy is having." They sat together, ate cereal and talked. "Ben and I decided we are going for a little walk after breakfast. Would you like to join us?" Ben was three years old, precocious and totally in love with his mother. "Yes, let's go."

He was in his study, reading, when he heard Marian call his name and ran to the kitchen to find Marian standing over Isabelle on the floor. "Mr. Siegel, she fainted and fell. Call the doctor." David spoke to Isabelle. "Can you hear me, are you all right?" Isabelle opened her eyes. "David, call the doctor." The ambulance arrived within ten minutes and they sped to the hospital. The doctor was waiting when they arrived and took Isabelle to the emergency room.

David stayed with her, held her hand, assured her everything would be fine. He was frightened. The doctor motioned for David to follow him outside the room. "David, I am going to perform a caesarian section and take the baby. Isabelle is suffering from hypoglycemic shock and the baby is at risk." David reached for the doctor's arm. "Is Isabelle okay? I don't care what it takes, bring in whoever you need. Will she be all right?"

"I think she will be fine. I want you to wait here." David sat in a chair with his head in his hands and prayed. Isabelle was his life, his reason for living. She had to survive. He paced the room, looked at the clock and his watch to compare seconds and waited for the door to open. He was looking out the window into the dark night sky when he felt a hand on his shoulder. "David, Isabelle and the baby are fine. You have a healthy daughter. Isabelle is in the recovery room and I will send for you in a few moments. Are you okay?" David reached for the doctor's hand with tears in his eyes. "I was so worried." The doctor placed his hand on David's shoulder. "We were all worried but now they are fine. You should get a breath of fresh air."

David walked outside and stared up at the sky to thank the heavens his wife was safe. He wiped his tears with his handkerchief and went to the men's room to splash some water on his face. A nurse was standing in the waiting room. "Mr. Siegel? You may see your wife now." David followed her through the doors and into the recovery room to Isabelle's bedside. As he leaned down to kiss her cheek, she opened her eyes and smiled at him, then drifted off to sleep. He pulled up a chair and sat beside her bed, watched the nurses as they monitored her blood pressure and oxygen. Two hours later Isabelle opened her eyes and squeezed his hand. "Hi, how long have you been here?" David breathed a sigh of relief. "How do you feel?"

"A little sore, but I'm okay. Where is our baby?" David told her the baby was fine. "She's in the nursery." The nurse told them they were moving Isabelle to her room. David followed as they wheeled the bed through the halls, into the elevator to a room on the sixth floor. Once she was settled, Isabelle asked the nurse if she could have some food. "Yes Mrs. Siegel. We will send breakfast."

She raised the head of her bed and looked at David. "You look so tired. Are you okay?" He squeezed her hand. "I have never been better." Breakfast arrived for both of them and they were famished. "We have a beautiful daughter, a little small, but the nurse told me we could see her." "Can we go now?" David rang for the nurse. "We want to see our baby." The nurse told them she would let them know. Twenty minutes later she wheeled the bassinette into the room. "Your daughter is here to see you. She is doing great." Isabelle began to cry as she looked at her daughter. The nurse handed the baby to Isabelle and she gently opened the blanket, counting her fingers and toes. "She has the same black curls as Ben and her little nose looks like Catherine's. She is perfect. How do you like the name Amanda?" David sat on the bed and smiled at Isabelle. "I like it, we have our ABCs, Amanda, Ben and Catherine." Isabelle laughed. "I guess you're right. We are so clever." David reached for her hand. "I believe this finally constitutes a gaggle. I do not want you to go through this ever again. I was afraid I had lost you." Isabelle had tears in her eyes, "Never. Look how lucky we are."

CHAPTER TWENTY-TWO

The Board of Directors met Wednesday morning at ten o'clock to talk about Clark Barnett's resignation. Arthur gave a brief synopsis of the events including the alleged ties to Bartel Corporation. Pete Preston requested the floor. "Arthur, I commend you for the manner in which you handled the Barnett situation. You offered him the chance to avoid the humiliation of sitting before us as we voted him off the Board. There was no other choice." The Board members applauded in agreement. "Thank you all. I would now like to ask for nominations to act as Barnett's replacement." Roy Jensen said he would like the Board to consider Ted Davidson, President of City Community College. He has an impressive knowledge of finances and is active in fundraising." David Siegel raised his hand. "Arthur, I would like to nominate Dr. Richard Anderson. I served on the capital campaign for the art museum with him. He is well-known in Chicago and would be an asset to our Board."

There were no other nominations. Arthur said he had two names for consideration. John Douglas asked that each nominee's qualifications be submitted to the Board as soon as possible for a vote at the annual meeting. They discussed the thumbprint credit card successful campaign and Mr. Douglas presented reports detailing the revenues for the first three months. Pete Preston raised his hand. "Has there been any sign of our competition duplicating our product?" Arthur spoke. "Not yet, and frankly I'm surprised it is taking them so long." The members laughed. "I expect one of them will announce a similar card soon. We have taken a substantial number of accounts from them which we aim to keep." John Douglas gave a brief report of reduced risk in foreclosures and a significant decline in personnel cost." Mr. Dunhill called for old business and the only discussion was related to the previous month's report on pre-tax income. The meeting was adjourned and the members dispersed.

"Arthur, do you have a minute?"

"Of course David. Let's go to my office."

"That was a positive meeting." Arthur nodded.

"Yes, we told them what they wanted to hear."

"I admire your patience Arthur. You must appease your Board of Directors, the New York analysts and your stockholders. I become impatient easily. Ask anyone who works for me. They will tell you I am a tyrant; I expect them to work long hours, at minimum wage and adhere to my corporate vision. Bonuses are paid on performance only. No one is considered unless I see extraordinary performance, above and beyond the norm." Arthur shook his head. "I wish I could get away with that. I have hundreds of employees who simply show up each day, totally uninterested in their jobs, who think they deserve an annual raise." David knew the problem all too well. "I know. I put in a program where they cannot hide. As soon as I know the bloodsuckers they are out. There will always be plenty of workers who would jump at a change to work at Siegel Enterprises. Arthur, we are planning a cruise from Palm Beach to Chesapeake Bay and back with three or four couples and we would like you and Ann to join us. We will be gone four days and I would like to go within the next month." Arthur looked at his calendar. "I will talk with Ann but it looks to me as though we will be available on the sixteenth or the twenty-third.

Sounds like fun, Ann will love it." David made a note. "Let me know and I'll make the arrangements."

George Cater phoned Arthur the next morning with news that the search firm had come back with two candidates to replace Diane Conlan. "Great, bring the resumes to me as soon as you can." George brought the resumes within the hour and briefed Arthur on the candidates. Arthur took his time reading the resumes and discounted the first name easily as their experience and background did not impress him. The next two caught his attention; one with the listing of twelve years as chief financial officer at B & E in New York, a respected financial institution. The candidate, a woman with her M.B.A. from Wharton, had an impressive record and was leaving B & E to come to Chicago to be near her elderly mother. The other was a man from Proctor Capital in California with his MBA in finance. "I want to meet with her, the sooner the better, and this one too." He handed the resumes back to George. "I will set up the meetings next week."

The first candidate, Beth Alton, flew in the next week to meet with Arthur. She was all business from her clothing to her demeanor, not flamboyant as Diane had been. Arthur listened carefully as she presented her qualifications, and took note of her poise, mannerisms and knowledge of finance. He was impressed and thought she could be a good fit but wanted to make sure he chose the right person for the job. "Thank you for coming in Beth. I feel you have the qualifications for this position, however as I am sure you understand, I am interviewing several candidates. Mr. Cater will be in touch."

The second candidate from California flew in two days later to meet with Arthur. Bruce Young was an energetic forty-something, full of self-confidence, with an engaging personality. He reminded Arthur of a younger Bill Lawrence. "Tell me about your job at Proctor." Bruce gave a concise description of his accomplishments; he increased profitability the second quarter of the year by four million and reduced staff by five percent that resulted in a three million one hundred thousand decline in personnel costs. Arthur watched and listened as Bruce spoke.

He stated his strong points in a matter-of-fact synopsis without appearing boastful. Arthur asked. "Why are you leaving Proctor?"

"There is only so much growth potential at Proctor. I want a position with more challenge and opportunity, a corporation like Barrington, with a solid reputation and a proven business model."

"I will be blunt with you Bruce. I want someone who can give me results not excuses. I do not want someone who cannot produce the results I expect." Bruce Young looked Arthur directly in the eyes. "Yes sir. I have read your annual reports and am aware of a weakness in the security corporation last year. Give me a chance and I feel I can turn it around and increase profitability." Arthur was impressed Bruce had done his research. He explained there would be another round of interviews and thanked him for coming. His intercom rang. "Mr. Barrington, I have a call from security, it's urgent."

"Put them through, Lillian."

"Mr. Barrington, we received an anonymous call saying a bomb has been planted in the building to detonate in thirty minutes. We are evacuating the building."

Arthur dropped the phone and walked to Bill Lawrence's office. "Bill, we have a bomb threat. Help me get everyone out of here." Arthur called Dan on his cell phone. "Bring the car to the back of the bank immediately." He told John Douglas, Lillian and Doug Swan. "Come with me, now, we have a bomb threat." They all met at the freight elevator. Arthur held the door as they filed in. "This is the quickest way to the ground floor." No one said a word in the elevator; it was as if they feared they would set off the bomb. They reached the lobby and went out the back door. Dan was waiting with Arthur's car. "Ladies, you go with Dan and John to the Ambassador Club. Dan will come back for us." Lillian protested but did as he said. Dan returned ten minutes later and took Arthur, Bill and Tom to the Club. They went to a dining room on the second floor where they could see the bank building from the windows. Arthur checked his watch. It had been twenty-seven minutes since security called him. Dan was on his cell phone with bank security getting updates. "At sixty minutes they are going in to search the building. They do not want anyone returning to the bank today."

Arthur looked at his watch. It was two-thirty-five. "Ladies, it looks to me as if you have a free afternoon. Dan will drive each of you to your car and we will see you at work in the morning. I'm sure there is nothing to be concerned about." Dan walked with them to the car and just as they drove away, they heard an explosion. Lillian gasped, "Oh, no, the bomb." Dan phoned Arthur. "Yes, we heard it, Dan. Get out of there. Keep me posted." Arthur called Ann to let her know he was okay, as the others also called home. They watched from the windows as fire trucks, police cars, bomb squads and ambulances sped toward the bank. John shook his head, "Arthur, our documents, our files."

"The building is still standing John."

CHAPTER TWENTY-THREE

David, Isabelle and Amanda went home four days later to the delighted squeals of Ben and Catherine at the sight of their mother. She held them on her lap, kissed them and told them how much she had missed them. "This is your sister Amanda, what do you think Catherine?" She hugged Isabelle and smiled. Ben frowned and looked up at his mother. "I think she is too little." He and Catherine ran upstairs to play.

David helped Isabelle to the elevator since she was not to climb stairs, and up to their bedroom. There were two vases of red roses, one on each side of their bed. "My roses" she bent to smell them. "Thank you, David." She sat on the sofa and he joined her. "How do you feel?" She reached for his hand. "I feel great, it is so good to be home." David reached in his pocket and handed a box to her. "For you, Isabelle. For our beautiful baby." She smiled, opened the box and gasped at the ring inside. "Oh, David, it is stunning."

The ring had a three-carat white diamond in the center with one carat yellow diamonds on either side. He slipped in on her hand. "The center stone is for Amanda and the yellow diamonds are for Ben and Catherine."

Nell and Marian took the baby to the nursery, put her in the crib and closed the shutters. Nell stayed in the nursery and Marian took Ben and Catherine with her to the kitchen to prepare lunch. She fed the children and took them outside to play ball in the yard.

Isabelle was confined to the second floor for ten days. She read books to the children and watched them play, helped Nell bathe and change Amanda, and rested whenever she could. David joined her for lunch and dinner in their room for the first few days. "David, I am feeling much better and think I could go downstairs now. You must be getting bored with this." He shook his head. "I am never bored when I'm with you, but I'll tell Marian we will have dinner tonight in the dining room. I'm sure you could use a change of scenery." They rode to the main floor in the elevator and sat at the table where Marian had placed salads, a dish of steamed asparagus and a seafood casserole.

They each had a glass of wine and talked as they enjoyed dinner together. "I have been thinking, we have plenty of acreage on the west side of the property. What would you think of building a stable?" Isabelle put down her glass. "What would I think? I would love it! Can we buy a horse, maybe two? The children could learn to ride as they grow up, I could teach them. We could ride together. I know you would learn to love horses." David shook his head and smiled. "Well, if you don't like the idea......" He laughed. "I didn't know you would be this excited."

"It is a wonderful idea, I love it. We have the perfect place to ride."

"Okay, think about it. I would want you to design the entire project from conception to completion, I know nothing of horses." She got up from the table and put her arms around David's shoulders. "You are the most wonderful man in the world." He stood and led her to the sofa. "I give you diamonds, sapphires, a house in Palm Beach, a yacht, and all you ever really wanted was a horse." She had to laugh. "Two horses."

Isabelle began to research stables, read design books and sketched layouts. She knew what she wanted, a version of the stable in Connecticut where she rode as a young girl. Within a month she showed her ideas to David and explained the details. "We will use the same fencing that surrounds the property. The stable will set back among the trees with four paddocks, an exercise area and an apartment above for a caretaker."

"Four paddocks?"

"Just in case, better to have too much room than not enough."

"It sounds great Isabelle. I think it's time for you to meet with an architect. I'll give you the name of the man who designed the house. He will take your ideas and draw up the blueprints."

Isabelle met with the architect the next week, took her sketches, some photos and a list of things she wanted in the stable. He listened carefully as she described what she wanted. This was obviously very important to her and he liked clients who did their homework. He made some suggestions and told her he would have the plans ready in two weeks.

The architect called for an appointment with Isabelle to show her the plans. She met him in his office, reviewed the blueprints and made some alterations. "I want the open area in the center of the stable, wider, where the horses can be led from their stalls without feeling confined. I prefer walnut tongue and groove stalls with individual fans for continuous air circulation, a tack room, water-fed grid floors, a padded washing room and an outside riding area." The architect made notes. "You know a lot about horses, much more than I. Please give me time to catch up with what you have told me and we will design the ultimate stable." Isabelle gave the architect detailed drawings of the stable she wanted with specific lists of utility needs from lighting to water and air conditioning. He began to see her vision. This was not to be an ordinary barn but rather a gentleman's stable in the style of an exceptional woman.

The final plans encompassed a twenty-foot high barn topped with a hand-crafted copper weathervane and anchored with massive beams.

The walnut tongue and groove stalls featured individual ceiling fans and the center aisle of the stable was enlarged and illuminated with bright light fixtures. There was a tack room for storing saddles, a room for washing the horses, padded to prevent injury, a state-of-the-art office with wireless internet connections, an apartment with a small kitchen and an outside fenced area for exercising and preparing the horses for riding. Isabelle reviewed the plans and was pleased. "When can we begin construction?"

"Whenever you give me the go-ahead to begin."

"Let's get started as soon as possible."

Once the ground was cleared and the foundation poured, Isabelle checked on the progress of the barn twice each week. It was thrilling to see it take shape into the dream she had held for years; her own stable with her own horses.

The barn neared completion at the end of four months with fences and landscaping yet to be installed. It was an elegant-looking stone building in the same style of the house with a beautifully crafted black iron gate at the entrance.

Isabelle, David, Ben and Catherine toured the barn and Isabelle pointed out the size of the stalls, the water-fed grid floors and the office. "When do we get a horse, mama?" David laughed. "Just like his mother, can't wait to have a horse." "Daddy and I are going to look at horses this weekend, would you like to come with us? Catherine, you too?" They both clapped their hands and ran around the stable in excitement.

They had an appointment at a horse farm in Wisconsin on Saturday afternoon. Isabelle knew what she wanted, a chestnut Arabian mare. She explained their characteristics to David, that the breed was known as being good-natured, quick to learn and willing to please. They were adaptable to pleasure riding as well as equestrian events. "In case the children ever want to show their horse."

The owner of the farm had selected six horses for them, three Arabians, two Appaloosas and one Morgan. They stood by the fence as the horses were led around the exercise area. The children jumped up and down wanting to ride the horses. Isabelle asked to see a chestnut filly, two years old and fourteen hands tall, she was a beauty with clear eyes and a friendly disposition.

The owner led her to Isabelle. "Her name is Lily". Isabelle looked in her eyes. "Hello Lily." She rubbed the filly's head and ran her hand over the back of the horse. "David, come and take a look, she is perfect." The owner led an ebony Arabian toward Isabelle. "This is her sister, Jessie, three years old and gentle as a lamb. David stepped inside the gate holding Catherine in his arms and Ben by the hand. The horses seemed to sense the children and lowered their heads for a pat on the nose. "The decision is yours Isabelle, they are beautiful horses." Isabelle placed her hand on the filly. "They will both be happier together. We will take them both."

The horses were delivered the next week and the family was nearly as excited as with a new baby. They were all there to greet them and show them the new barn. The tack room was neatly arranged with halters, tack sets, blankets and western saddles. Brad had worked for David for six years as security guard and jumped at the chance to live at the barn and take care of the horses.

Isabelle couldn't wait to ride and went to the barn the next morning with apples for Lily and Jessie. She talked with them as she put the saddle and halter on Jessie, climbed on her back and they walked into the exercise area. Brad led Lily outside in the sun and tied her to the fence as she looked around her new surroundings. "They did fine their first night, slept like babies." Isabelle had nearly forgotten how much she loved horses. "I'm so glad to have them here together." Jessie was gentle, well-trained and obeyed the slightest movement of her rider. She rode along the back of the property, thick with trees, and toward the stream where Jessie stopped for a drink. They returned to the barn and Isabelle looked up to see David's car coming up the drive. She got down from Jessie and walked her back inside the fence, turning to wave to David. "Are you having fun?" She went to him and put her arms around his neck. "I cannot tell you how wonderful she is, so gentle and smart. You must get to know them both."

"I will, but right now I have to go to work."

"I know, I'm heading back to the house now. Amanda was up two times during the night and Nell could use a break."

CHAPTER TWENTY-FOUR

Arthur paced the floor waiting for word of the damage to the bank building. Finally, the building security guard called his cell phone. "Mr. Barrington, it's Fred, they found where the bomb went off. No one was hurt. It was hidden in a cabinet on the fourth floor. The explosion blew out the walls and windows on the southeast side of the fourth and fifth floors. Everything is a mess up there. The bomb squad says it could have been a lot worse, the damage was pretty isolated." Arthur listened intently. "I'm coming there now." He hung up the phone and relayed the information to the others. "Why don't you go on home, there's nothing we can do today with the police investigation in process. I'll call you later once I have talked with them. Come on Dan, I want to see my bank."

They drove to the back alley filled with fire trucks and talked with a policeman who led them into the lobby where they had set-up a command center.

"We think this was an amateur, someone who wanted to scare everyone and shut down the bank. The damage was limited to the southeast side on two floors." Arthur asked to view the areas but was told he could not. "We are still investigating and checking the damage. The building will be shut down for at least the next week."

Arthur and Dan returned to the car and Arthur began making calls. "Get the disaster management crew together, the bank will be closed tomorrow, we need to set-up temporary offices for the fourth and fifth floors. Call Burt and Dick and have them ready to implement the emergency measures. They need to notify their staffs and recall records from storage facilities." He called John Douglas and asked him to notify the Board of Directors and his executive team of the situation.

Arthur's phone rang all evening with calls from colleagues and concerned friends. The next morning he returned to the bank building and met with the police, the F.B.I. and the bomb squad.

They explained if the bomb had been placed in an elevator shaft, the entire building would have imploded resulting in total destruction. "We feel we have someone out for revenge, someone who wanted to shut you down for a while. They gave you thirty minutes to evacuate, they weren't looking to kill everyone, but put fear in your mind. The placement of the bomb was in a secured area with firewalls that forced the explosion forward and upward. We need to know of anyone who may have reason for revenge against you, someone who works for you or the bank. What offices were on the fourth floor?" Arthur told them the fourth floor housed the trust and investment offices of the corporation. "I recently dismissed a director from our corporate Board and fired the Chairman of our holding companies but I do not suspect either of them." The policeman took notes. "It is our job to determine motives and opportunities. We need to talk with the employees who worked on those floors." He played the recorded phone call from the bomb caller for Arthur. "Do you recognize the voice?" Arthur did not. "Okay, we will keep in touch with you."

"I need to go to my office on the twenty-first floor." The policeman allowed him to go with a police escort and only for one hour.

The next few days were exhausting with the news media covering the explosion, calling his home and hounding his employees for any information. They set-up temporary offices for the trust company in a nearby utility building, installed computers, telephones and trucked in customer files from their storage facility. It was three days before the bank was fully operational and Arthur returned to his office. His number one concern was for his staff and secondly for his customers. Arthur held a meeting with the entire staff of the twenty-first floor, re-assured them the building was safe and the police were investigating the bomb. "I want to commend you all for your actions the day of the explosion. You were all calm and orderly. I have made arrangements for you each to receive what I am calling a 'hazardous duty' bonus in your next pay. Now, let's get back to work."

The bank placed ads in all of the major newspapers announcing they were open for business as usual following an unfortunate accident.

They offered a one-hundred dollar credit to all checking account customers for their inconvenience and promised to waive any overdraft charges incurred.

It was three weeks before construction began to repair the damages to the fourth and fifth floors of the building. Both floors were completely gutted, windows replaced, firewalls repaired, new sprinklers and electrical work had to be done first. The offices were ready for occupancy nine weeks after the bomb had gone off. The work of packing-up the temporary offices and moving back into the bank building was accomplished in twenty-four hours, with computers and phone lines up and running. Arthur toured the new offices the next morning with Carl Kincaid, making sure everyone had what they needed to get back to work and thanked the employees for their patience.

He noticed Leslie at her desk. "Leslie, hello, we miss you upstairs but I'm glad to see you are still with the bank."

"Thank you, Mr. Barrington. Mr. Kincaid is a pleasure to work with." Arthur smiled, acknowledging the innuendo towards Diane Conlan.

"You will be a big help to Carl." They returned to Carl's office. "Carl, this was not the easiest way to begin your work in Chicago, we really welcomed you with a bang." Carl laughed. "Yes, it was, I'm just glad no one was hurt. The staff has been great Arthur, everyone pitched in to get things in order and make sure our clients were re-assured their accounts were safe." Arthur placed his hand on Carl's back. "Good job, Carl. Let me know if there's anything you need, and take good care of Leslie."

An emergency Board meeting was called to discuss the bombing and the fallout of business having been suspended for three days. Mark Dunhill called the meeting to order and Arthur took the floor. "Gentlemen, I am pleased to announce our offices are up and running again. We are fortunate that the damages were relatively confined and no one was injured. The building security team did an excellent job of evacuating the building in less than thirty minutes. The FBI and Homeland Security have been called in to investigate the bombing and Police Chief Campbell will update you on the status."

CHAPTER TWENTY-FIVE

David, Isabelle, the children, Nell and Marian flew to Palm Beach two days before the other guests were to fly in for the weekend. Isabelle wanted the children to have a couple of days in the house to feel comfortable before she and David left on the boat. She made sure they had everything they would need and David hired a security guard at Isabelle's insistence.

They greeted their guests aboard the yacht on Friday morning; Arthur and Ann Barrington, Bill and Grace Lawrence and David's CFO, Alan Blake and his wife Jenny. David gave them a tour of the yacht as they headed out to sea and north toward the Chesapeake Bay. Arthur and Bill were impressed with the 'boat' as David referred to it; luxurious furnishings, polished rails, gleaming mahogany cabinets and a crew who attended to their every wish.

The weather was ideal and the scenery breathtaking as they glided effortlessly through the water.

The chef prepared a grand buffet lunch, worthy of a cruise ship, with selections of seafood, chicken, pasta, salads and fresh fruit for dessert. Isabelle, Ann, Jenny and Grace spent the afternoon on the top deck while Arthur and Alan played cards on the rear platform. David took Bill up to the bridge for a bird's eye view of the open water. "How do you stay away from this? I would want to be out here every day."

"You know, Bill, work comes first, but I love this too. I want to take the boat down to the Bahamas in the fall and cruise around the islands. I'll let you know when we're going and we would love for you to join us. Does Grace like being on the water?"

"Absolutely, on a yacht like this? Who wouldn't? Have you heard any more from the F.B.I. on the investigation?"

"No, evidently they haven't found who planted the bomb and I wonder if they ever will. I just hope it's over."

They all returned to their cabins late in the afternoon to rest and dress for dinner. They met in the salon at six for cocktails and the steward called them to dinner in the dining room at seven o'clock.

They had a sumptuous meal topped off with a choice of cheesecake or fresh peach cobbler. Ann took a bite of the cheesecake. "Isabelle, David, your chef is outstanding, creating all of this delicious food. I'm going to get up early and jog around the deck so I can enjoy breakfast!"

"We will set-up skeet shooting on the rear deck in the morning if anyone is interested, about nine o'clock." Grace spoke up. "Bill and I will be there, David. I used to shoot with my father and I now have Bill interested. We sometimes go on weekends."

"Grace is an expert marksman. She was the number one woman in the country three years ago. I just carry her bullets."

The next morning everyone except Isabelle and Jenny were out on deck to try their hand at skeet shooting. Isabelle was on the phone with Nell to check-up on what the children were up to and Jenny slept late. They met in the dining room at eleven o'clock for a brunch of fresh salmon, frittatas, sausages, pastries and juice. "We will be in Maryland by one o'clock and docked by two or two-thirty. There will be transportation into the city if anyone wants to shop or sightsee.

The ladies decided to go into town to browse among the galleries but the men wanted to stay on board and see the port.

As they slowed to enter the harbor two Ospreys came to greet them and swooned above the yacht as Arthur and Ann took pictures. The harbor was filled with yachts of every description from as far away as Africa and Jamaica. David, Bill and Arthur walked along the pier, surveyed the other boats and talked with the owners. Alan was the quiet one of the group and checked his cell phone constantly for business calls.

The ladies returned to the yacht at five-thirty. Grace had four shopping bags, Jenny a water color painting and Ann a book on the area. "Poor Isabelle, you didn't see anything you liked?" She smiled and reached into her purse. "I did find books for Ben and Catherine and this little hat for Amanda."

Saturday evening they took a car across the Bay Bridge to the Annapolis Yacht Club for dinner. David had reservations in The Commodore's dining room on the third deck with the best view in all of Annapolis. They dined on an array of shrimp, oysters, scallops and sea bass.

Monday morning they left port and headed south. Once they were at sea the captain gave the wheel to David. Isabelle watched as he stood at the helm looking very in charge of the boat as he checked the instruments and turned on the radio. "Would you like to try it?" Isabelle held up her hand. "No, thank you, I am happy being a passenger." She stood beside David and pointed to a group of sailboats off to their left. "Chesapeake really is a boating paradise, isn't it? We've seen schooners, kayaks, fishing boats and yachts of every description." Just then there was a new flash on the radio. 'Trading has been suspended on the New York Stock Exchange as the Dow dropped three hundred points in the first hour of trading today. The U.S. dollar sank to a record low as currency traders panicked buying up gold. The President will hold a news conference at two o'clock eastern time today.' "Isabelle, come with me, we need to tell the others." Alan, his wife, Arthur and Ann were in the salon playing cards. "Where is Bill?" Arthur spoke up. "He and Grace are outside. Is something wrong?" "Wait here. I want Bill to hear this too."

Arthur found Bill and Grace on the sun deck and brought them inside. "We just heard on the radio that trading has been suspended on the stock exchange." He repeated what he had heard on the radio. "The President is holding a news conference at two o'clock today. Alan, call headquarters and find out what's going on."

Arthur called the bank and spoke with his chief financial officer who told him the bank stock had dropped twenty points. "It's across the board, Arthur, every industry took a hit. I'm looking at anything we can do to stay afloat." Arthur hung up the phone and looked at Bill. "We're down twenty points, it doesn't look good."

David turned on the television. Every news channel was covering the market with continuous updates. The President began his news conference with the announcement of the suspension of trading on the N.Y.S.E. "The crash began overnight in Asia as the Hong Kong index dropped six percent. The losses spread to the European markets when London's index fell ninety-seven points.

The U.S. markets, the Dow, NASDAQ and S&P 500 all dropped three hundred-fifty points. Trading was halted for sixty minutes. When trading resumed, stocks continued their immense slide eventually pushing the Dow through the NYSE's second halt in trading at five hundred-fifty points. The New York Stock Exchange had no choice but to take the controversial action of closing the Exchange early. The U.S. markets will open tomorrow morning on time and we fully expect trading to stabilize." The President did not take questions but left immediately following his address. The major news networks continued coverage of the story throughout the day, citing more in-depth coverage of the cause of the crash. 'The market decline is directly linked to the derivative trading by the Tokyo Commodities Exchange. As foreign investors attempted to withdraw their money, the exchange market was flooded with the currencies of the crisis countries, putting pressure on their exchange rates. Twenty-five percent of the nine-trillion in commodity contracts are traded in Tokyo.

The International Monetary Fund has stepped in with sanctions against Tokyo as well as funds to stabilize the currencies of South Korea, Thailand and Indonesia.'

Arthur turned down the volume. "They're offering bailout money to countries with excess debt and failure to ensure profitability. The South Korea banking sector is burdened with non-performing loans. We would be hung for those business practices." David checked his watch. "The South Korean businesses, pretty much controlled by the government, incurred enormous debt that led to major failures. Now the world is supposed to run to their rescue." Bill stood up and stretched. "The President can't point his finger at South Korea on national television, I know, but you can bet there will be some repercussions for this."

The next morning the U.S. stock market continued to drop from the previous day but by ten a.m. began to climb. Thirty minutes later the Dow began climbing, up nearly fifty points. Ten minutes later it advanced over one hundred points and by the close of trading at four o'clock, finished with a sixty percent gain from the previous day's loss.

One billion shares were traded on the exchange for the first time ever.

The stock of Barrington Bank had dropped thirty-eight points but rebounded to a positive gain of fifteen points placing in the top ten banks in the country.

The entire group flew back to Chicago the next morning. Arthur met with his executive team late in the day. "I want a full report on our exposure in derivatives. The risk is something I want to reduce as much as possible, as soon as possible. Our retail operations are solid, the holding companies are improving and our stock is at an all-time high. I am seriously looking at an acquisition that could take us to number four in the country, a pretty impressive slot. We should know more by this time next week. I want each of you to keep me updated on any areas of concern. I don't want any of this middle management complacency or oversight, any questions?" Bill Lawrence raised his hand. "I have a concern Arthur. Did you realize your fly is open?" The room exploded in a roar of laughter as Arthur looked down. "Very funny, Bill, but actually that is just what I mean. Tell me the facts even if you don't think I want to know."

CHAPTER TWENTY-SIX

Isabelle was in David's study using his computer as hers was in the shop for new upgrades. Nell had taken the children for a walk down to the stable to feed the horses. Isabelle picked up the phone. "Hello?"

"Mrs. Siegel, it is Helen Montgomery from Lakeside Village."

"Hello, Helen, is Allison ready for her big debut in the play?"

"Mrs. Siegel, there has been a terrible accident. Allison was swimming when she had a seizure." Isabelle stood frozen, her mind reeling. 'There *was* an accident, Allison *was* swimming'...

"Millie was with her but wasn't strong enough to help." Isabelle held her breath. "They pulled her from the water but it was too late. She is gone, Mrs. Siegel."

"NO!" Isabelle dropped the phone as if to refuse the information. Marian came running to the study. "Mrs. Siegel, what is it?" Isabelle was standing, leaning on the desk, her arms trembling and tears running down her face.

"Here, sit down." She pulled up a chair, Isabelle sank into it and covered her eyes with her hands. Marian picked up the phone from the floor. "Hello? Who is this?" Mrs. Montgomery told her what had happened. Marian looked at Isabelle, pale as a ghost and shaking. She hung up the phone and immediately called David's office. "Mr. Siegel, I must speak with him at once. Mrs. Siegel needs him now!" David came on the phone. "Isabelle?"

"No, it's Marian. We just had a call. Mrs. Siegel's sister had an accident. Please come home right away."

Marian met David at the front door. "Where's Isabelle?"

"She is in your study. Her sister died Mr. Siegel." David went to Isabelle who sat quietly staring out the window. He knelt down before her and took her hands in his. "Darling, I am so sorry." She looked into his eyes and tears streamed down her face. "Marian, call Dr. Warren and tell him what has happened."

David stood and helped Isabelle to stand. "Come with me." He helped her up the stairs to their room and closed the door.

She turned to him, wrapped her arms around his neck and began to sob. He held her silently searching for something to say or do to calm her. He reached for his handkerchief and released her arms, dabbed her eyes now red and swollen. "Let's sit, here."

David heard the doorbell, then a soft knock on their door. Marian came in holding a package. "The pharmacy just delivered this from Dr. Warren."

"Thank you, Marian. Please bring us some water."

"Isabelle, here, take this. You need to rest." He helped her to the bed and brought a damp cloth from the bathroom that he placed on her eyes. He closed the drapes and sat beside her as she drifted off to sleep. He silently left the room and looked back toward her as he closed the door.

He went directly to his study and phoned Allison's school. "This is David Siegel. I must talk with Helen Montgomery at once." She came on the phone and told David about the accident. "We had a barbeque lunch by the lake today. Several of the girls wanted to swim before eating. Allison and Millie were partners, we insist they have partners.

Four instructors were supervising as they watched the girls swim to the platform in the middle of the lake. Allison waved to them and called out that she and Millie were going to race. They dove into the water and began to swim. Allison was such a strong swimmer and was ahead of Millie when she began to thrash about in the water. Millie turned and tried to help but couldn't. Three of the instructors dove in to get her and brought her up on the bank. They tried to resuscitate her but it was too late. The ambulance took her to Seton Hospital. I am so very sorry. Is Mrs. Siegel alright?" David winced at the question. "No, Mrs. Siegel is not alright. She is inconsolable in her loss. I will be in touch with you Mrs. Montgomery." He called out to Marian. "Where in the hell is everyone? Where are the children?"

"Nell took them for a walk, down to the stable to see the horses. They should be back any minute."

Nell and the children returned. Amanda ran ahead of the others when she saw David. "Daddy's home, yeah!" He placed his finger to his lips. "Let's be quiet and go in the kitchen."

They sat at the table and David told them Mommy was resting. "We had some bad news today. Aunt Allison had a terrible accident, a thing called a seizure, and she is gone. Mommy is very sad so we all must be well behaved and make her feel happy." Catherine began to cry. "It's okay, Cathy, we will all miss Aunt Allison." Amanda frowned. "Where did she go?" "She went to heaven, darling, to be with the angels. Nell, why don't you take the children outside, I think the fish are hungry."

David went to check on Isabelle who was resting peacefully. He went back downstairs and called Dr. Warren. "Thank you for the medication." He described the news of Isabelle's sister. "David, she will need the sedatives to get through this. Please let me know if there is anything I can do. My sympathies to you both."

David sat at his desk and looked at his photograph of Isabelle. His heart ached for the agony she was going through. She needs some sense of roots, of family history, he thought, and decided to call her friend Joan in New York. He told her what had happened to Allison. "Oh no, how awful. I'll fly in tomorrow. I'll be there by one."

Marian prepared dinner for the family. "Shall I make a tray for Mrs. Siegel?"

"No thank you, Marian, it is more important that she rest now." David read stories to the children, kissed them goodnight and slipped into bed beside Isabelle. He heard her get up and looked at the clock, it was five a.m. "Come with me." They quietly went downstairs to the kitchen. "How are you feeling?"

"Better, now." He held her for a moment. "I'll make coffee. Here, have a glass of juice." They talked about Allison. "It was such a senseless accident, David. She was only thirty-four years old. She could have lived much longer." David listened as Isabelle told stories about Allison when they were little girls; birthday parties, trips to the zoo, baking cookies with mother. "Everything was so perfect, for a while." They watched the sun come up and heard Marian stirring about in her room. "I talked with the children and I called Joan. She is flying in this morning." Isabelle reached for his hands. "Thank you, David. You always know just what I need."

Nell and David took the children to a matinee movie for the afternoon to allow Isabelle and Joan some time alone. They went for a long walk around the property, talked about old times, their youth and Allison. "I know it sounds cliché, but you wouldn't have wanted her to suffer through a long illness or forget who you were. She was fun-loving and happy to the end and she would want you to be happy too, you know that." They returned to the house and Joan suggested Isabelle lie down for a while. "I have some errands. Do you mind if I borrow your car?"

Isabelle went upstairs and Joan scurried off on a mission. She returned a few hours later and met up with Marian in the kitchen. "I know this is last minute, but do you think we could have a cookout for dinner? I brought everything we will need." Marian looked through the bags. "Well, yes, I guess you have. Sure, why not, the children will like that."

David returned with his brood of sleepy children late in the afternoon and Nell put them down for a nap. He went to the kitchen where Joan was waiting to talk with him. "Isabelle and I had a great conversation this afternoon and she seems much more relaxed.

I want to ask your help with a little surprise for this evening." She told him what she wanted to do and David was skeptical. "Joan, I don't know. I don't think Isabelle would agree with you." "Trust me, David. This is your children's' first experience with a death in the family. It is a horrible loss, I know, but Isabelle will go on. I want to try to help make this easier for you all."

Isabelle walked downstairs holding hands with Catherine and Ben. She had talked with them about Allison. "These two tell me the movie was great, a jungle story?" David looked up from his work. "Yes, it was pretty good. Of course, Amanda slept through the entire thing." She smiled. "You are a lucky man."

David took charge of the barbeque grill and Marian called everyone outside to the veranda when the food was ready. The table was covered with a pink and white striped cloth, with pink dishes and a large vase of pink roses. There were large pink balloons tied to the back of each chair. Isabelle realized what Joan was up to and gave her a sly glance. Joan ignored her and poured lemonade for Catherine. "This looks like a party, mother."

Isabelle smiled and touched her hand as Joan spoke up. "It *is* a party to show you how much I love being here with all of you!" They had hamburgers, hot dogs, salads, fruit and a beautiful cake covered in fluffy pink frosting for dessert. Joan stood and held up her glass. "Let's have a toast to Allison, our sister, our aunt and our friend. Because she is up in heaven, looking down on us, I think she would like this surprise. So, as a tribute to her, let's send her our love. Everyone get your balloon from your chair. Now, on three, let them go!" They stood and watched as the pink balloons rose in the sky. They watched and pointed to the balloons as they soared along the currents of wind, higher and higher. Isabelle smiled as she watched Ben and Catherine wave toward the sky, they were saying goodbye to Allison. She put her arm around Joan's waist. "Your methods are a little unconventional but that was very special, a wonderful remembrance for the children. Thank you."

The next morning Isabelle, David and Joan flew to Connecticut where Allison was laid to rest next to her mother and father. Isabelle wanted a small service at the cemetery, nothing more.

CHAPTER TWENTY-SEVEN

Ben had his father's drive and determination to succeed in everything he tried. He was bright, the first to be chosen in school projects, and displayed an uncanny ability for math. He played rugby and soccer at school and pushed himself and his teammates to excel. Isabelle and David watched him on the playing field with his friends and it was apparent Ben had leadership skills. The other boys followed his lead and looked toward him for signals. He was growing quickly. His little boy features had become more defined and he looked more and more like David, except for his black curly hair. He had a spontaneous nature and a charming smile that lit up his face. He and Catherine had impeccable manners thanks to Isabelle's gentle reminders to sit up straight and remember to say please and thank you. They grew up knowing to keep their rooms neat, which fork to use and to write thank you notes for any and all gifts large or small. Isabelle expected these things as part of growing into a responsible, courteous adult.

Isabelle began to show Catherine how to ride. She showed her the proper way to place her feet in the stirrups, toes pointed in and knees hugging the horse. Catherine rode Lilly because she was gentler and Isabelle rode Jessie alongside. Catherine loved the horses as much as Isabelle and the two of them spent hours riding around the property, talking about school and her friends. Isabelle treasured their time together as Catherine was so open. She told her everything, sometimes surprising perceptions of her classmates. She was an intuitive child, aware of the strengths and weaknesses of others her age.

Catherine was a voracious reader from the time she was five and read well above her age level. Isabelle made sure she had all of the classic children's books as well as new and exciting stories she found. She would stand in the kitchen looking out the window at Catherine sitting on the veranda, totally lost in her book, submerged in tales of adventure and far off lands. Her dark brown hair fell over her shoulders as she sat curled up in the chair, long legs folded to one side, oblivious to anyone around her. She reminded Isabelle of herself at that age and remembered her own childhood.

Her sister, away in a special school, her mother depressed and withdrawn, her father immersed in his work as his means of coping with it all, Isabelle had been on her own. Catherine didn't have those issues in her life, thank goodness. Isabelle was thankful Ben, Catherine and Amanda had each other and would never be alone in the world.

Catherine attended ballet class every Saturday morning at a dance school near their home. She and her best friend, Sarah, had matching pink leotards and shoes and both tied their long brown hair into sleek buns at the back of their heads. They looked quite the part of ballerinas and envisioned themselves performing in The Nutcracker or Swan Lake one day. Isabelle was less optimistic about her stardom but appreciated the poise and grace Catherine developed through the dance lessons.

She enrolled Catherine in Cotillion Class when she turned twelve, a monthly event in which children learned ballroom dancing, proper introductions and dining etiquette

The night of the first class, Catherine slowly walked down the stairs toward the smiling face of her father.

She was dressed in a pink and white striped taffeta dress, pink leather ballet flats and a white satin ribbon in her hair. "Catherine, you look like a princess." David kissed her gently on the cheek. Catherine held out her hands. "Look Daddy, my gloves match my dress." David held her hands and looked at the pink striped fabric on the back of the gloves. "Very chic." Isabelle reminded them it was time to go. Have a good time darling." She and Amanda stood at the door and watched as David held the car door for Catherine to step into the back seat and they drove away. "You will be going to Cotillion in a couple of years, Amanda." She smiled up at her mother. "Okay, but promise me I won't have to wear pink." Isabelle closed the door. "You shall have some very pretty dresses, I promise. Now, let's go see if Ben wants to watch a movie with us."

Amanda had definite ideas about what she liked. Ben and Catherine were both very easy to please but Amanda marched to a different beat. She preferred trendy clothes, mix-matched socks and funky sweaters, much to Isabelle's dismay.

She took Amanda shopping, directed her toward classic styles suitable for her age but Amanda begged for the fads she saw on mannequins. She chose library books about fantastical adventures featuring brave heroes and heroines, deadly monsters, lost treasures, and immersed herself in the stories. She loved the horses and rode with Isabelle as often as possible. She wasn't content with a leisurely pace but challenged her mother to races, jumped fences and streams and galloped as fast as Jessie would go until they were both short of breath.

CHAPTER TWENTY-EIGHT

Barrington Bank's stock price held steady through news of the bombing and kept it's ranking as one of the top four banks in the country. Arthur's course of keeping the bank strictly an end user of derivatives to hedge business risk, not a dealer, had paid off handsomely. David Siegel had convinced Arthur to take a calculated risk in the swap market. He had made millions timing the ups and downs of interest rates. His strategy was to do swaps in which the bank received fixed interest rates and paid floating rates because he expected rates to go down. It worked and made Barrington a huge winner in its zero-sum swaps with dealers during the past two years.

Tom Morrison met with Arthur to give him an update on the Missouri bank he had been checking into. He handed a report to Arthur. "Their investors rating was cut and Cunningham shifted millions in derivatives to the retail side of the bank in a Hail Mary move, basically risking the federally insured deposits of their customers.

The Federal Reserve initially supported the move but is now reconsidering depositor exposure. It is good timing for us. Their Chairman is legendary in St. Louis as a real dictator in running the bank. It's his way or no way and it seems his decisions have placed them in a compromising position." "This sounds almost too good to be true. Okay, Tom, get started on it and keep me posted."

Arthur looked over Tom's report on Caldwell Bank after he left and knew it was a target for acquisition. Their rating cut and the bungled derivative move left the door of opportunity wide open. They had also made critical errors in not reducing mortgage exposure and not concentrating more on consumer lending, the bread and butter of Barrington Bank. Arthur was proud of Barrington's retail lending success on loans for cars, recreational vehicles, home equity lines of credit and signature loans, as well as secured loans on certificates of deposit, stocks and mutual funds.

The Senate Committee on Banking had met with the top ten banks and was ready to vote on proposed legislation. Arthur sent his corporate governance team to Washington to join powerful lobbying groups for the banking industry.

They paid congressional representatives handsomely in the days before they voted on an important consumer-friendly credit card bill the banking industry strongly opposed. Several of the House lawmakers who received contributions voted "no" on the Credit Cardholders' Bill of Rights Act which placed a number of restrictions on interest rates and fees that issuers could charge cardholders. The Act was defeated. The banks were free to continue their fee structures without intervention.

The shareholders voted on the slate of three candidates to replace Clark Barnett. Walter Morris had withdrawn his name from the nomination citing his wife's poor health. Howard Driscoll was unanimously elected.

Arthur announced to his directors he had hired Bruce Young to head-up the holding companies as a replacement for Diane Conlan. "I was impressed with Bruce from the start. He has the vision, experience and track record needed to grow our business and he is a good fit with our senior staff." Bill Lawrence chuckled at the subtle reference to the explosive personality of Mrs. Conlan.

Tom presented a synopsis of the due diligence findings at Cunningham Bank. "It has built a solid reputation in Missouri and future prospects should carry the customer base. Of course, we'll face some resentment as the new guy in town but we can overcome that with integration resources and marketing. Their information technology is compatible with ours which will save huge amounts of time, money and resources. The report includes examination of their financial statements, accounts receivable, inventories, workers' compensation and employee benefits. There is no pending litigation and the risk is low for potential lawsuits. Their exposure with mortgage defaults has hit them hard, a key soft spot with the directors who totally blame the CEO. Jack Cunningham has a forceful personality and exercised too much influence over the Board. There was a culture of not rocking the boat at their meetings and no one challenged his judgment."

Cunningham Bank suffered more than $70 million in losses in real estate loans that resulted in a stock price drop of nearly half at the close of the fourth quarter. Arthur called a meeting of his directors and presented the latest figures in his proposal. "Now is the time to go forward with our offer to merge with Cunningham." Howard Driscoll asked to speak. "I feel we are overpaying in this deal at the expense of our shareholders. You cannot deny the impact of the merger on our customers in higher fees, closed branch offices and less customer service. This 'greater efficiency' and 'economics of scale' you talk about simply means reducing costs by cutting jobs. Do you all realize the outcome of this merger will mean a fifteen percent reduction in the combined workforce? The publicity we will face in this economy will not be positive. We risk a significant decline in our own corporate value and I do not see any benefit in merging with Cunningham Bank at this time." The silence in the room was deafening as Driscoll took his seat. David Siegel stood. "I disagree with you Howard. The due diligence report clearly supports the value of this merger for Barrington Bank.

The world markets are changing every moment and we must align ourselves to compete globally for corporate finance deals in Singapore and London if we want to increase our shareholder value. I openly agree with Arthur and support the merger." Mark Dunhill asked for further comments and called for a vote. The Board approved the offer to merge. The directors filed out of the room congratulating Arthur on approval of the merger. He asked David Siegel to join him in his office and closed the door.

"Thank you for your support in there. I was frankly surprised by Howard's stance and persistence. He was elected to the Board just five months ago and thinks he knows better than I what is best for Barrington? He clearly has no future on the Board."

"I couldn't agree more Arthur. He seemed to have a deep-lying antagonistic opposition on the merger, why I don't know. The other Directors agree and support the deal. Congratulations."

Arthur called Jack Cunningham the next morning. "Cunningham, Arthur Barrington here. I have an offer to discuss with you on the merger of our banks."

They made arrangements for Arthur to fly to St. Louis to meet with Cunningham at his home to discuss the terms of the deal. Arthur was prepared. He knew the weakness Cunningham was up against and had met with his advisors who prompted him on how best to approach the issues. Jack would not make it an easy meeting. He was egotistical, proud and demanding. "You will need to show him you are willing to make concessions and enable him to look good to his shareholders. Image is all-important to him." Arthur was prepared for a tough sell and ready for Cunningham's aggressive style.

Jack met him at the door, shook hands and led Arthur to his study. The room was dark and pretentious with heavy velvet drapes and a dark mural that wrapped around the room. It resembled something in a Scottish castle not suburban St. Louis. Cunningham showed Arthur to a chair opposite his seat of power behind the carved mahogany desk. Arthur was not intimidated. "Let's get down to business, Jack. I am here to make you an offer to merge with Barrington Bank. What is your main concern?" Jack leaned forward with his arms on the desk.

"Leadership. I want to know who would run the bank."

"I am offering you the Chairmanship. I will be CEO and president." Jack made notes, obviously pleased with the title. "Next, I want to know exactly what cuts will be made in personnel and staff. My people have been with me for years and I won't have them kicked out of their jobs." Arthur looked down at his folder thinking of the best way to approach the delicate subject. "Jack, we both have people we want to keep but there are only so many positions to be filled. We may each need to compromise there. We will have a redundancy of personnel and product offerings. Here is a list of the senior staff I am willing to offer retirement or buy-out. We will pool our directors, each keeping five of our choice." Jack shook his head. "I disagree. We need an uneven number of directors for voting purposes. I want six of my directors." Arthur made a note. He handed Jack a paper from his folder that illustrated an exchange of Barrington stock for each share of Cunningham Bank.

The rate of exchange would be beneficial for Cunningham shareholders. He felt certain that would seal the deal. Jack scribbled notes on the offer and cautiously told Arthur he was receptive. "Now the big question, what will be the name of the bank?" Arthur was ready for a fight on this one. "The bank will be named BNB for Barrington National Bank. He would cede the title of Chairman but he would not remove his name from the bank. Jack slapped the table with his hand. "Damn good Arthur. I like it! I always wanted to get 'national' into our name. It defines our geographic presence throughout the country." He wrote in on his legal pad in large letters. Arthur noted the condescending lapse of mentioning Barrington in the name but let it slide. Jack saved pride by focusing on 'national' instead of the omission of the Cunningham name. "I like the offer Arthur but I can't give my okay until I present it to my Board next week." They toasted the proposal with a drink and Arthur left to return to Chicago, pleased with the meeting. He knew it was a deal they wouldn't refuse.

Jack Cunningham phoned Arthur Wednesday afternoon. "The Board approved it Art. The merger is a go."

"Congratulations Jack. I will give the go-ahead to our mergers and acquisitions team to set the wheels in motion. They will present it to the Federal Reserve within the next few weeks. I would like you to come to Chicago to meet my staff and get a feel for how we operate. Let me know when it is convenient for you."

"Thank you, Art. I will be in touch."

The merger was approved by the Federal Reserve six months later and BNB officially opened its doors for business the next year.

Cunningham kept his home in St. Louis as his 'escape' as he called it and flew there every other

weekend. He lived alone except for his two hunting dogs and hired a caretaker to look after them. Jack lost his wife in a car accident five years before and his dogs were like the children they never had. His passions were pheasant, duck and deer hunting and he flew to Wyoming once each year to hunt elk. He wasn't interested in private clubs or golf, boring and a waste of time in his estimation.

Jack Cunningham moved into an upscale condominium on North Shore Drive in Chicago.

He took over a conference room at the end of the hallway on the twenty-first floor of the bank as his office. Lillian selected furnishings from a storage facility filled with desks, credenzas, sofas and chairs. She had a selection of artwork delivered to his office for him to choose among. "I will keep this country landscape and the one with the lake, the rest can go. I want them hung by morning." He walked to the corner of the room and grabbed the branch of a silk plant. "Find a trashcan for this fake tree. I'll need a coat rack and another lamp by that chair." Lillian made notes as he spoke. "Will there by anything else?" Arthur tapped on the doorframe. "Wow, it looks great in here. Lillian has made sure you have the best." She turned to leave and rolled her eyes toward Arthur. She was fuming. How dare he order her around like a lackey. She returned to her desk and looked down at her notepad with the list of demands. Jack Cunningham had taken the wrong road with her. Lillian had agreed to help in setting-up his office until he could hire an assistant. She picked-up the phone and called George Cater.

"George, Lillian here. Do you have the interviews scheduled yet for Mr. Cunningham's assistant?"

"As a matter of fact, I have two resumes I want to pursue."

"Great. Let's get them in next week. I will meet with them first and if they're suitable I will introduce them to Mr. Cunningham."

"I will call them today and set it up."

"Thank you, George. Please let me know so I can put the interviews on the calendar." Lillian hung up the phone, sat back and smiled. Jack Cunningham would soon have someone else to order around.

Arthur stopped by Lillian's desk. "Are you okay? I take it Jack gave you a hard time." She set down her pen and folded her hands on the notepad. "Nothing I can't handle Mr. Barrington." Arthur laughed. "I am sure of that. Don't take his attitude personally; he talks to everyone in the same charming manner. We will get used to him." Lillian shook her head and shrugged. "Perhaps."

CHAPTER TWENTY-NINE

Arthur decided it was time to replace Doug Swan. He had shown weakness, a quality not acceptable in his position. Arthur encouraged him to take advantage of early retirement as part of the merger. "You will receive a substantial severance package that will enable you to live a very comfortable life." Doug knew it was over. Once the Chairman of the bank made an offer of retirement there was no hope of keeping your job. He accepted his fate and returned to his home state of Michigan where he had friends and relatives.

John Douglas was one Arthur would miss. He had been chief legal counsel of Barrington for fourteen years and Art valued his friendship. John's wife had medical issues and he saw the re-organization of the bank as a time to leave and take care of her.

Jack Cunningham brought three of his senior staff to Chicago; the new legal counsel, a credit card executive and Arthur's favorite, Margaret Wise in corporate finance.

She had expertise Arthur appreciated and he liked her style. She was smart, savvy and didn't try to act like a man to get the job done. In her early fifties, Margaret was stylish, gracious and sophisticated with a dry sense of humor.

The two former Boards combined, Jack brought six of his directors and Arthur kept five from Barrington.

Arthur hosted a dinner meeting at his club to welcome the Cunningham Bank executives to Chicago. He made every effort to keep the evening relaxed and informal for them to get to know one another. David Siegel talked with Margaret Wise during dinner and was impressed with her knowledge of corporate finance. Jack Cunningham sat next to Tom Morrison and took the opportunity to grill him on his knowledge of major league baseball statistics, a subject he knew extensively. The next morning Tom called Arthur on his way to work. "Next time we have a dinner meeting I refuse to sit beside Cunningham. He did his best to intimidate me with his knowledge of baseball; earned run averages and scores from games played thirty years ago. Who the hell cares! I'd like to get him in a corner to explain how his bank lost $60 million in mortgages.

What an ass."

"Calm down Tom. He can be oppressive, I know. He likes to hear himself boast."

Tensions at the bank were strained with Jack Cunningham in charge. The integration process of the two banks was met with obstacles every day. Each faction resented the change in management and culture. Cunningham employees resented new business practices and job descriptions. Barrington employees disliked the militaristic environment of Cunningham's demands, referring to him as J.C., their savior.

As part of the consolidation process the decision was made to sell-off the mortgage portfolio of Cunningham Bank and Jack retaliated by adding stiff fees to the new credit card division. Customers left in droves as the bank fought to overcome the losses. The competition had come out with their brands of thumb reader credit cards and customers no longer felt an allegiance to BNB. By the end of the fourth quarter it was clear the division would not meet their projections and the earnings announcement was met with a sizeable decline on Wall Street. Jack Cunningham had been a banker long enough to know his position was in jeopardy.

The Board of BNB viewed him as an albatross to their future endeavors. Even the Board members he had brought along did not support him. Someone had to go. He was the outsider, not privy to the inner sanctum of Chicago politics and business associates. Arthur and the Board agreed to force Cunningham's resignation and replace him with Bill Lawrence as president and CEO. Arthur regained the title of Chairman. Cunningham accepted his fate, along with an enormous buy-out and returned to St. Louis to hunt birds and form his second venture in life, a capital management firm with his longtime friends.

The first of the year Arthur announced a restructuring strategy to increase profitability. BNB made the decision to create a new business unit to house the $70 million in troubled assets of the former Cunningham Bank. "The unit will be named Community Asset Servicing. We need to get these loans off the books. All new mortgages must meet our stricter lending standards." He gave his staff the task of defining customer issues. "We will meet the first of next month to hear your results."

Bruce Young was chosen to give the recommendations of the group. "Many former Cunningham Bank customers have been with them since their days as a small community bank. They knew their bankers and made deals on handshakes and one another's word. They don't like change and resent our role in the closing of offices and job loses. They complain about the new statement format, investment options and new personnel. Our first recommendation is a step you have already taken in aligning the senior management of the bank into one cohesive voice. Now it is imperative to show customers we value their business. We need to build a visible presence in the Missouri communities, sponsor marathons, senior citizen outings and little league teams, contribute to their charities and participate in county fairs giving out BNB tee shirts, ball caps and golf balls. Get the name in front of the public and give them a reason to want to bank with BNB. In house we must re-design the credit card division to reduce fees and institute a reward program. We need to develop a marketing campaign to promote the mutual funds and set-up kiosks in branch offices staffed with investment officers to explain the products and services.

In short, reach out to the consumer and build their trust." Arthur looked around the room as Bruce spoke. Everyone seemed to be in agreement on the objectives. "Does anyone have something to add?" Margaret Wise stood. "I agree with each of the suggestions and would like to add that our farming communities would appreciate an occasional pig roast." The room erupted into laughter. "Good idea Margaret. We'll let you make the arrangements." Arthur stood. "I also agree with the ideas and want each business unit to get moving to implement the plans. Burt Williams can work on publicity campaigns, marketing materials and the kiosks. I want each of you to report to me in your monthly meeting on the progress. Let's get started."

Within the next six months Arthur saw results. The number of new investment accounts had risen significantly in southern Missouri, boosting their mutual fund numbers and absorbing the cost of the kiosks. The credit card division had a record number of applications that more than made up for the reduced fee structure. His division heads reported less resentment among former Cunningham employees as well as an increased rate of job satisfaction.

CHAPTER THIRTY

Isabelle sat at the kitchen table and talked with Marian as she prepared lunch. "Ben has a rugby game after school today and Catherine is going with her friend to dance practice. I will take Amanda with me to the game and we should all be home by six-thirty. David has a meeting at the club so you can make something easy for dinner." Marian shook her head. "I don't know how you keep up with everyone's schedule. The children are so involved in activities." She handed Isabelle a bowl of soup and a sandwich and turned on the television. "Thank you. Nell will be back tomorrow from visiting her family and she's a big help. Come sit with me and have some lunch." A news bulletin flashed across the screen just as the news program began. 'A shooting on the north side of Chicago this morning has sent two victims to hospitals. Prominent businessman Arthur Barrington and his driver Dan Wilson were gunned down outside the Hermitage Country Club at ten-thirty this morning.'

Isabelle stared at the television in disbelief. "Oh no!" She went to turn up the volume. 'An eye witness told us a gray van drove up alongside Mr. Barrington's car as his driver held the door for him. A gunman opened fire and shot them both as the van sped away. Sources at Chicago Medical Center told us Mr. Barrington and Mr. Wilson are both in critical condition.' Isabelle jumped as the telephone rang. "Isabelle, it's David, have you seen the news?

"I'm watching it now. I can't believe it."

"Jordan Banks just called me. Arthur was pronounced dead thirty minutes ago. Jordan is devastated."

"David, that's horrible! Poor Ann, she will be lost without Arthur. Do they know more about what happened?"

"Not yet. I'll be home in a couple of hours. Love you."

"I love you too. Please call me as soon as you know any more information."

Marian cleaned up the kitchen while Isabelle went to the study to watch the news. She thought of Ann Barrington and what a terrible shock Arthur's death would be for her.

Isabelle was reading with Amanda when David came home. "I'm so glad to see you. Have you heard anything new?" David kissed her and Amanda. "Bill Lawrence called me. He said the police have talked with the entire executive staff and asked that the Board of Directors be notified. They're asking if anyone knows of threats against Arthur or the bank. The bombing at the bank may be related. He said Arthur's secretary, Lillian, collapsed when she heard the news. She is at the hospital now with Ann."

"I just cannot believe Arthur is gone. He was such a good man. What about his driver? Is he going to be okay?" David turned to the television news. "Let's hope so. Jordan said he is married and has two young children." The cameras showed pictures of Ann Barrington leaving the hospital amid swarms of photographers. "There's Ann. Why don't they leave her alone? I hate it when news crews hound people. David, I'm going to drive to her house. I want to see her."

"My car is waiting. Let's go together." Isabelle asked Nell to take Amanda for a walk. "We'll be back within a couple of hours."

The driveway was full of cars as they approached the house. A woman came to the door, introduced herself as a neighbor, Mary, and showed them inside to the living room where Ann was sitting. She looked up as they entered the room. "Isabelle, David, how good of you to come. Mary, please bring some tea for our guests." David's cell phone rang and he excused himself to take the call. Isabelle sat with Ann and listened as she described Arthur's injuries. "It all happened so quickly. They didn't have time to react. Arthur never did anything to harm anyone. Who would do this to him?" Tears rolled down her face and she shook her head. "I'm sorry, Isabelle. I can't seem to control myself." David returned from outside and went to Ann. "Is there anything you need Ann, anything at all." She reached for his hand. "Arthur thought so much of you David. I may need some advice as far as the bank is concerned. I would appreciate your help with decisions of the Board." He covered her hand with his. "You have my promise, but I don't want you to worry about that just now. Isabelle and I want to help with whatever you need.

Our home is open for any out-of-town friends who will be coming for the services and I would like to provide a car and driver for you until this is all over." Ann dabbed at the tears on her face. "Thank you, David. That would be helpful. What would I do without such wonderful friends?" Isabelle kissed her on the cheek. "We love you, Ann. Will you be all right here tonight?"

"Yes, thank you. My neighbor has offered to stay and help take phone messages. So many people are calling. There is one more favor I would like to ask. David, would you come with me to make the funeral arrangements? Arthur and I didn't discuss what he would want and I could use your help."

"Of course, call me tomorrow and let me know when you would like to go. I will be home all day." They said their goodbyes and gave their number to the neighbor. "Please don't hesitate to call if there is anything we can do." As they drove home David told Isabelle the phone call he had was from Jordan Banks. Dan Wilson had died.

The funeral for Arthur was held three days later at the Lutheran Church he and Ann had attended for years. The church was filled with friends and business associates as well as community leaders, all shocked by Arthur's death. Ann had decided the casket would be closed. Arthur's dear friend from New York, John Meier, gave a eulogy that brought both tears and laughter as he recalled the years of their friendship. Ann sat with Isabelle, David and Lillian. The caravan of cars in the funeral procession lined the streets for over a mile as police escorts lead the way to the cemetery. Following the burial, guests were invited to Isabelle and David's home where caterers and servers provided food and desserts.

John Meier stayed at Isabelle's and David's home and Isabelle insisted Ann spend the night with them. "You can go home whenever you want but we would like to be with you tonight." Isabelle was especially sensitive to Lillian who was still in shock from Arthur's death. She was pale and her voice was raspy from the stress. She had been his right hand for many years as well as a friend to him and Ann. John Meier spent time talking with her and tried to convince her to try some food.

Jordan Banks and Bill Lawrence talked with David on the veranda. "Have you heard any more from the police?"

"They have stationed armed plain-clothes officers in the lobby of the bank and on the executive floor. They say it is a precautionary measure until they know more about the shootings. They don't have many clues. The eyewitness at the club didn't get the license number of the van. He did tell them it was gray with the name of a florist on the side." Bill Lawrence told David that Dunhill had called an emergency meeting of the Board for the next week. "The job of naming a new chief executive officer of the bank is at hand. I only hope it is someone who knows the bank, not an outsider. Arthur would hate that." David brought up the publicity the newspapers were exploiting, tying the bombing to the shootings. "There is going to be a lot of customer defection, people will want to know why Barrington is being targeted. The police need to get to the bottom of this quickly."

After the guests had gone, Isabelle, David, Ann and John Meier sat in the living room and visited. They reminisced with stories about Arthur.

"He would like this, you know, being the center of our attention. He loved you all and we had such good times together." Ann decided to turn in for the night. She thanked Isabelle and David for all they had done and asked John to go with her to her house the next morning before heading to the airport.

Ann went upstairs when they got to the house. "I'll be right back, please make yourself at home John." She returned to the kitchen with a box she set on the table. "This is for you. Arthur would want you to have it." John opened the box and took out Arthur's fishing vest. "Ann, I can't take this."

"Of course you can. Remember all of the fun we had at the lake over the years? I want you to use it and remember Arthur and the good times." He hugged her. "Thank you, Ann. I shall take good care of it. Maybe we'll go fishing together one of these days. Are you going to be okay here alone?" She looked around the large kitchen. "Yes, I will be fine. We had a wonderful life together and this house is filled with happy memories that will keep me company.

CHAPTER THIRTY-ONE

The directors of the bank met in executive session promptly at nine o'clock as Lillian recorded minutes of the meeting. The mood in the room was solemn, the first time the directors had been together since Arthur's death. His chair remained empty. Mr. Dunhill called the meeting to order and asked for a moment of silence in memory of Arthur. "Our task at hand, unfortunately, is to name a new Chairman of BNB. I ask for nominations from you now." Roy Jensen spoke up. "Mr. Chairman, I will nominate Bill Lawrence for the position. He worked closely with Arthur for the last fifteen years and knows the job." Hiram Baker seconded the nomination. Pete Preston raised his hand. "I will nominate Tom Morrison who has been the key to our mergers and acquisitions success." The directors waited for a second to the Morrison nomination. Howard Mitchel, the newest member of the Board, seconded the nomination. All heads turned toward David Siegel who had not spoken.

"I move that we close the nominations." Hiram Baker seconded the motion. Mr. Dunhill handed a note with the nominations on it to Lillian. "Please prepare the ballot for us."

Lillian returned to the room, walked around the table and handed each Director an envelope containing the ballot. "Are there any questions before you cast your vote?" The room was silent. "Please mark your ballot and pass your envelope to the head of the table." Lillian sat quietly beside Mr. Dunhill, secretly praying for Mr. Lawrence to win the vote. Dunhill opened the envelopes one by one and announced the vote within. "The vote is seven votes for Bill Lawrence and four votes for Tom Morrison. The Chairman of Barrington Bank is now Bill Lawrence." He picked-up the phone and rang Mr. Lawrence's office. "Bill, will you please come to the Boardroom at once?"

Lillian breathed a sigh of relief. Bill Lawrence was the only reasonable choice to head the bank, the only person Arthur would have chosen himself. Bill Lawrence walked into the room to a round of applause. "Bill, we have voted and I am happy to announce you have been elected Chairman and CEO of BNB."

Bill addressed the Directors. "Thank you for your vote of confidence in naming me Chairman of Barrington. Arthur was my friend and my mentor. His are big shoes to fill but I plan to follow the business practices we have found to be successful in continuing our stature in the industry. I do have one request." He turned to Lillian who was looking down at her notebook. "I would like to ask Lillian Conrad to work with me as my assistant." She looked up toward Bill who was smiling at her. "Mr. Lawrence, it will be my honor." There was another round of applause lead by Bill.

Mr. Dunhill asked if there was any other business, and the meeting was adjourned.

Bill went to Lillian, gave her a hug and whispered in her ear. "I now have my own KGB agent." She squeezed his hand and returned to her desk, relieved and most pleased that she would be working with Bill Lawrence.

David Siegel was the first to shake Bill's hand. "Congratulations, Bill. Please don't hesitate to call if I can be of help in any way. We'll have to take another boat trip one of these days." Tom Morrison came to Bill's office immediately following the meeting.

"Congratulations, Bill. You are the best man for the job and you have my full support." News of the meeting spread throughout the bank like wildfire as people called to offer their congratulations. He waited until the end of the day and phoned Ann Barrington. "Ann, its Bill Lawrence. I wanted to call you personally to let you know I was chosen today as the CEO of Barrington."

"Bill. How nice of you to think of calling me. Congratulations, I know Arthur would be pleased."

"I think of him every day and plan to try and live up to his reputation."

"You will do fine, Bill. Please keep in touch with me and thank you for calling." Bill stopped by Lillian's desk on his way out. "We had quite a day, didn't we?" She looked up at him. "I couldn't be happier for you, Mr. Lawrence. You are the one person Mr. Barrington would want to replace him."

"Thank you, but we need to get something straight. I want you to call me Bill, not Mr. Lawrence. Okay?" She stood and shook his hand. "Okay."

The transition process included meeting with the entire executive staff, planning the news release, contacting community leaders and schedule changes. Bill met with Lillian first thing the next day. "I need to see Burt as soon as possible about publicity and I want to meet with the team tomorrow morning at nine o'clock for updates from each business sector. Please call Jordan Banks' office and schedule lunch when it is convenient for him." Lillian took notes. "I will need to see Arthur's files." Lillian looked up at him. "Are you moving into his office?"

"No, not yet, I want to give Mrs. Barrington time to collect Arthur's personal belongings." Lillian paused and looked down at her notepad. "Lillian, I know how difficult this has been for you. Do you need to take some time off?"

"No, I would rather stay busy. It's just sometimes difficult to think of going on without Mr. Barrington. I will talk with Ann and arrange to have everything delivered to her house. It would be easier for her than coming here."

"I understand. We can conduct business just fine right here for now. Is there anything pending I should know about?"

Lillian smiled. "I will bring Mr. Barrington's personal files. He kept important documents in a special drawer only he and I knew about."

Lillian called Burt Williams' office and asked him to come see Mr. Lawrence as soon as possible. She alerted the executive staff to be in the Boardroom at nine o'clock the next morning prepared with business updates for Mr. Lawrence. She scheduled lunch with Jordan Banks on Wednesday in the east dining room and alerted Della that Mr. Lawrence was the new CEO. She went to Arthur's office, collected the contents of the file drawer and took it to Bill. "These are the files Arthur kept as top on his priority list. This notebook lists passwords and pin numbers he couldn't remember. I will forward it on to Mrs. Barrington along with his personal letters." "Thank you, Lillian." They went over Bill's calendar for the next month, cleared whatever necessary and scheduled meetings with key advisors. "I need to plan a road trip to meet with the regional offices as soon as possible. Here is a list of locations I want to visit, Missouri, Indiana, Michigan, Wisconsin, you know the list. Work on a time schedule where I can be here in the office three days a week and on the road two."

Lillian took notes. "I will get on it today. Is anyone going with you?"

"Yes, count one more person depending on which location I'm visiting. I will take Morrison, Williams or Young with me." He turned to his computer. "I see you scheduled lunch with Jordan on Wednesday. I am adding dinner at the club this Saturday, Grace and me with Isabelle and David Siegel. Between you and me, Grace is a wreck over what to wear. She says Isabelle Siegel is the most stylish woman in Chicago. Now, there's one more date I want on my calendar. When is your birthday Lillian?" She blushed. "That is not necessary, Bill."

"That's not what I asked. The date?" Lillian put down her pen. "April twenty-fifth. But do not even think about asking my age." He held up his hands. "I may not be the brightest star on the tree but I'm not crazy." Burt Williams knocked on the side of the door. "Hi Bill, are you ready for me?" Lillian stood. "You have perfect timing, Burt. I was just leaving." Burt brought drafts of the press releases he had prepared for Bill's approval. "Good job, Burt. They look fine. Let's get them out as soon as possible."

Lillian returned to her desk and looked through the personal items from Arthur's desk. She ran her hand over the pebbled leather cover of his appointment book as if to re-connect with something he had touched. It was still difficult to believe he was gone. She somctimes woke in the morning and hoped it had all been a bad dream, but reality dawned all too quickly and the pain of his loss came creeping back. She opened the book and smiled at his notes. He always used the same password for everything, much to securities' dismay. "Ann.One." He was a hopeless romantic when it came to his wife. She took a deep breath and placed the items in a box.

Bill looked over the files from Arthur's office. Tom Morrison's file on Caldwell Bank in Missouri caught his attention. It contained the entire report on the due diligence investigation. There was a file on Bruce Young who replaced Diane Conlan with his resume, the cover letter he had written and Arthur's notes about their meeting. A folder marked 'Confidential' caught Bill's attention. Inside he found a crumpled note and a detailed account of a threat against Barrington Bank and specifically, Arthur.

A disgruntled customer had walked into a branch office in Wisconsin and asked to talk with someone in the investment department. He contended the bank had stolen funds from his account and covered up the proof. He ranted that he would get his revenge one way or another.

Bill couldn't believe what he was reading. There was a phone message from Tim Turner dated a year before. Bill picked-up the phone and called him. "Tim, Bill Lawrence here."

"Bill, congratulations, I just heard the news. What can I do for you?"

"Tim, I want to know everything about the customer you had who threatened Arthur last year." Tim relayed the entire story to Bill. "I called Arthur right away and told him what the man said. Arthur asked me to fax a copy of the investment agreement, account statements and all written documentation. We did an audit of the account from the original meeting notes and list of assets. He took regular monthly withdrawals and depleted the account. I told Arthur the man was erratic and dangerous but Arthur said he wasn't concerned, he had threats like that every day and not to worry about it."

"Has the customer been back in the bank?"

"No. We monitored the security videos for six months with nothing. I told the bank to let me know if there was any further communication from him." Bill stared out the window as Tim talked. "That was over a year ago. You don't think this guy had anything to do with Arthur's death, do you?"

"I don't know, Tim, but I am going to talk with the police about the threat. Thanks for the information." Bill phoned Jordan Banks and told him about his conversation with Tim. "I want to meet with the police chief in private. I don't want the news media getting any ideas. Can you arrange a meeting in your office?"

"Of course, Bill. I'll call you in twenty minutes."

"Lillian, I have a meeting with the mayor at two o'clock." The chief of police was in Jordan's office when Bill arrived. "Thank you for seeing me so soon. I just learned about a threat against Arthur Barrington. It was over a year ago but could still be important." Bill showed the documentation to him. "This could be a lead. We'll run a check on him and find out where he was the day Mr. Barrington was killed.

We have video of him in Wisconsin on the security cameras showing him in the bank." "Do you have copies of the file?" Bill handed him a folder. "Good. I'll take these with me. I also want the security video. I will be in touch as soon as we know something. Thanks for your help."

The announcement of Bill Lawrence to the office of CEO of BNB was the front-page story in newspapers around the country. The stories gave Bill's background with the bank and included endorsements of business leaders as well as the mayor of Chicago. "Bill Lawrence has been instrumental in the success of the bank for the past fifteen years. He brings a wealth of experience and a commitment to the city of Chicago to provide outstanding financial improvements to our communities." Bill phoned Jordan as soon as he read the story. "Thank you for your support Jordan. I appreciate your confidence and applaud your reference to community investments. Your supporters will be our best customers."
"I sincerely feel you have the qualities it takes to head up a bank the size of BNB. I am here to assist in whatever I may do to be of help."

Calls of congratulations came into the office for the next week from Chicago, New York and Washington. Lillian was exhausted trying to field off reporters while ensuring Bill received the important calls. She sorted telegrams and notes into separate folders, one for business associates and one for personal friends and piled them in his in-basket. "What's all of this?" "Your fan club has spoken. There are telegrams and notes of congratulations from all over the country. You could have warned me, when the President's brother called, I nearly had a heart attack." Bill laughed. "Dan and I played on the same basketball team at Duke and we've known each other for years. I could tell you a lot of stories about 'the dipper' as we called him." Lillian shook her head. "I presume you will let me know if I should expect a call from the Vatican."

"I sincerely doubt that. I was baptized Presbyterian." She looked at the stack of papers on his desk. "I don't know when you will have time to read all of this but there it is."

Bill turned to his computer. "Look at this. It's an email from John Meier in New York, Arthur's friend. He not only congratulates my appointment but says he will be in Chicago to visit Ann Barrington next weekend and wants to see me. Have you talked with Ann?"

"Yes, we had lunch last Saturday at the club. She looks good and tells me she is keeping busy playing tennis and volunteering. She didn't mention John Meier."

"Well, it's good of John to stay in touch with her. You don't think there something more to this do you?" Lillian frowned. "Of course not, Ann and Arthur were friends with John for years. They used to take him along on fishing trips and skiing in Montana."

"Okay, if you say so, but I have a suspicious feeling about this. What else do you have for me?" Lillian went over phone messages for him. "Isabelle Siegel called. She is Chairperson on the fundraising campaign for the girls' club. She wants to come in sometime over the next two weeks to talk with you about a donation. I checked your schedule and you have time on the twelfth or the fifteenth." Bill opened his online calendar. "Let's make it the twelfth at ten-thirty."

342

He typed in the entry. "Grace and I are going to New York Friday evening, the sixteenth, for a play and of course, shopping. We will return Sunday evening." Lillian made a note. "I want to schedule lunch with Burt Williams next week to discuss a media release. Call George Cater and ask him to bring the employment agreement on Margaret Wise. Tomorrow at nine-thirty looks good." Bill leaned back in his chair. "Now, how is my favorite KGB agent getting along? Anything I should know?" Lillian looked up from her notepad. "Actually, everything has been running smoothly, much more relaxed since Mr. Cunningham was here. There is a noticeable air of relief."

"Good, all clear on the home front. Thank you Lillian."

Bill wasted no time in meeting with his senior staff and outlining his expectations. Fortunately, Arthur had kept him up to speed on most of the issues, good and bad, during the last few months. Lillian set-up a schedule for the regional office visits and the first trip was to Detroit and Lansing.

Bill took Bruce Young along as he had demonstrated outstanding leadership skills in increasing morale and productivity among the operations units in Detroit. He was hands on, open to questions and suggestions from his staff, not inaccessible as Diane Conlan had been. Bill was impressed at the changes he saw and the increased profit margins.

The next week he took Burt Williams and Bruce with him to tour the Missouri locations. The employees did not respond as enthusiastically to their visits. They sat quietly, avoided eye contact and participation in the presentation. It was clear the former Cunningham Bank employees still resented the merger and Bill Cunningham's expulsion from the bank. On the flight home Bill told Burt to step up the conversion efforts. "Get Margaret Wise involved in this. The people know her and she can spread the love but I want to make it clear these employees have three months to improve attitudes or they will be replaced."

The police chief phoned Bill Lawrence. "We have reviewed the files and the surveillance video.

The customer is Richard Davis. He is five feet six inches tall, one hundred and eighty pounds, has brown hair, a mustache and wears glasses. He has a history of mental illness and was institutionalized for four years in Indiana. He now works in a discount store outside of Bloomington. He was in a two-hour sales meeting on the morning of the shootings, there is no way he could be in Chicago at ten a.m. We ran a background check on him and found he has an identical twin, Robert Davis who lives in Valparaiso. Robert is a paramedic who works mostly nights. He called in sick and was out for two days surrounding the murder. We are working on a search warrant to check his apartment for evidence and he is being monitored. We'll contact you when we have more information."

Bill phoned Jordan Banks to give him an update from his conversation with the chief of police. "It might just be the lead they need." "Let's hope so. Whoever did this must be caught. I want you to watch your step Bill until they get this guy off the streets."

Bill glanced at the picture of his wife on his desk. "We have plain clothed officers in the bank and one outside our home twenty-four hours a day. Grace is a little edgy about all of this."

"I'm sure she is, which unfortunately can be a good thing, it keeps you on your toes. I wish Arthur had paid closer attention to the threat against him and maybe this could have been prevented. Keep me posted on any news."

CHAPTER THIRTY-TWO

"We sent two detectives to the apartment building where Robert Davis lives to talk with neighbors. A woman told us she was walking her dog at seven-thirty that morning and saw a van pull up at the side of the building. She saw a man come out of his apartment, get in the van and it drove away. The driving distance from Valparaiso to the scene of the shootings near Highland Park is fifty-eight miles. He could have easily been there at ten o'clock. It was enough to issue the search warrant and bring him in for questioning. Robert swears he was home in bed with the flu for two days. We checked his cell phone records. He regularly talks with his brother Richard once a week, usually on Monday evenings. The records show he received two calls from Richard the morning of the shootings, once at nine o'clock and another at ten thirty-four. When we asked him about the calls, he told us Richard was checking see how he felt." Bill shook his head. "What about the van?"

"We ran down the van in Gary, Indiana. It was found in a wooded area behind an abandoned barn, burned and without tags. Whoever set it on fire left too soon as there was enough identity to trace it back to a body shop in Valparaiso, some coincidence, eh? The missing piece of the puzzle is who drove the van."

"So, Robert is being held in jail?"

"Yes. We are holding him on suspicion for now."

"What about Richard? He is the one who threatened Arthur. He must be involved in all of this."

"Sure he is, but with his alibi we have to stand back for now." The police chief stood and shook Bill's hand. "I need to get back to work. Remember don't make any comments to the press. We don't want to blow this."

"I understand. Thank you."

The phone call records gave police reason to question Richard about the day of the shootings. Richard was picked-up by the Bloomington police and taken in for questioning with two detectives from Chicago. He was noticeably irritated as he sat in the interrogation room. A stenographer recorded the conversation.

"Mr. Davis, where were you on Wednesday the twenty-fourth?

"What is this all about? Why am I here?"

"We just want to ask you some questions. Where were you that day?"

"I was at work at the Discount Mart. I demand to know why I am being questioned."

"What hours do you work?" Richard pounded his fist on the table. "Look, I don't have to answer your questions." The detective stood and went to the door. "Bring an officer in here now." A policeman came in the room and stood by the door. The detective returned to the table and leaned down in front of Richard. "Now, Mr. Davis, I will inform you that if you do not cooperate you will be charged with resisting arrest. You are being questioned as a suspect in the shootings of Arthur Barrington and Dan Wilson." He read Richard his rights and sat down. Richard laughed. "I don't want an attorney. I don't trust them. They're all alike and side with the likes of the rich guys."

"Do you know the name Arthur Barrington?" He watched Richard's face turn red.

"Yea, I'm afraid I do. He and his bank stole the money my father left to me! They stole thousands of dollars and they won't admit what they did. They have a conspiracy going to cover up their tracks. They lie for each other and destroy records. I have to work in a discount store to have enough money to live because of them!" He was screaming and breathing hard. "Do you know how much money they make? Millions! They don't need to take my money but they all want more and more and more. They walk on the dark side of the law with the devil as their guide and they get away with it because they're rich and powerful." He started to recite scripture and ranted about the evil corruption of the bank, then broke down and cried. The detective poured Richard a glass of water. "Do you have a cell phone Mr. Davis?" Richard handed it to him. The detective gave it to the policeman at the door. "We just want to check something." Richard took a drink of water and asked to use the men's room. When he returned the detective held up the cell phone. "Mr. Davis, we checked the GPS on your phone.

You placed two calls on your cell phone that morning, one from Chicago and one from Highland Park, Illinois. You were not in Bloomington that morning." Richard looked at his phone in disbelief, as if it had betrayed him. "You drove to Highland Park, Illinois to The Hermitage Country Club that morning, didn't you? You drove there for one reason, to shoot Arthur Barrington and get your revenge." Richard stared at the detective and broke down sobbing. "I told you what they did to me. They shouldn't be allowed to get away with that. Someone had to show them." He told them he wanted to scare Arthur Barrington. "I read a story in the Chicago newspaper that Barrington won first place in his Wednesday morning golf league at The Hermitage Country Club in Highland Park. Every Wednesday he played golf there, it was too easy. I studied maps of the club, right off of an interstate highway for a quick exit, safer than trying anything in the traffic of downtown Chicago. I thought it would be an easy place to surprise him, to show him how I knew he was a crook." He laughed. "Those rich guys think they can get away with anything, you know?"

The detective nodded. "Then what happened?" Richard's eyes lit up. "We were parked behind some trees when we saw this car with Chicago tags pull up to the pro shop. A guy got out of the car and opened the back door. A man got out and I knew it had to be Barrington, I recognized him from the newspaper. We sped toward the car and I thought I would yell at him and tell him what I thought, but I've tried that before and got nowhere."

"You tried before?" Richard nodded. "I went to the bank and yelled at them but they ignored me. I tried everything I could think of to scare them."

"Is that when you decided to plant the bomb?" Richard's eyes widened and his mouth fell open. "Who said I planted a bomb?" The detective stared at him. "Okay, yeah it was me. I shut down their bank!"

"But it wasn't enough was it?"

"No. I wanted to get to the big boss, the guy in charge of everything. That day at the country club I decided to fire my gun to really scare him. I pulled the trigger, again and again and we sped away laughing."

He grinned and nodded his head.

The detective stared at Richard. "They both died Mr. Davis, Arthur Barrington and his driver Dan Wilson." Richard grimaced and looked down at his hands. The detective sat back in his chair. "Who was with you Richard, who drove the van?"

"A guy I work with. He didn't have anything to do with it."

"We need his name Richard."

"I don't want to get him into trouble." The detective handed him a paper and pencil. "What is the name, Mr. Davis." Richard scribbled on the paper and pushed it toward the detective. "Thank you." He handed the paper to the officer at the door. "Now, Mr. Davis, where was your brother on the day of the shootings?" Richard turned pale. "How do you know about him? Robert has nothing to do with this." The detective smiled. "Did Robert go to your job that morning as you?" Richard shook his head. "How did you know that? We do things like that all the time. People can't tell us apart. I told Robert I was going to get even with Barrington Bank and he should cover for me. Nobody at work knew it wasn't me that morning."

The chief of police met with Bill the next week in Jordan Bank's office. "Richard Davis confessed to the shootings." The chief gave them the details surrounding the murders, how Richard's brother provided him with an alibi that day, the stolen van and the driver who drove Richard to Highland Park. Bill and Jordan sat stunned as they listened to Richard Davis' plan to kill Arthur. "It was premeditated murder. Richard has been charged with two counts of first-degree murder, his brother and the driver of the van have been charged as accessories to commit murder. They're all three being held without bail." He told them about Richard's erratic behavior during questioning, the anger, the crying and the biblical ranting. "He's a real nut case." Bill let out a sigh of relief. "I'm relieved he is off the streets."

"I will go see Mrs. Barrington and Mrs. Wilson later today before the news hits the papers." Bill nodded. "I would like to go with you to see Mrs. Wilson but if you don't mind, I would like to talk to Mrs. Barrington privately about the arrests." The police chief agreed. Jordan congratulated him on the arrests and thanked him for coming to give them the news.

Bill asked David Siegel to go with him to talk with Ann Barrington. Ann had been friends with David and Isabelle for years. He did not go into details of the plot but simply told her the man had confessed and was in jail awaiting trial. Ann listened quietly and glanced out the window as Bill finished speaking. "He has no idea how his actions have affected so many people. Have you talked with Dan Wilson's wife?"

"Yes, I went with the chief of police to meet with her."

"Thank you both for coming to talk to me. I really don't care to see the police; they remind me too much of that day." David asked her about the event planned by the Chicago Foundation to honor Arthur. "It is wonderful of them to dedicate the evening to his achievements; Arthur would be very pleased."

"We look forward to it. We'll see you Saturday night."

Jordan Banks attended the ceremonies honoring Arthur Barrington. He made sure to say hello to Ann who sat with Bill and Grace Lawrence and David and Isabelle Siegel.

"Bill, I want to get together with you next week to discuss an opportunity. I would like to ask David to be there also. I'll call you." Jordan did call the next week and arranged to meet with Bill and David on Wednesday in Bill's office. "Thank you both for taking the time to be here today. I have been approached by the President's search team as a potential Vice Presidential candidate in the upcoming election. I have met with the Chairman of the Democratic party of Chicago and he assured me they support my nomination. I wanted to go over this with both of you and ask if I can count on your endorsements. You are both key figures who can be instrumental for me to secure the nomination." Bill leaned back in his chair. "What do you think David? Do you suppose this mid-western mayor could make it to the White House?" David paused and looked intently at Jordan. "I am sure of it. Jordan, you have my full support." Bill put his hand on Jordan's shoulder. "We are behind you 100%. I went to college with the President's brother. I will give him a call." Jordan held up his hand. "Thank you Bill, but it is far from a done deal.

They will run background checks on all potential candidates before offering a nomination."

"Are there skeletons in your closet you're concerned about?"

"No, nothing criminal or incestuous, but we're all human you know. I have run two campaigns for mayor of Chicago without any serious fallout and I do not anticipate a problem."

"Good. Let me know what you hear. Congratulations Jordan." David stood and shook Jordan's hand. "Congratulations. I feel positive about your nomination. You have a stellar reputation as mayor of Chicago with a long list of accomplishments I am sure will be of interest to the selection committee and the President. Keep us informed." Jordan thanked Bill and David for their support. "You will know as soon as I hear from them."

The next week Jordan received a call from the President who invited him to the White House. "My advisors have searched your background thoroughly for the slightest reason to disqualify your nomination. One point in question is that you never married. The only relationship they could find was a three-year connection while you were in college."

"Yes sir. That expired while I was serving my country overseas. When I returned to the states, I decided to further my service to our country and immersed myself in politics. I never looked back." The President removed his glasses and set aside the reports. "Jordan, with your credentials as a West Point graduate and your stellar military service record, I know you are an honorable man I can trust."

"Mr. President, I have nothing to hide. I still believe in ready to lead, ready to follow, never quit."

Three days later the President phoned Jordan's office. "Congratulations, Jordan. The committee has approved your nomination. I expect you here next week ready to run." Jordan took a deep breath. "Thank you, Mr. President. It is my honor to serve with you."

Jordan immediately phoned Bill Lawrence and David Siegel to tell them before they heard it on the news. Bill was elated for Jordan. "That's great. You know I cannot come out in full force behind you but I am here to help with your campaign finances and rally supporters.
I need to be careful not to alienate our Republican customers."

Jordan laughed. "I understand. I appreciate any help you can offer." David Siegel was every bit as enthused. "I knew it. Congratulations Jordan. Tell your people to call and let me know what they need. I will get together with you to brainstorm on how best to approach the business leaders in New York and California. I have some favors to call into action."

The news of Jordan Banks as the nominee for Vice President of the United States hit the news media the same day. Jordan flew to Washington to appear with the President in a press conference at the White House followed by a closed-door meeting in the oval office. The President outlined what Jordan could expect in the coming weeks and months. "The press will hound you continuously, photographers, reporters and television personalities will question your every move. They will pick up on the smallest quirk in your behavior and blow it out of proportion mimicking you in the media. They will try to interview your high school English teacher, your ex-girlfriends and your mother. Our opponents will criticize, challenge and lie about statements you make in public." Jordan listened intently as the President spoke.

"Yes sir, I understand. The windy city has given me similar challenges over the years." The President laughed. "Yes, I am sure it has. Chicago politics is a good training ground for this job."

Jordan sprang out on the campaign trail with the President on an exhausting schedule of town hall meetings and appearances before labor unions and community groups. An interim Mayor was appointed and Jordan turned his full attention to the campaign trail.

David Siegel was an ally of immeasurable capacity in fundraising events. He summoned influential friends who volunteered their exclusive homes for wealthy contributors to dine with Jordan Banks. He rallied political support in major cities to stir volunteers into action and provided financial support for campaign expenses. Bill Lawrence was equally as effective with his support. He personally donated the ultimate limit he was allowed for campaign donations. He phoned friends across the country to ask their support of the ticket and attended all fundraisers in Chicago, New York and Los Angeles.

Election night was the crescendo of the campaign as the Democrats won the election and Jordan Banks was elected Vice President of the United States. It was nearly two o'clock in the morning when he telephoned Bill Lawrence. "Bill, its Jordan. Sorry to wake you old man, but I had to say thank you. We won!" Bill looked at the clock and rubbed his eyes. "I will have you know I already have a credit card and do not need another." Jordan roared with laughter. "But we can give you a great deal."

"I am happy for you. Good night."

Bill and Grace Lawrence and David and Isabelle Siegel were invited to the inauguration and the parties that followed. Bill was mesmerized with all of the pomp and circumstance. "I haven't seen this much pageantry since my first trip to the Kentucky Derby." They were given VIP treatment and met the President and First Lady for brunch the next day at the White House. Isabelle was fascinated with the decorum of Washington and David was equally spellbound. "My father would not believe I had breakfast with the President in the White House. His dream was one day I would own a delicatessen."

CHAPTER THIRTY-THREE

Ann and Isabelle met for a game of tennis every Tuesday morning either at the club in good weather or at an indoor facility during the winter months. It had been over two years since Arthur's death and they had remained close friends. They freshened up and walked to the patio for lunch. "You look absolutely glowing Ann, the tan looks good on you."
"I have been playing a lot of tennis in this wonderful weather." Isabelle watched as Ann nervously turned the wedding ring on her hand.
"Is something wrong Ann?"
She smiled and took a sip of tea. "I would like to confide something to you. I have been seeing quite a lot of John Meier." Isabelle reached out and touched her arm. "That is wonderful Ann. He is such a nice man."
"Yes, he is. We all graduated together from Northwestern so I've known him for a long time. Isabelle, it isn't until one is alone that you realize the world is totally made up of pairs. I watch the ducks swimming in the lake, always in twos.

I see young lovers holding hands as they window shop, I watch elderly couples help one another across the street. I miss that connection."

Isabelle listened quietly as her friend struggled with her thoughts. "You and David have been wonderful, inviting me to dinners and charity events but it is difficult always being the third person." She took a deep breath. "John has asked me to marry him." Isabelle looked into Ann's eyes. "Have you given him an answer?"

"Yes, I told him yes." Isabelle stood and hugged Ann. "What wonderful news! David will be thrilled for you both."

"Do you think so? I have worried that Arthur's friends will think I am foolish and impulsive." Isabelle squeezed Ann's hand. "Absolutely no one would ever think that of you Ann. You have no idea how much people have admired you for years. Everyone on the 21st floor wants only the best for you. Have you made plans?"

"No, nothing definite, we are not making any rash decisions at this point. John will keep his home in New York and I intend to keep my home here. We plan to travel, go fishing and have fun. Sounds a little childish, doesn't it?"

"It sounds absolutely fabulous. What about the actual ceremony?"

"I know that I want a small, private ceremony. I'm too old to play the bride."

"Don't be silly. You deserve a very special day. David and I would be honored to host a reception at our house. I promise to keep it intimate and simply done."

"That would be lovely Isabelle, to share our day with dear friends. I know John will agree."

Isabelle orchestrated the entire reception with elegant simplicity, true to her style. Vases of white flowers were scattered throughout the public rooms of the house emitting the subtle fragrance of phlox and roses. She told the caterers she wanted round tables covered in white linen where they would serve hors d'oeuvres. She insisted on tables filled with small individual bites of food easily managed while holding a glass of champagne; food stations of seafood, pastry appetizers, fruit and decadent bite size desserts. The house filled with friends of Ann and John, all there to celebrate their union and happiness. Bill noticed Lillian arrive and went to meet her. He handed her a glass of wine.

"You look lovely tonight Lillian. Come with me, I can't wait to introduce you to the newlyweds. I told you I knew there was more to their friendship." Lillian whispered to him. "Don't be smug, it doesn't become you."

David had kept an announcement from Isabelle and their guests. An hour into the party the Siegel home became a bevy of secret servicemen and hoards of police cars as Jordan Banks made a surprise entrance at the reception. Ben, Catherine and Amanda were in awe as Mr. Banks, the Vice President of the United States, arrived at their home. He made a special effort to talk with each of them and gave them White House souvenirs. He led a toast to Ann and John with his best wishes as well as those of the President.

David took John Meier aside and handed him an envelope. "Inside are the keys to our home in Palm Beach. It is at your disposal for the next month along with the yacht harbored nearby. We hope you and Ann will accept its use with our compliments." John shook David's hand. "Ann will be delighted. You and Isabelle have made this evening very special. Thank you both for your friendship."

Jordan Banks did not forget his Chicago friends who had been staunch supporters of his candidacy. He invited Bill and Grace and David and Isabelle to White House receptions and dinners where they met international politicians, socialites and entertainers, all of whom were quite taken with the beautiful American ladies. Foreign dignitaries vied for a seat beside the flawless Grace Lawrence and Isabelle charmed the President of France with her fluent command of his language.

Occasionally they were invited to Jordan's home in Washington where they relaxed with their friend and could talk candidly. Bill discussed the regulatory restrictions pending in the senate. "I will do what I can to stall passage but ultimately some things will change."
"I appreciate your interest Jordan. We have taken steps to block passage of the bill and have instituted changes at the bank to override our leverage in fees and interest charges. What we need now is help with mortgage defaults. We are faced with millions of dollars in credit losses because of the devaluation in real estate. We hope you will urge the President to back a program to intercede with the crisis."

The interim Mayor of Chicago wasted no time stirring controversy in office. He was determined to demonstrate the ability to get things done quickly and apologize to his critics later. He expressed little concern for the interests of the business leaders of the city but chose rather to champion the cause of urban development, privatization of city-owned property and restraints on the police department. His latest battle was over a report that he received a kick-back of $40,000 from an attorney whose client wanted land in the fourteenth ward rezoned for a grocery store.

The business leaders of Chicago were outraged by the lack of influence they held with the new Mayor. They had the inside track when Jordan Banks was in office; labor contracts were quietly negotiated, lucrative bids were thrown their way, tax incentives were prioritized and zoning requests sailed through unfettered. The new administration had to go.

A secretive meeting was called to discuss a course of action for the upcoming election. Two trusted city commissioners, influential business leaders, financiers and political bosses made up the group.

It was a well-oiled secret society that held tightly to the reigns of the city. The members told no one of their activities, not their wives, attorneys or priests and trusted each other explicitly. Jim Ramsey, CEO of National Insurance, spoke first. "Charlie Jarvis is in major trouble. No mayor has ever had this much controversy surrounding his administration so early in the game. We need an all-out effort to throw our support behind the campaign of Jack Baker in the upcoming election. You all know him and his family. They have been instrumental in the success of many Chicago charitable events and their philanthropic contributions to the university are monumental. Jack will support the business community in much the same way as did Jordan Banks. We can get him elected with the right financial and political support." Others spoke about how the mayor's reputation affected their efforts to attract new businesses to the city. Bill told the group he had spoken to Jordan Banks about Charlie Jarvis. "Jordan is furious over the actions of Jarvis. He pulled funding Jordan had secured for George Tomlin's highway project on the south side and has earmarked the money to upgrade the El stations.

It cost Tomlin Construction $400 million. Jordan will wield the political support necessary to undermine Jarvis' campaign." David Siegel was the first to commit funds to the Baker campaign with a pledge of $100,000 that was followed by pledges from everyone in the room. The group formed committees to move forward immediately with action plans; political fundraisers, endorsements and a smear attack on Jarvis.

The race for Mayor was an all-out war of personal accusations and in the end Jack Baker was elected in a landslide victory of seventy-three percent of the vote, unprecedented in Chicago politics. Bill and Grace Lawrence hosted a gala at the Hermitage Country Club to celebrate his victory.

Jack Baker took office and immediately began to implement a pro-business stance favorable to his supporters. He had political aspirations far beyond the Mayor's office and knew how critical it was to stay in favor with those who championed his election. He became a confidant and friend to Bill Lawrence and accompanied him to pro basketball games and golf outings in Silver Springs, off the radar as Bill joked, in private limos and the corporate jet.

They maintained a low profile to avoid the press. Jack Baker was named to the University Board of Directors at the suggestion of David Siegel, a prestigious position with influential contacts. Members of group insured the Mayor held prominent liaisons with all the right people.

Bill met with Tom Morrison to discuss plans he had for an aggressive expansion of BNB. "I project a new corporate headquarters and several branch locations. I want one at Siegel's Brighton complex. He is showing remarkable success. Take a look at our demographics and let me know other areas you think will be a good fit." Tom was cautious. "How many branches are you considering?"

"We have nothing in Niles and only one office in Peoria. Get back to me with what you find." He called a meeting with the entire senior staff to discuss the plans. "It is time for us to move up. I have met with one of Chicago's leading architects on plans and possible site development. I talked with David Siegel about it and he agrees a new corporate image will be impressive to the competition." Tom Morrison spoke up. "What about our inner-city clients?"

"We can lease any number of spaces on Michigan Avenue to put in a glitzy branch office to service them. They don't need to bank at the corporate offices." Tom decided to back off. He didn't want to antagonize Bill.

The architect met again with Bill and brought the results of his study. "The site on the north shore is going to be pricy. Demolition of the existing building will easily be $4 million before construction begins. There are height restrictions, setback restrictions and a budget to work within. I know of another site more reasonably priced west of Lincoln Park. I have prepared some preliminary projections I foresee at somewhere close to $150 to $200 million depending on the details. Here are two designs for you to review." Bill studied the blue prints the architect left for him to review. He had insisted they limit the building height to twenty-one floors. "It's my good luck number; my birthday is the 21st; I wore 21 on my college basketball jersey, I have worked on the 21st floor of Barrington Bank for years and I married Grace on December 21st."

He took David Siegel with him to scout out the locations and David agreed the north shore site was preferable. "You must look beyond the initial cost to the impact the building will have on the city of Chicago. Although not the tallest structure in the city, it will still command a presence on the north shore as an iconic landmark. If I had listened to my critics I wouldn't be where I am today. People told me Brighton was too big, too costly and too extravagant to be profitable, but look at its success. You bankers are conservative by nature I know. I have the curse of being dogmatic in my resolve. Once I make a decision I move forward in my belief. You have two options Bill. Go big or don't go at all."

Bill narrowed his preference of blueprints and presented a slideshow at the next meeting of his senior staff. They were awed by the modernistic appearance of the structure; twenty-one stories of matte aluminum steel holding up ethereal glass walls to reflect a vivid play of clouds. Barrington corporate offices would be housed on floors ten through twenty-one and the bottom floors leased out to a large brokerage firm.

The staff congratulated Bill with praises of approval and jokes about which office they wanted. Tom Morrison was reserved as always. "What do you think Tom?"

"It is spectacular, but you know me, always on the conservative side." The room erupted in laughter as Tom was a notorious miser. "I wouldn't get any work done. I would always be looking out those windows wishing I was sailing on Lake Michigan." He felt the new headquarters was a mistake, too extravagant, too costly and he worried that Bill was becoming a bit star struck in his new position.

It was clear Bill had his sights set on the new building. The architect produced a three-dimensional model of the structure that took center stage in Bill's office for all to see. He knew every nuance of the building and reveled in explaining details of the design. He drove by the site weekly to check on the progress of demolition of the existing building and the beginning of construction.

Two years later the building was completed and ready for final inspection.

There were minor changes to be made that caused another month delay and the actual move of the offices took another month to complete. The final cost came in $2 million over budget.

Lillian had her first office with a door much to her delight. Usually those offices were restricted to officers of the bank. The executive staff was elated with the building. It was elegant with the finest of furnishings and appointments and even Tom Morrison was pleased with his office view of Lake Michigan.

Bill's office was an opulent suite of floor-to-ceiling glass soaring fifteen-feet that gave the impression it was suspended in mid-air. The color scheme of creamy taupe and dove gray gave a calm sophisticated feel. A thickly sculpted carpet of silk and wool anchored six cushy suede club chairs around a low table of glass and steel which rose to table height with the push of a button. The room featured a custom-built unit of gray cabinets that housed flat screen televisions and a hidden safe. The office had a large private washroom with a shower and changing room with fresh shirts and ties. He kept Arthur's mahogany desk, the only piece of wood in the room, and the aged patina made an impressive contrast.

The twenty-first floor was a sumptuous enclave of security and secrecy open only to invited guests and executive staff. The average bank employee could spend their entire career at BNB without ever seeing the rumored elegance of the executive suites.

CHAPTER THIRTY-SIX

Lillian's age was catching up with her and Bill insisted she take more time off. She turned seventy-five in April and seemed to tire more easily much to her disdain. However, she still monitored his phone calls and visitors with the icy will of a border guard and maintained her position as matriarch of the twenty-first floor. Bill's gift to her was a white gold necklace sprinkled with seven one carat diamonds, her birthstone. "For all you do for me, Happy Birthday Lillian."

"Bill, it is lovely. Thank you so much. Please help me put it on." She looked down as she touched the necklace. "Very elegant for a secretary."

"It is very elegant for a very elegant lady. Lillian, I want you to think about something. What do you think of hiring an assistant to help out with some of the mundane work?" Lillian removed her glasses and looked sternly at Bill. "Are you trying to tell me something?"

"No, don't get defensive. I know how time consuming it is to schedule the company planes and all of my travel. Wouldn't it be helpful to give that to someone else?"

"It would not. I would spend more time monitoring their work and correcting their mistakes. You see how some of the secretaries come in late, call in sick and take too much time for lunch. I will not waste my time training some young woman who has other things on her mind than work." Bill shook his head. "Feel free to tell me how you really feel! Sorry I brought it up."

"When you think I cannot perform my work sufficiently you can feel free to fire me. Until then I will continue to do my job as I have for the past thirty-four years." Bill knew he had pushed the wrong button with her, the last thing he intended. "What is that saying, hell hath no fury like an angry woman?" Lillian laughed. "Yes, it is something like that. I apologize for my outburst." Bill looked at his watch. "Come on, let's get out of here." He walked with Lillian to the elevator as they left work for the day. He gave her a hug. "Make sure you are here on time tomorrow or you're fired." She smiled. "Yes sir.

Lillian did not show up for work the next day and no one had heard from her. Bill called his driver. "Bring the car around. I want to check-up on Lillian." They drove to her townhouse and knocked but there was no answer. There was mail in the box from the day before, unlike something she would do. Bill knocked on a neighbor's door and explained who he was. "Do you know Lillian Conrad?"

"Of course, she is such a nice lady. There were no lights in her house last night and we thought she might be out of town." Bill thanked them and returned to the car. "You call the hospitals. I'll call the police. Something has happened to Lillian." They learned a woman named Lillian Conrad was admitted to the hospital the night before and was in the intensive care unit. Her condition was listed as critical but that was all they would say. They drove to the hospital where Bill asked to speak with someone about Lillian. He explained who he was to the nurse. "What happened?" The nurse explained Miss Conrad had been in a car accident the night before and was brought to the emergency room. "She is in very serious condition Mr. Lawrence.

Do you know how to contact her family?"
"I will find their number. May I see Lillian?"
"Sorry, family only for now. Leave your number with us and I will call you if there are any changes in her condition." Bill called Grace on his way back to the bank and told her about Lillian. "Meet me at the hospital in an hour. I don't want her to be alone." He went to Lillian's desk and looked through her address book. He found the number and phoned her niece, Janice, in Milwaukee. "She is in critical condition. Will you be able to come to Chicago?" The niece was crying. "Yes, I will be there as soon as I can. Thank you for calling me." Bill went to his office and sat down. He picked-up the phone and called the police chief who he had met with when Arthur was killed. He explained what had happened. "I need to know what happened to her. I would appreciate your help." Bill held the phone while the chief checked on the accident. "Here we are Mr. Lawrence. Your secretary's car was hit head-on last night at six-fifteen. The driver of the other car was killed immediately. Miss Conrad had to be removed from her car with the Jaws of Life and she has multiple injuries."

Bill listened intently. "Where did it happen?"
"The accident was on the corner of State and Benton. How is she doing?"
"Not well. She is in ICU in critical condition. Thank you very much for the information." Bill sat back and thought about the accident. It must have happened on her way home from work. He thought about their conversation and hoped she hadn't been distracted while driving. He went to Tom Morrison's office and told him what happened. "I'm going back to the hospital Tom. Cover for me until I get back."

Bill returned to the hospital and gave them the phone number of Lillian's niece. "She is on her way from Milwaukee. Has there been any change?" The nurse told him no. "The doctor is with her now. I will ask him to talk with you when he comes out. You can wait at the end of the hall."

A doctor came in the waiting room. "Mr. Lawrence? I understand Miss Conrad is your secretary?"
"Yes, as well as a good friend."
"She has been in a coma since she arrived last night.

Both legs were crushed in the accident and she has a severe head injury with swelling of the brain I am most concerned with for now. She is a very frail woman. The next twenty-four hours are extremely critical." Bill thanked him for the information. "Please let me know if there is any way I can help, anything at all."

Grace arrived just as the doctor was leaving the room. She hugged Bill. He repeated what the doctor had told him. "How awful, how are you?" Bill told her about his conversation the day before with Lillian and how guilty he felt. "Nonsense, you and Lillian always spar like that, she enjoys your teasing."

Two women walked into the waiting room. "Are you Mr. Lawrence?" Bill stood. "Yes, are you Janice?" The younger woman said yes. "Thank you so much for calling me. This is my mother Betty." Bill shook their hands. The mother looked very much like Lillian. "Are you Lillian's sister?"
"Yes. You see the resemblance I'm sure." He introduced them to Grace and they sat together as Bill told them about what the doctor said. "Poor Lillian, what an awful accident.

I am not surprised she never mentioned me to you. We have not spoken for several years, and now this." She began to tremble. Bill handed the niece Lillian's address book from work. "I brought this for you in case there are others you want to contact. Here is my number. Please let us know if there is anything we can do to be of help while you're here. Lillian is very special to me."

Bill's phone rang at two o'clock in the morning. It was Janice telling him Lillian had passed away. He paced the house the rest of the night as he thought of her. The next morning he called Janice. "I would like to meet with you and your mother when you feel up to it. I want to take care of the cost of final arrangements for Lillian."

CHAPTER THIRTY-SEVEN

Bill's advisors warned him to be prepared for opposition to his expansion plans at the upcoming annual shareholder meeting. The hotel conference room was filled to capacity with a crowd of nearly five hundred people when he stepped on stage to a round of applause. He began with an upbeat video presentation of community development programs the bank had led during the past year with hundreds of smiling bank employees participating. He began his year in review executive summary when suddenly he was interrupted by one of the guests. "Mr. Lawrence, we want to know how much was spent on the new bank building. The newspaper says it was $200 million, is that right?" Bill peered over his glasses as the man spoke. "The total figures are not complete. We have outstanding invoices that have not been counted." Another man stood. "You must have some idea of the cost. You are avoiding our question."

"I do not want to give you an incorrect figure at this point. Our next quarter numbers will list the final costs. I will tell you we budgeted $200 million that included the land, permits, architect fees and construction cost." There were noisy comments throughout the room. "We hear you are now planning to build new branch offices in the state. We think you are spending too much money." The crowd erupted in shouts of agreement. "Our dividends are at risk with this excessive spending and we want to voice our opposition to any new expansion of the bank. Arthur Barrington didn't run it this way, he was conservative and made sure his stockholders' investments were safe." Bill looked down at the faces of his Directors sitting in the front seats. Their pained expressions spoke volumes and he knew he had to get control of the audience. He removed his glasses, stepped aside of the podium and held the microphone. "I assure you our plans are well within budget. We owe it to you, our shareholders, to stay competitive by providing our banking services to a wide area of customers. You watch the market and you know our stock price is up 12% from this time last year. I wish I could offer that percentage on C.D.s."

The crowd laughed. "That is an impressive rise in this economy. I assure you that your dividends are safe, in fact the Board has voted to continue the current dividend rate for the coming year. I understand your concerns but am here to tell you we have the leverage to make these investments in the future of BNB. I ask for your continued confidence and support of our direction. Thank you all for being here today." He introduced Margaret Wise to a round of applause and walked off the stage immediately before they could corner him with more questions.

He looked at Burt Williams who was standing backstage. "Tough crowd, I thought they were going to tar and feather me. I feel like I have thrown Margaret to the wolves." Burt laughed. "She can handle them. You did fine Bill. You reassured them and asked for their support. I knew there would be comments but I didn't expect this."

Margaret was followed by Bruce Young who gave a presentation on each of the holding companies. The meeting ended with rousing music as hundreds of balloons dropped from the ceiling.

Bill and David Siegel rode back to the bank together. "Have you ever had stockholders attack you like that?" David smiled. "No. I think they're afraid of me."

"You heard them. They act as if I'm reaching into their wallets to fund the expansion. It simply is not their decision as to how I run the bank."

"No, it is not, but you can't say that to them. They think if they own ten shares of your business, they can tell you what to do. They have little understanding of the complexities of the financial world. Arthur would have loved the comments immortalizing him as the good guy but you and I know he was a tenacious businessman behind the scenes. You bankers all want to project a good guy image and it sometimes comes back to bite you in the ass. Shake off the negative comments and do what you feel is right."

Bill phoned Carl Kincaid the next morning. "Carl, I have a question for you. How do you like your secretary?"

"Leslie has been great Bill. Why?"

"Frankly, I am thinking of pulling rank on you and offering her a job as my assistant.

Lillian was my right hand and I need a seasoned secretary who can pick up the pieces and run the show. Leslie worked on the executive floor and knows the protocol. Lillian was fond of her and I can't think of a higher compliment. What do you think?"

"I think she will be thrilled. Not many have the chance to work for the CEO." Bill smiled into the phone. "Great. I will have George call her and set up an appointment. Thank you, Carl. I owe you one."

Tom Morrison gave Bill the results of his study on sites for new branch offices. "I agree with you on the addition of an office in Peoria. The city is growing and can benefit from a second location. I suggest an in-store office for Niles. We can get into the grocery chain there and it would be more cost efficient for us. We could put in two offices there for less than the cost of a brick and mortar building. The Brighton location is a high rent district but David may be willing to cut us a deal for the presence of BNB. I will continue looking at other locations but frankly Bill, my recommendation is to limit the expansion for now."

"Did you get cold feet from the annual meeting comments?"

"No, I simply feel we are in no hurry to do more." Bill was well aware of Tom's conservative approach but did not agree on the delay. Tom stood. "I had a phone call yesterday from a friend in New York, pumping me for information on BNB. He is with an investment firm on Wall Street but I know he has close ties with Joe Fisher of Reade Street Bank. I evaded his questions but whenever I get rumblings from New York I get suspicious of who is behind the scenes. Someone may be scouting us."

"You are a suspicious character Tom. Keep your ears open and let me know if you have any more calls."

Bill gave the go ahead with his development team to get started on the new branch offices. David Siegel gave him a deal on office space and offered him a prime location just inside the entrance of Brighton. "They can stop there for extra cash to spend in my hotel. We'll both win".

Leslie jumped at the chance to work as senior executive assistant to Bill Lawrence and moved into Lillian's office.

The surroundings were bittersweet as it all reminded her of her friend and mentor. Leslie thought back to the first time she met Lillian. She had been nervous on the day of her interview, arrived fifteen minutes early and sat anxiously in the hushed oval waiting room as the receptionist announced her. Two glass doors quietly opened and an intimidating looking woman walked toward Leslie and introduced herself as Lillian Conrad. She wore an expensive-looking red wool dress of impeccable quality and her silvery gray hair was pinned into a perfect chignon at the nape of her neck. It was as if a celebrity had entered the room. That first impression of Lillian would stay with Leslie always. They had become friends over the years and Leslie had seen a glimpse behind the stern, controlled exterior Lillian portrayed to the rest of the world to a woman with the same complexities as all other women she knew and loved.

Lillian's niece had removed her personal belongings but left Lillian's private telephone book, her bible as she called it, with listings of politicians and business leaders from Washington to Hollywood and their private phone numbers.

CHAPTER THIRTY-EIGHT

David and Isabelle accompanied Bill and Grace to the World Economic Forum in Geneva. David chartered a jet comfortable for the four of them with sleeping berths so the ladies could rest on the ten-hour flight. He and Bill talked about business, politics and family. David brought up the need for security with Bill. "It's a different world Bill. People used to write threatening letters, now they resort to guns, bombs and extortion. You need to take security measures now that you are high profile." Bill agreed. "We're thinking about moving to a more secure home. The bank security team is on call twenty-four-seven but Grace is still uneasy after Arthur's death."

"Women have a sixth sense. Listen to her concerns Bill."

They had reservations at the Beau Rivage Hotel, an elegant historical site with panoramic views of Lake Geneva. It was the first week of June and the weather was perfect at seventy-three degrees and sunny.

The hotel was on the shores of Lake Geneva with a magnificent view of the Alps. It was an elegant hotel of refined luxury and subtle discretion that made it one of the most distinguished hotels in Switzerland. It was located opposite the Mont-Blanc Grand-Rue, the birthplace of Rousseau, a street graced with mansions built in the eighteenth century by Geneva's wealthiest families.

The first day they visited Geneva's Art Museum. It was a gigantic space covering Western culture from antiquity to the present. A romantic sculpture of Venus and Adonis carved in marble stood alone, lit by skylight at the top of the grand staircase. David and Isabelle held hands as they gazed at it for several minutes. They viewed Rembrandts, Dutch and Flemish artists, Pissarros, Cezannes and Renoirs and were both in awe at the paintings.

The next morning Bill and David attended the symposium. The event was hosted by Japan's Minister of Finance who took the stage to welcome the attendees.

He expressed his thanks to a professor of Cambridge University, the president of the World Bank Group, the managing director of a prominent financial group, Bill Lawrence of BNB Corporation, David Siegel, CEO of Siegel Enterprises and participants from various parts of the world. They listened to the speeches of international businessmen as they discussed measures to ensure stable growth of the world economy in the new millennium.

The ladies went off to investigate the shopping possibilities of Geneva. The hotel concierge directed them to High Heel, a contemporary space of white and silver with the most elegant, incredible shoes to be found in the city. From there they visited the Left Bank boutiques with designer lines of haute couture fashion and attentive staff eager to assist foreign shoppers. Grace was a perfect size six and ordered several dresses to be sent to her home in Chicago. Isabelle chose two dinner suits in her favorite colors of graphite gray and steel blue. They met up with Bill and David at the hotel for a cocktail before dinner.

The symposium ended the second day and they flew on to Rome for a week of exploration in Florence and Naples before heading back to Chicago. Grace was enchanted by Naples. The architecture, the food and views of Mt. Vesuvius in the Mediterranean Sea were awe inspiring. They attended the San Carlo opera in Naples, a theater unequaled for the majesty of its architecture and the perfection of its acoustics.

They shopped the Galleria Umberto with the most stunning interior, architecturally, in all of southern Italy with a beautiful arched dome and amazing mosaics. The men managed to find time to be fitted for custom, handmade suits by a premier tailor. David enjoyed the comparisons between the Italian shopping areas and his Brighton complex. "The shoppers are definitely better looking in Naples. I am getting hungry. We are in Italy, where can we get some spaghetti?" They found a charming restaurant near the water where they enjoyed a late lunch with wine, bread, cheese and pasta. The next day they flew back to Chicago rested and rejuvenated by their trip.

Bill and Grace enjoyed the limelight and the attention from their newfound celebrity status. They received preferential treatment wherever they went and were sought out as VIP guests. They moved from the stately home they shared in the suburbs to a penthouse condominium atop one of Chicago's most noteworthy buildings. Grace spent money freely on designer clothing and expensive furnishings. She encouraged Bill to participate in philanthropic activities where they would be honored for their commitment in promoting everything from the arts to education to society events. Bill enjoyed seeing how much attention Grace received when they attended the extravagant galas and opulent events. She was star material and knew how to promote both his image and her own. They were hounded by the press who vied for a glimpse into the lives of the rich and famous.

In four years at the helm of BNB Bill had taken the bank and himself on an upward spiral of success. His ties to Washington had catapulted him into the cloistered private clubs of Arlington, Palm Beach and the Hamptons where he and Grace were welcomed warmly.

He had a circle of influential contacts privy to insider information on everything from Wall Street to Saigon. Titans of industry confided in him and asked his advice. He lost some of his Kentucky charm along the way, gave in to the world around him and acquired the blasé attitude of being difficult to impress. Jordan Banks noticed the change in Bill from their conversations and was the one person who knew he could speak openly with him. He invited Bill on a quail hunting trip in Chevy Chase for the weekend and they sat at the dining room table in Jordan's home as they reminisced and shared stories of Chicago and the bank for hours. Finally, Jordan spoke up. "Bill, forgive me if I am overstepping my bounds, but are you losing touch with the people who supported your rise in BNB? Your focus seems to have changed." Bill laughed. "Are you trying to tell me I have become a snob? I am simply playing the game Jordan, a big game with big stakes. I work twelve-hour days, travel four days a week and spend countless weekends at benefits and boring dinners with Ivy Leaguers whose biggest worry is managing the trust account left by their fathers.

They attended private schools, fell into top notch jobs and have sailed through life by simply standing above others on stacks of family money. I came up through the ranks, from a small town in Kentucky to a penthouse office on the north shore. I have fought off two attempts to buy out BNB and one offer to merge with the largest bank in the country. I will admit that a weekend of deep-sea fishing with Stewart Simons off the coast of Nantucket beats the annual Fourth of July party on Navy Pier. Guilty as charged. Yes, I like all the trappings. I have earned every luxury and fully intend to enjoy them." He looked around the elegantly furnished room. "You too have come a long way from your humble beginnings in Chicago. Has your focus changed?" Jordan raised his glass. "You're right. I guess we have both risen to the challenges before us. Be careful Bill and consider potential security leaks from your newfound friends." Bill paused and looked into his glass. "Don't worry. I'm sure I have more on them than they have on me and I do not intend to share the skeletons in my closet with any of them.

They all boast about the inside information they have on lucrative government contracts, their political favors and corporate conquests. It is part of doing business today. Fortunes are made by seizing opportunities, not by chance, and every successful businessman is guilty of some sort of crime. You know, Abraham Lincoln once said that banking was conceived in iniquity and born in sin. Can you imagine what he would say if he saw inside the banks of today? He would be shocked. You know as well as I that our government favors the rich, big business, big banks and big corporations. If the general public understood economics, we would all be out of jobs."

"There's little danger of that." Bill nodded in agreement. "I have convinced enough big-time investors to buy up all of the BNB stock they can find and I can now manipulate our market price with a phone call, up or down, to conform to Wall Street. I am in a position of strength few can duplicate." Jordan smiled and shook his head. "You are in an enviable but dangerous position my friend. Remember the S.E.C. has eyes and ears everywhere and modern technology has made all forms of communication traceable."

Bill pushed aside his plate and folded his hands on the table. "I know what I'm doing. You will be surprised to know I have been approached to run for Senator of Illinois." Jordan listened intently as Bill spoke. "Are you interested?" "Hell no, the one reason I would consider running would be to kick Barnett out of his Senate seat but I'll let someone else take the pleasure of ousting him. I am far too impulsive for politics and the pay scale is less than enticing to me. I have all of the power and notoriety I need. My sole focus is to make BNB the number one bank in the country, whatever it takes, and if ingratiating the rich and famous paves the way, so be it."

CHAPTER THIRTY-NINE

Tom Morrison rushed into Bill's office Friday morning. "My brother just called to tell me the President has died! He had a massive heart attack this morning. He's dead!"

"What? My God, what happened?"

"It's all over the internet. He was speaking at a town hall meeting when he collapsed. The Secret Service tried CPR but he didn't respond. He died immediately." Bill turned on the television in his office. Headlines scrolled across the screen that the President had died. Newsmen reported events from Orlando, Florida where the attack occurred. They interviewed people who had witnessed the President fall, still in shock and disbelief at what they had seen. "The entire world mourns the loss of President Sanborn. Jordan Banks was sworn in as President in the Oval Office moments before the First Lady boarded Air Force One for Orlando."

Bill buzzed Leslie's intercom. "Get my staff in here at once. The President has died."

They watched the news reports in silence and shock. News crews filmed Air Force One as it landed in Orlando and followed the motorcade from helicopters as it made its way to the hospital. National Guard troops were everywhere as well as Orlando police and the President's Secret Service. Bill turned down the volume and looked at his watch. "Let's get out of here. I know you all want to go home and watch the news."

Bill and Grace had dinner in front of the television as they watched reports of the tragedy. The President had a complete physical in the past month and there were no signs of heart disease. Grace reached for Bill's hand.
"That is very scary to be healthy and active one minute and gone the next. Unbelievable."

The next morning Bill watched as cameras followed the motorcade from the hospital to Air Force One for the flight to Washington with the President's body. The First Lady was engulfed by Secret Service Agents as they shielded her from photographers.

The President's body was taken to the Capitol Rotunda to lie in state as hundreds of thousands lined up to view the guarded casket.

The funeral procession to Arlington National Cemetery was covered live around the world and Bill watched as he saw Jordan and the Secretary of State. He didn't envy his friend's sudden thrust into the Presidency and could only imagine what he must be going through.

Bill was surprised with a phone call from the President a month later on a Sunday evening. "Bill, its Jordan. I need your help."

"My help? You must be up to your ears in help. Sorry, Mr. President, how may I assist?"

"First of all, I need you to address me as Jordan in private. Secondly, I want to talk with you. Can you come to the White House Saturday for dinner, low profile?"

"Of course, I'll be there, if they'll let me in."

"Don't worry about that. I promise lobster bisque for dinner and I'll put you up in the Lincoln bedroom. I will have a driver waiting for your plane. Shall I tell them two o'clock?"

"Yes sir, I'll be there." He understood what Jordan meant by 'low profile', not to mention their meeting.

Bill told Grace he was going on a fishing trip with some friends in Maryland. He knew she wouldn't mind as she hated fishing.

He arrived in Washington Saturday afternoon, was driven to the White House and escorted to the private residence of the President. The Chief of Staff showed Bill to the living room. "Make yourself at home. The President will join you shortly." Bill looked around the formally furnished room and sat down with a book on White House history until Jordan arrived. "It's about time. This is the most boring book I have seen in years." Jordan offered him a drink and chose soda water for himself. "One glass of wine with dinner and that's it. I never know when the next crisis will occur." Jordan filled him in on the course of events during the past month. "I never expected this. The change in command was so sudden. I'm still struggling with it. I felt as though the First Lady was kicked out of her home when she was moved to Arlington three weeks after the President's death. She had dealt not only with the loss of her husband, but the exhausting funeral and all of the decisions that followed. Bill listened intently as Jordan vented his frustrations. "I'm sure it hasn't been an easy transition." Jordan refilled Bill's drink. "Let me get down to the reason I wanted you here.

I have major misgivings with one of Sanborn's cabinet members. I had issues as Vice President but now that he reports to me, it is an entirely different scenario. I am going to replace the Secretary of the Treasury. He is one of the most powerful members of the presidential team but clearly has his own agenda. The Secretary of the Treasury is the principal economic advisor to the President and plays a critical role in policy-making by bringing an economic and government financial policy perspective to issues facing the government. He serves as Chairman of my Economic Policy Council and formulates fiscal policies in Social Security and Medicare trust funds." Jordan paused as his assistant appeared in the doorway. "Excuse me for a moment." She handed a note to him. "Come with me, I guess dinner is ready." Bill followed Jordan to the dining room and sat opposite him. A server appeared and poured them each a glass of chardonnay. "I promised you lobster bisque and you won't be disappointed. It's magnificent." Bill tasted the soup and had to agree. The next course was grilled shrimp and rice pilaf. Bill sat back and raised his glass. "My compliments to the chef, I'll have to come here more often."

Jordan suggested they go outside for a walk. "I understand you would not be interested in a long, drawn-out campaign for a political office but this is an appointment. Granted, the candidate I choose must be confirmed by the Senate but your financial credentials and position as head of BNB more than qualify you for the job. I know you once told me you were not interested in politics because of the pay scale. Government salaries are not nearly as lucrative as private business but the position comes in at about $400,000 a year, plus perks. It comes with a private car, free transportation, a generous housing allowance and free meals at the White House whenever you are available." He watched Bill's expression. "I'm not offering you a fortune, you already have that, but what I am offering you is power, real power to make decisive economic policy. Don't give me an answer now, think about what I said. Bill, I need a trusted advisor who will be honest with me, not tell me what he thinks I want to hear. It is a service to your country and a favor to your friend."

"God, I thought you were going to ask me to sign up for the Marines."

Jordan smiled. "I need a few good men here too."

Jordan showed Bill to his bedroom. "I'll see you in the morning." Bill looked around. He was in the Lincoln bedroom, emancipation proclamation and all. He couldn't believe Jordan's offer of a job. It was the last thing he expected. His initial reaction was no, he wasn't interested in leaving BNB and certainly not for $400,000 a year, but he decided to take Jordan's advice and think about it overnight.

The next morning, he awoke at his usual time of six-thirty, showered, dressed and wandered into the living room where Jordan sat with a cup of coffee. "Good morning Bill, I hope you slept well." Bill looked around him and shook his head. "Slept? I was up all night listening to ghosts discuss politics!" Jordan poured him a cup of coffee and showed him into the dining room where breakfast was set on the sideboard.

Bill asked Jordan about his schedule. "Do you have any time to yourself?" Jordan laughed. "I do, but I never know when it will be. If the red phone rings I run.

Actually, I sometimes wander around here learning the ins and outs of the White House. The staff is great and they try to give me privacy whenever possible. Now for the million dollar question, did you think about what I said last night?" Bill took a drink of juice. "Are you kidding? It was all I thought of. I must admit I am curious and I would like more details." Jordan excused himself. "I'll be right back." Bill wandered around the private living quarters of the White House and looked out the window at the bustling city of Washington. Jordan returned with a leather-bound book he handed to Bill. "This should answer many of your questions. I will direct my Chief of Staff to provide any other information you might need. It is usually easier to contact him than me." Jordan looked at his watch. "Sorry Bill but I have a reception to attend." Bill shook his hand. "Thank you for your confidence, Jordan. I will think about the position. When do you need an answer?" Jordan laughed, "Yesterday, of course. Take your time, it's a big decision."

Bill read the policy manual on the plane back to Chicago. It detailed the duties of the Chief Executive of the Treasury Department.

The scope of the power of the office enticed him, the number one financial advisor to the nation.

Bill decided not to mention his conversation with Jordan to anyone, including Grace, until he considered his options. The first consideration was the future of BNB. His goal of taking it to the number one bank in the country could only be reached by one means if he took the job in Washington, by reconsidering the idea of a merger. He decided to confide in David Siegel.

He met David at his office and told him about the trip to Washington and his conversation with Jordan. David was impressed. "Bill, this is the opportunity of a lifetime you must consider. You would be a leader on the world stage of financial economic policy decisions." Bill agreed it was an exciting prospect. He asked David's views on the future of BNB if he accepted the job. "As a director of the bank I am committed to the shareholders. Your leadership has increased profitability thirty percent in the past four years, a significant accomplishment. As your friend I will tell you the bank will survive, it is a drop in the bucket compared to the scope of what you have been offered.

This is a seat of power and influence opened to few people. My advice is for you to call Jordan and accept his proposition."

David had validated what Bill already knew, that he had decided to seize the opportunity. He discussed it with Grace the next evening. "How exciting, I would love to live in Washington." He smiled. "I knew you would like the idea."

"Have you given Jordan an answer?"

"Of course not, I wanted to get your opinion first." She kissed him, "Secretary of the Treasury and advisor to the President. You must feel very proud."

"I do. Not bad for a guy from Kentucky." She looked around the room. "We will need to find a home there."

"Whoa, one step at a time, Jordan will nominate me for the position and it will go to the Senate for confirmation. Jordan seems confident I will be confirmed."

"I know you will be. Congratulations darling."

Bill phoned Jordan the next day to give his decision. "That's great! I couldn't be happier. You had me worried there for a while, it's been a week since we talked."

"It was a big decision but an opportunity I couldn't decline." Jordan was delighted. "Why don't you and Grace fly here next weekend and we will discuss it further. I will have my Chief of Staff coordinate your plans. Thank you, Bill. You will not regret this choice."

They arrived in Washington Saturday morning, checked into their hotel and arrived at the White House at noon where they joined Jordan for lunch in his private quarters. "Thank you both for coming, we have quite a lot to discuss." He asked if there was anything particular they wanted to see at the White House. Grace spoke up immediately. "I would like a tour. There is so much here to see."

"I will arrange for someone to give you a private tour after lunch while Bill and I talk business." Bill told him they planned to go to the Kennedy Center that night for a performance of the Washington Symphony. "You will enjoy it. They put on a great program. I do hope you will join me for brunch tomorrow. I would like to give you the nickel tour of Washington in the afternoon and I need to be back here by four to prepare for a speech."

"We appreciate your time Jordan."

They discussed the treasury job in detail and Jordan gave Bill information on where the office was located and the size of staff he would lead. "Of course, you will have a driver to shuttle you between meetings. It is the only way to get through the traffic on DuPont Circle." Bill asked questions about the infrastructure of the department and the international scope of the position. They talked for three hours.

Grace returned from her tour excited. "Jordan, thank you so much. I learned more today about the White House than I possibly would have guessed. The rose garden is beautiful and, Bill, they have their own flower shop in the basement where they make all of the fabulous bouquets. It is amazing." They thanked Jordan and returned to their hotel to dress for dinner and the theater.

They returned to the White House the next morning for a wonderful brunch of cheese soufflé and baked ham. "You're in for a treat now, a little bit of White House espionage. I will be escorted to the basement and into an unmarked car that will pick you up by the East Wing entrance.

It's the only way I can get out of here undetected by the press." Grace loved being part of the undercover plan. They drove around the city as Jordan pointed out federal offices, the Smithsonian Museum, the National Theater and presidential monuments. They returned to the East Wing entrance while the presidential limousine distracted the news corps. "I can see you've played this game before. Thanks for the tour Jordan. We'll talk soon."

Bill met with his senior staff the next week to announce his news. They were stunned as he told them of his meeting with the President and his nomination as Treasury Secretary. "It came as a surprise to me also. You all know what BNB means to me. The twenty-first floor has been my home away from home for many, many years, but after careful consideration I have accepted the President's offer." They all stood to congratulate Bill with a round of applause. He explained the Senate confirmation process. "I won't know for sure until their decision but if confirmed I will step down as Chairman of BNB." Tom Morrison spoke. "Congratulations Bill. The President must feel confident of your confirmation."

"Thank you, Tom. Jordan plans to make the announcement the first of the month. I have called a Board meeting for next week to alert our Directors. For now, it is business as usual."

News of the President's announcement brought in hundreds of phone calls, telegrams and letters from across the country. The next few weeks were tumultuous as the news media tracked Bill's every move while he tried to remain focused on the bank.

Two months later he received a call from the President. "Bill, the Senate notified me in writing today of your confirmation. Congratulations." Bill was relieved. "Thank you Jordan, that's a relief."

"Now the real fun begins. How soon can you be here?"

"I will fly in Monday morning."

Bill set-up temporary housing and met with Jordan Monday evening. "Your confirmation signaled an immediate exit for the current Treasury Secretary. Your offices will be cleared for you by Friday and you can get to work. I meant to tell you, your confirmation by the Senate was unanimous. You will be a welcome sight in Washington."

Bill met his Washington staff the next week and outlined the transition process. They were a seasoned group, savvy in how to cut through bureaucratic red tape and battle opposition forces. Their support would essential to the transference of leadership.

His apartment was nearby and he plunged into educating himself on the job. Bill hit the ground running. He initiated meetings with federal agencies under his direction, toured the treasury building and talked with world financial leaders to discuss global monetary concerns. It was a fast-paced schedule but he reveled in his role of power and authority on economic and financial issues and basked in the attention of the press.

Grace found a house she adored in Bethesda, Maryland just ten miles from the White House. She had it completely redecorated and they moved in six months later. Their lives were filled with political receptions, charitable balls, preferred seating at theatrical premiers and invitations to foreign embassies. Their luxurious lifestyle had been elevated to new heights of importance in which they reveled.

Bill shelved thoughts about BNB and Chicago. What had once been his driving force seemed insignificant compared to his new world. The friends who had been central in his life became distant acquaintances seldom heard from. He had moved onto bigger fields. Bill had walked away from BNB with a severance package worth $200 million; he was a wealthy man who focused his attention solely on his role in Washington.

He did keep in touch with David Siegel, a confidant and valued mentor. Isabelle and David visited Grace and Bill at their home for a weekend of society festivities in the fall. Bill and David sat up late one night after the ladies had retired and talked about world events. "You know, David, you gave me the best advice of my life. I recall you once told me to go big or don't go at all. I took the advice and look where I landed. Now I can't imagine anything less than the Washington lifestyle and the power that comes with commanding the entire nation's purse strings."

David set down his drink and looked intently at Bill. "I remember a quote by George Mason where he said, "in all our associations; in all our agreements let us never lose sight of this fundamental maxim – that all power was originally lodged in, and consequently is derived from, the people." In short Bill, your success will center on remembering your origins and how you encourage the progress of our nation and our people. I have faith you will achieve significant distinction."

416

417

Books by Kathleen Ormond

THE TOSS of a COIN
OCEAN ROAD

Available through Amazon.com

Made in the USA
Monee, IL
08 January 2020